Enjoy!
F. Haywood Gle
2016

The Vance Legacy

F. HAYWOOD GLENN

The Vance Legacy

A Novel

Ambiance Publishing Company
Philadelphia, Pennsylvania
U.S.A.

This book is a work of fiction. Names, characters, places and incidents are products of the author's imagination or are used fictitiously. Any resemblance to actual events, locales or persons, living or dead is entirely coincidental.

THE VANCE LEGACY.
Copyright © 2008 by
F. Haywood Glenn

All rights are reserved. Without limiting the rights under the copyright reserved above, no part of this publication may be reproduced, stored in or introduced into a retrieval system, or transmitted, in any form, or by any means (electronic, mechanical, photocopying, recording or otherwise), without prior written permission of both the copyright owner and the publisher of this book.

ISBN 978-0-9820101-0-5

Cover art by LaReine Nixon

ACKNOWLEDGEMENTS

For my mother, Jessie Marie Haywood, who was a constant source of encouragement throughout my life. She lived to see this novel completed, but unfortunately departed this life before the novel could be published.

I extend sincere thanks and appreciation to my family, friends and associates, and all those who contributed to the publishing of this novel.

Special thanks to Patricia Cash, who served as my editor. Also, special thanks to LaReine Nixon who painted the cover art. It was her decision to use an old photo of my Great-great grandmother as the model for this fantastic portrait.

Prologue

January 1832
GLORIA

The Vance Plantation
Richmond, Virginia

ig Bill's once bright green eyes had become pale and near blind, leaving him only able to see shapes and shadows. However, his hearing was as keen as ever. He sat up in bed listening to the soft paddle of footsteps in the corridor just outside his bedroom. When the door opened, the old man leaned forward trying to make out the shadowy figure that entered his room. "Who's there?" he yelled. Then, not waiting for an answer, the insistent old tyrant shouted again. "Who is it, damn it? What the hell do you want?" His once booming voice was now weak and shaky, void of the commanding bluster he once possessed.

Lillian held her breath as she quietly entered the sick room, which is what everyone on the plantation had taken to calling Massa's bedroom. The room smelled of death. Decaying flesh, medication, and soiled linen all contributed to the stench. Lillian hated her duty in the sick room almost as much as she hated her patient. "It's me, Massa. It's Lillian. I come to tend you for a time. Now, don't you go getting yourself all riled up? You just be a good old boy and mind your manners while I tidy up this room a bit."

"Stop talking to me like I'm one of your pick-a-ninnies, girl. I may be sick but I ain't dumb," Bill bellowed in his usual ornery manner. Suddenly racked by an attack of coughing, his body quaked and convulsed for several minutes. He leaned over the side of the bed to a tin basin and spat out the phlegm and blood brought up from his diseased lungs. The attack lasted for several minutes and when it was finally over, he laid back against the pillows breathless and wet with perspiration.

Lillian watched the attack not knowing what, if anything she should do. "Are you alright, massa? Should I ask massa James to send for the doctor?"

"No! I don't need a damn doctor. What I need is a touch of brandy."

"Oh no, sir," Lillian was horrified. "The doctor says you can't ever have brandy no more, sir."

"To hell with the damn doctor! You do as I say girl. Now run on down stairs and get me a bottle of brandy." Lillian hadn't heeded the old man's demands, standing still and knowing that Big Bill would not be denied. "Do you hear me, girl? Do as you're told, now!"

"Yes sir," Lillian whispered as she sat a pitcher of fresh water on the bedside table and began to collect the soiled linen. She glanced down at the sick old man that she had hated for most of her life. How pitiful he looked now, but still she could find no sympathy for the dying man.

William Vance, known as Big Bill to most, was once a robust and powerful man. He was tall with broad shoulders, a barrel chest and a square jaw, a very imposing figure and the obvious reason for his acquired nickname, 'Big Bill.' He'd led a life of privilege and wealth as owner of one of the richest tobacco plantations in the state of Virginia. Some say that the sprawling green acres of Gloria began as little more than a farm won in a poker game by William's grandfather. But it was William's father, Delvin who had cared for and cultivated the land. The first crop of tobacco was planted in 1780. It was the result of his diligence that the powerful Vance dynasty was born. By the time Big Bill was born the Vance family was one of the wealthiest families in the country.

Unfortunately, Bill did not inherit his father's passion for the land. He did, however, thoroughly enjoy the wealth and power that the land provided. By the time William was fifteen, Gloria had grown to over 200 acres and the family owned hundreds of slaves.

Delvin died in 1798 leaving his vast fortune to his only son William. Big Bill ruled the plantation with an iron fist and rigid authority. He was hated by almost everyone who ever had an occasion to meet him and feared by just as many. The only soft spot in Bill's heart was for his deceased wife, Gloria, for whom the plantation was eventually named.

In his youth Bill's good looks and wealth made him the most sought after bachelor in the county. Bill was known to have shared his charms with several young ladies in the county but he was content as a bachelor and never once considered marriage.

His past experiences with the opposite sex were legendary but did little to prepare him for the all-consuming love that would besiege him upon meeting Miss Gloria Beauford of Georgia. The two met at a social gathering of a neighboring plantation. Miss Beauford was a slight young woman with a pale complexion and large, round blue eyes which contributed to her childlike beauty. Bill was completely taken with her from their very first meeting. She was unlike any woman he had ever known. Bill thought her more than just beautiful, to him she was exquisite. Everything about her was pleasing to him. He adored her sweet scent, her corn flower colored hair, and the way she demurely looked down trying to avoid eye contact whenever he spoke to her directly. He often couldn't take his eyes away from her soft face. He even found something appealing about her fragility. Her mere presence ignited in him a need to protect her from the world.

Their courtship was short and to the delight of Gloria's parents, they were married soon after their first meeting. Bill was happier than he'd ever been in his life. He never imagined that he could love a woman as completely as he loved Gloria.

Unfortunately the couple's happiness would be short lived. From the moment they arrived at his tobacco plantation home, Bill knew that they would never enjoy the blissful marriage he had anticipated. Gloria was indeed fragile. She was ill much of the time, sometimes even too weak to leave her bed for days on end. She hated the smell of tobacco and complained that she wasn't comfortable with the house slaves quartered in their own rooms on the ground floor of the mansion. She even boldly told her new husband that she found their lovemaking distasteful and would only oblige Bill until she could conceive an heir. Bill, usually not a patient man by any means, took all of this in stride. He loved his wife more than anything on earth and would do anything to make her happy.

Bill mellowed somewhat during his years with Gloria but when she died it left him bitter and angry. He was in his mid forty's when he was diagnosed with a lung ailment that was expected to shorten his own life. However, he chose not to heed the warnings of his very well paid physicians and continued to live a life of indulgence. His condition continued to deteriorate over the years and in the past two years he had become considerably worst. Now at age fifty-six, Big Bill Vance was completely convalescent. He was as obstinate in his waning years as he had been in his youth, and to the dismay of his family, he had refused to give in to the call of death and lingered far past his time.

Lillian quietly slipped out of the room as fast as she could. She had no intention of bringing the old man brandy as he had ordered. She was sure that if she waited a little while he would probably fall asleep and forget all about the brandy, after all, this wasn't the first time the old man had demanded brandy.

James, Big Bill's youngest son, was on his way to his father's room when he saw Lillian leaving the room. "How is he?" he asked.

"Oh he ain't changed none sir. He's hardly breathing at all and done stop eating too. Only he keeps asking for bandy. Only time I get a word out of him is when he's cussin bout eating or asking for brandy."

"You pay no attention to his cursing, Lillian. The doctor says that he must eat to keep up his strength. You just go right on feeding him no matter what he says."

"Yes sir," Lillian said as she wondered just how she was supposed to feed the man if he didn't want to eat.

A short time later, holding her breath again, Lillian brought a tray of chicken broth and bread to the sick room to feed the old man. She sat the tray down and pulled a chair close to the bed. The old man had fallen asleep just as she expected and she let out a breath of gratitude. She sat down beside the bed watching the old man as he slept. His breath came in shallow but steady gasps. Occasionally his frail body would shiver as if a cold wind had blown straight through his soul. He didn't look so much like the monster that she had feared most of her life. There was no evil force emanating from his presence as she had once believed, but Lillian would not be fooled. She knew all too well that the demons still lived and they still possessed the man, Big Bill Vance. As he lay there, so close to death, Lillian couldn't help but remember how she had come to hate the old tyrant.

She remembered the first time she had laid with the old man and how it had made her sick to her stomach. She was just a girl then, maybe thirteen or fourteen, she wasn't exactly sure. But she remembered that her mother had come to wake her and was so excited with the news that massa Vance wanted a virgin. She was asleep when her mother had come for her, calling and pulling at her arms to wake her. "Lillian! Wake up child. Mamma's got good news for you girl. Wake up now." Lillian sat up on the tiny cot, wiping the sleep from her eyes. "Massa be wantin a virgin tonight," her mother said. "That be you, girl. Ain't you happy? You gone be massa's virgin tonight."

"But Mamma, I don't want to be with massa. He's old and wrinkly. Please don't make me go, Mamma. Etta says he do awful things to the girls that go to the big house. Please don't make me go. I don't want to go."

"Yes you does!" Her mother was suddenly angry. "Even if you don't know it yet girl, you does want to go." Lillian remembered how the excitement had faded from her mother's face. Before she even knew what was happening, her mother took her by the arms and pulled her into a sitting position. "Look at my hands, girl," Mamie said as she held out her hands with crippled fingers for her daughter to see. "These here fingers will never be as pretty as yours. They all bent and crooked and they gone stay this way till I'm in my grave, and my back, I can't even remember standing when I didn't feel like there was something pressing down my back right through to my legs. Most days I got an ache in some bone or another and there ain't a damn thing anybody can do about it." Lillian looked away. "Look at me girl," Mamie screamed. "What you see is what them tobacco fields does to a person. My own Mamma died when she was just about my age and I don't expect I'll out live her by too long. But you," she stopped to look at her pretty daughter. "Lillian you have a chance to have a better life. No tobacco fields for my daughter. You gone live in the big house! Do you hear what I'm saying to you, girl?"

"Yes Mamma, but I don't want to go to the big house and I

don't want to live in the big house. I just want to stay here in our cabin with you Mamma." Lillian hadn't fully understood what her mother was trying to tell her at that time. Mamie reached out and wiped the tears from her daughter's soft brown cheeks. "You may not want to go now Lillian, but I know that this is the best thing for you. If you don't want to spend your whole life in those damn tobacco fields, if you don't want your body to bend and twist up so painful that it sometimes hurts to take a breath, you'll go to the big house and sleep with that old white man. You do everything he tells you. If you act like you likes it, you won't ever have to sleep in this leaky old shack again. If the old man likes you, you'll be able to sleep in a real bed in the big house, get a pretty new dress every now and again and eat in that big warm kitchen. Now don't you want those things honey?"

"No Mamma, I just want to stay here."

"Belonging to a man ain't no peach no matter how you looks at it, but some of us get a chance to make life just a little easier. Do you understand, Lil? Ain't nothing gone happen in that big house that can change who you are inside. They can't ever change that."

Lillian didn't care about pretty dresses or sleeping in the big house. She only cared that her not wanting to go was making her Mamma unhappy. "Yes, Mamma, I understand." Lillian finally whispered. She really didn't understand but she would go without a fuss if it would make her Mamma happy.

"Then get yourself ready, child. You be massa's virgin tonight."

Lillian did as she was told and every time the old man took her, she would close her eyes very tight and ask God to take massa Vance away so he could never do this to her again. But there was always a next time and after each time she would feel sick and dirty.

Eventually she was assigned duties in the big house so that she could be near whenever Big Bill wanted her again. She quickly learned that the more pleasure she gave in the bedroom, the more privilege she was awarded around the plantation. Lillian became skilled at fulfilling the old man's lustful desires and was rewarded likewise. She was given new clothes and considered herself lucky to own three dresses when most of the other slaves were given only one for winter and one for summer. The rest of their clothes were usually crudely stitched together from any scraps of fabric found discarded by the Vance's. Just as her mother said, she was allowed to eat in the kitchen house and Massa always brought her some small gift when he returned from his end of the month shopping trips to Richmond. Once he'd even bought her a shinny new mirror. Though she cherished that little mirror she could never forget the things Massa made her do for such a gift.

After a while Lillian no longer cringed when the old man touched her. Of course she could never love Big Bill and she never looked forward to being with him but she learned to accept her place on Gloria with complacency. The things he made her do, even now, the thought made her sick to her stomach. She had hated old man Vance for as long as she could remember. Now as he lay there as helpless as the child she had been when he had taken her the first time, she couldn't even feel pity for the dying man.

"Massa," she whispered. "It's time to eat. Sit up, now." The old man opened his eyes but did not move. "Bell fixed some good chicken stock and fresh bread for you. Massa James says the doctor wants you to keep up your strength." Lillian tried to coax the old man into eating. As she lifted the spoon full of steamy broth to his dry lips, the old man opened his eyes and glared at her.

"Get that watery stuff out of my face, girl," he sneered as he swung his arm through the air knocking the spoon from Lillian's hand and causing the hot broth to splash her in the face. "You hard of hearing, are you girl? I told you to go and get me some brandy," he yelled.

"Brandy is the last thing you need right now massa. The doctor says you need to eat." Lillian chose to ignore his outburst. After wiping her face she bent down to pick up the spoon and wipe the spill from the floor. As soon as she lifted her head, Big Bill raised himself on his weakened elbows and spat in Lillian's face. She jumped to her feet and for a moment she just stared down at the old man, wishing him dead again as she had so many times before.

"I told you I don't give a damn what the doctor says. Now, do as you are told and get me a bottle of brandy or I swear I'll take a whip to you."

"If its brandy you want, sir, I'd be glad to get if for you. You can't die soon enough for me."

"You can't talk to me that way girl," he screeched. "What you need is a good whipping. That will teach you to mind your tongue. I should have whipped you long ago."

Lillian was fed up with this tantrum. She gathered the dishes back onto the tray and started for the door.

"Yes, a whipping, that's what you need . . ." the old man's words were chocked away by another violent attack of coughing. When Lillian reached the door she turned to look back at Big Bill. His face had become red and bloated as the attack took his breath away. His eyes rolled back in his head so that his pupils could no longer be seen and Lillian thought he looked like the devil himself. She knew that she should do something, anything, but she just stood there watching, secretly rejoicing in his agony.

The old man could not catch his breath. He raised a weakened hand toward Lillian, silently pleading for her help and forgiveness, but Lillian had no forgiveness to give. As if rooted where she stood, Lillian watched as death slowly closed around Big Bill Vance. Suddenly his body was jerked forward and blood began to run from his nose and mouth. He regained his breath only to lose it again as he choked on the blood that the attack brought up from his diseased lungs. "Die, old man," Lillian whispered. "Die and go straight to hell where you belong."

Big bill coughed deep within his chest one last time. A small trickle of blood began to stream from the corners of his mouth and then, it was over. Lillian gently closed the door and stood for a moment in the quiet of the corridor. The whole world seemed to have stopped for that one moment, as if the passing of evil needed to be acknowledged, recognized but not mourned. Big Bill Vance was dead.

Lillian inhaled, holding the stale air of the old mansion in her lungs for a few seconds. It was almost as if she thought that exhaling too soon would revive the demon. When she realized that Big Bill was finally dead she fell back against the wall as if she had just received divine absolution. "Now David can come home," she whispered.

Part One

Deliverance

"For reason, ruling alone is a force confining;
and passion, unattended,
is a flame that burns to its own destruction."

Kahilil Gibran,
The Prophet, 1923

Chapter 1

❧

February 1832
Philadelphia, Pennsylvania

*M*adam Renee's experienced eye took in the creamy unblemished complexion and perfectly manicured hands as she considered the young woman before her.

"Madam, this is my last hope. I beg you to just give me a chance," Beth pleaded. "I promise you, I won't be any trouble to you."

"By the looks of you, I'm not sure you can make such a promise. A genteel lady like yourself could bring me more than a little trouble."

"I assure you, Madam. I will bring you no trouble."

It was Madam Renee's business to know people and she knew that the young woman's promises were ones that neither of them could guarantee. "You've never done a days work in your life, have you, Miss?"

"No Ma'am," Beth confessed. "But that doesn't mean that I won't work very hard for my keep. I can sew a little and I'm sure I can learn to do most anything."

"I've no doubt," Madam Renee smiled. "And that's all very nice but I'm not hiring a seamstress or a housekeeper. Do you even know what my girls do here?"

"Yes Ma'am but I thought that with all the people living here, you might need someone to perform," Beth paused looking for just the right words, ". . . more domestic services."

Madam Renee was a large woman, nearly six feet with strong arms and an ample bosom which she did little to conceal. Her blond curly hair was piled high on her large head and her lips were painted in the same shade of ruby as the red in her velvet dress. She leaned closer to Beth as if to speak some confidence. Her whispered words reeked of old whiskey and stale tobacco. "My customers pay for services of a more personal nature, sweetie. Besides, I'm not looking for a housekeeper." Satisfied that her words had shed new light on the situation, Madam Renee leaned back in her chair and searched Beth's face for the look of shock that she was sure would come. Finding that the young woman was not in the least deterred, she continued. "But, I like you Miss Beth. Not many women like yourself would have the guts to come into the Chateau, let alone seek the kind of employment you're looking for." Madam Renee smiled. "You've got a certain presence, if you know what I mean." Beth didn't. "I'll make a deal with you," Madam went on. "I'll hire you on to help with the housekeeping and such but if any of my customers should take a fancy to you and want to spend some time with you, you'll oblige or you will be asked to leave my house. How's that?"

It wasn't exactly the proposition Beth had hoped for but at least it was a job. All she needed to do was keep out of sight of Madam Renee's customers. "I can't thank you enough Madam. I promise you, you won't regret this decision."

"I've already warned you about making promises you can't keep. I may very well regret this decision but I'm willing to take that chance. It's a very sad thing to see a young woman like you in such circumstances." With great effort, Madam Renee heaved her large body from the chair, nearly toppling the tea table. Beth watched in awe as the old Madam sashayed across her lavishly decorated parlor. "It might surprise you to know that I knew your father Ernest quite well."

"No Ma'am. I don't think I would be surprised at anything about my father. Since his death I've learned that Ernest Gable was a very different man than the man I knew as my father. My mother and I probably never saw the man you knew as Ernest Gable."

Madam Renee smiled as if she understood more than she was willing to say and Beth wondered if a woman like Madam Renee could really understand her loss. She wasn't just left alone after her father's death; her entire life had been forever changed.

Before her parents died Beth's world was filled with parties, the theater and the Baptist Church. Her dreams were filled with romantic adventures, a home of her own with a husband who would adore her and the family she expected to have one day. The life that Beth once led was akin to perfumed candles. Though the sweet scent of a privileged life lingered, in just a few short months it had all melted away. Although Madam Renee could certainly sympathize with Beth's unusual circumstances, Beth doubted if she could really understand Beth's devastation. How could she know that just being in her presence was one of the most humiliating experiences of Beth's life? How could Madam Renee know that although the Gables weren't rich by any stretch of the imagination, money was a topic never discussed in their household and Beth and her mother never had a single worry about their well-being? Madam certainly couldn't know or understand that Beth's entire life had prepared her to be a good Christian wife and little else.

Beth, born Elizabeth Gable, was the only daughter of Ernest Avery and Esther Gable. Her parents, though not wealthy people, had both come from good families. Her father had worked very hard most of his life to provide a very comfortable living for his small family. The Gables lived on a country estate just outside of Philadelphia.

Beth had been educated by the best tutors her family could afford and at eighteen her parents were hopeful that a suitable young man would one day marry their only daughter. But in late September in the year 1831 Ernest was killed in a logging accident in Western Pennsylvania. Four months after her father's death her mother, suffering from a broken heart, had taken her own life. In the midst of her grief Beth was to learn that she was penniless. The news was brought by Mr. Whitt Thornton, one of her father's oldest friends, his lawyer for more than a decade and the one man who knew Ernest Gable best.

Mr. Thornton was a portly man with white hair and steel gray eyes. "Beth," he'd begun. He cleared his throat and pushed a stray gray hair from his face. "I came by because there are some very pressing matters that we should discuss."

Beth was appalled. "Mr. Thornton, I'm sure you mean well but this is simply not the proper time!" she protested.

"I apologize if I seem insensitive to your grief dear but this is of the utmost importance." He went on to tell Beth that her parent's death had left her impoverished. What little money the family had was squandered away by her father's obsessive gambling habits and instead of leaving their only daughter an inheritance Beth was left in serious debt. Her father had even lost the lumber company that he had worked so hard to build over the years. Everything on the estate, including the house and a small collection of art and antiques that her mother had acquired over the years, must be sold to pay off a long list of creditors. "To put it bluntly dear, you're broke."

Feeling assaulted and defeated, Beth sank into the leather armchair behind her father's desk. The image of her father, the man she had loved and respected all of her life would be forever tarnished. The man she called father was an illusion. Her eyes stung as she blinked back the tears that threatened to spill onto her cheeks. "How could he?" she softly whispered.

"I'm sorry Elizabeth," Mr. Thornton said. "Now, do you understand why I could not wait to tell you these things? Believe me I only have your best interest at heart."

"I understand Mr. Thornton."

"Now my dear, you have some very important decisions to make over the next few weeks. I just want to assure you that I'll do whatever I can to help. You are not alone dear. I may even be able to help you secure a position with a good family."

"Are things really so bad that I am forced to look for work so soon?"

"I'm afraid so. But, I'm sure that a girl of your background should be able to find a position as a governess or teacher with a respectable family."

Beth was on her feet again pacing. "I'm sure you mean well, Mr. Thornton and I do appreciate your concern but I'm not sure that I'd be any good at teaching nor is that something to which I aspire. I wasn't the best student with my own tutors. How could I hope to be a good teacher?"

"You haven't understood a thing I've been saying, have you Elizabeth?"

"Yes, I have listened to you Mr. Thornton. I just don't want to think about it now. This is all such a shock to me. I'm having difficulty just dealing with my parent's death. Now you tell me that I'm broke, my parents left me destitute. This is all too much to absorb so quickly. Besides, I've no wish to plant myself in the middle of some family as a servant or a poor distant relative. I just can't do it, Mr. Thornton."

Mr. Thornton leaned back in his chair and eyed Beth thoughtfully. "I think, my dear, if you seriously examine your situation you'll find that you are capable of doing many things that you probably would have never dreamed possible but for your profound situation." Mr. Thornton sighed, shrugging his shoulders and Beth could see that he was losing his patience. "I'm sure that this has all been quite traumatic for you dear, but you are not a child and you unfortunately don't have the luxury of time. My suggestion is that you try to sell everything in this house that is worth anything. This of course includes your mother's antique collection. That should give you enough income to survive until you can find work. I urge you to do this as quickly as possible as your father's creditors will foreclose on the house in the very near future."

Broke and in serious debt Beth was forced to discharge the few servants in her parent's employ. She sold most of her family's possessions as Mr. Thornton suggested. He had been right about everything as the foreclosure papers were delivered to her door only a couple of weeks after her meeting with Mr. Thornton. She was given no more than thirty days to vacate the property.

With the money she'd earned from the sale of her family's possessions she was able to rent a room in a respectable boarding house in Philadelphia. Day and night she searched for work and was turned away time and time again.

Finally she was offered a position in the Briscoe Confectionery Shop. Mrs. Briscoe was a cruel old woman in her fifty's while her husband was a least fifteen years her junior. The job paid two dollars a week, which was barely enough to pay for Beth's room and board. She was expected to be in the shop by seven each morning to help with the candy making. The afternoons were spent selling candy in the shop. It was grueling. Some days Beth was on her feet for more than twelve hours. Besides enduring the hardships of making and selling candy, she spent her days fending off the sexual advances from Mr. Briscoe whenever his wife left them alone. Mrs. Briscoe treated Beth as if she were a dim witted child. Every order was delivered with her voice pitched high enough to shatter a crystal glass and coupled with the cruelest insults Beth had ever heard. Mrs. Briscoe had even gone so far as to ask Beth if she were just stupid or a complete moron.

It would be well after eight o'clock in the evenings when Beth would finally be released and she would drag herself to the boarding house where after her supper she would fall asleep almost as soon as her head touched the pillow.

Beth wanted desperately to find other employment but how could she when the candy shop monopolized all of her time. She couldn't very well go knocking on doors, seeking employment after eight in the evenings or before seven in the morning, people would think she was daft. After six months in the candy shop Beth had come to accept the fact that she would probably always live in the boarding house and work in the Briscoe Confectionery Shop.

Sundays had become Beth's favorite day of the week. The candy shop was closed so she could actually sleep until ten in the morning. Mrs. Lena, who owed the boarding house, spent Sunday mornings at the Presbyterian Church. Breakfast would not be served until she was back from morning services, usually about eleven. Beth and some of the other women in the house would help Mrs. Lena clean her kitchen after breakfast and begin preparing for Supper. It was just such a Sunday when Beth overheard a conversation be-tween two of the boarding house maids. The younger of the two boasted about turning in her apron for the finery she would wear working for Madam Renee' at the Chateau Pleasure near the water-front. Beth didn't wait to hear the end of the conversation. She'd never even heard of Madam Renee or the Chateau Pleasure. It wasn't until she stood at the front door that she realized that she was apply-ing for work in a brothel. For one fleeting moment she considered returning to the boarding house but suddenly the door opened and there stood Madam Renee.

Now feeling somewhat awkward, Beth followed Madam Renee to a small room behind the kitchen. "You'll sleep here. The other housekeeper sleeps in the next room. If you get a customer, you'll move to a better room on the second floor." Madam paused momentarily just to make sure the young woman understood. "I keep late hours," she went on. "I never wake before ten and I expect my breakfast to be served in my room at half past ten. My girls eat their breakfast in the dinning room and we all have supper in the dinning room no later than seven. Other than that Sarah, the other housekeeper, will show you everything else you need to know. Any questions?"

"No, Madam," Beth stuttered. The room wasn't nearly as nice as Beth's room in the boarding house but at least she would not have to work at Briscoe's any more. After meeting the other housekeeper Sarah, who gave Beth a brief tour of the Chateau and a description of her duties, Beth returned to the boarding house to collect her things. She thanked Mrs. Lena for her kindness and settled her rent bill before leaving again for the Chateau.

For the first couple of months Beth was content. The work wasn't nearly as hard as she imagined but it gave her little time to dwell on her misfortune. Sarah was a pleasant enough woman and Madam Renee, despite her harsh appearance, was sympathetic and understanding of all of her employees. The other women in the house were also kind to Beth. In fact, they were so nice that Beth suspected that Madam Renee might have shared the details of her dilemma with the women. It was almost as if they were welcoming her into the fold. Beth returned their kindness but she never lost sight of the fact that they were whores and she had no desire to share in their chosen profession. She was always careful to dress modestly, so as not to attract any notice from Madam Renee's customers. She used the back door and stairs whenever possible and came and went as indiscernible as possible.

Evenings at the Chateau were chaotic. The entire house was a bustle of activity. People came and went so often it could make your head swarm. The women were all decked out in their finery.

The front parlor was awash with silk, lace, ruffles and feathers of every imaginable color. Politicians, clergymen, bankers, solicitors, conductors and even farmers, were all discreetly escorted to the upstairs rooms by the lady of their choice. It was all done so subtly that the Chateau could almost be mistaken for a social club instead of a brothel.

Beth hated working the evenings. Sarah, on the other hand, loved the evenings and this arrangement worked perfectly for both women for a while. However, the perfect arrangement ended abruptly when Sarah ran off with one of Madam Renee's regular customers, leaving Beth as the only housekeeper at the Chateau.

The very first night Beth worked the evening she was summoned to bring fresh linen to room eight, which was on the third floor of the house. The narrow corridors on the third and fourth floors looked very different at night. Beth tried to suppress the uneasy feeling the crept up her spine as she moved quickly down the corridor. Strange noises came from some of the rooms as she passed. Just as she passed room seven Beth was startled as something smashed against the door causing her to jump. She tapped lightly on the door of room eight and moments later the door swung open and there in the doorway stood David Vance. He was the most exquisite man Beth had ever seen. He was tall, over six feet Beth guessed, with a muscular build. He was covered in dark olive skin while piercing green eyes peered through a mass of thick charcoal hair. He stood there as brazen as a cat, making no attempt to cover his nakedness. "Your towels, sir." Beth stammered. She knew that she should look away but no matter how hard she willed her eyes in another direction, she simply could not take them away from his bulging masculinity. Silent, uncomfortable moments passed as he stood in the door and Beth waited in the dim light of the corridor, for what she didn't know.

"Well, well," he said. His smile was broad and sensual as he stroked at the smooth beard that covered his jaw and chin. "It seems that Madam Renee' is picking her girls a bit more carefully these days."

The spell was immediately broken. "I am not one of Madam's girls."

"Pity, I'd be willing to pay a good price for the company of a young woman as beautiful as you, Miss."

"If you meant that as a compliment, thank you, but I'm not for sale. Your towels, sir," Beth said as she thrust the pile of towels at his chest. "I've already told you, I am not one of Madam's girls," Beth curtly said. As soon as he reached forward and relieved Beth of her bundle she turned and walked quickly away.

A few days later Beth was summoned to Madam Renee's parlor. "It seems that you have acquired an admirer, Miss Beth. I can't say that I'm surprised. You are quite an attractive young woman. I knew that it wouldn't be long before you started to attract attention."

"Madam, it was not my intention to attract anyone."

"That may be dear. However you've managed to attract at least one of my very best customers. Mr. David Vance has requested to spend an evening with you."

Beth pulled her spine up and stood as straight as she possibly could. She looked down on Madam Renee as she spoke. "Please tell Mr. Vance that I am unavailable."

Madam Renee glanced up in surprise as she let out a little giggle. "But my dear, you are quite available."

"I thought we agreed that I was to be hired as a housekeeper. You don't really expect me to spend an evening with that man."

"That is exactly what I expect and I seem to remember a little more to our agreement, Miss Beth. Have you forgotten?"

Beth hadn't forgotten she simply never thought that she would have to honor such an agreement. "No Madam, I haven't forgotten."

"Good. I've put you in room ten on the third floor. I've already had a pretty dress laid out for you. You'll find matching slippers and everything else you'll need. You will have one hour to bath and dress before Mr. Vance comes to your room. Any questions?"

"How could this happen?"

"Fate, honey. Some of us are blessed while others, for reasons no one could possibly know, are cursed no matter what they do or where they come from. If you're smart, and I think you are, you'll learn to take whatever life throws your way and make the best of it. Do you know what I mean?"

"No. I haven't the faintest idea."

"Mr. Vance is a very rich man Miss Beth. You could do worst. If you had met Mr. Vance a year ago, you and your family would have welcomed him as a proper suitor."

"He doesn't want to court me, Madam. He wants to ruin me. I can't let that happen."

"Look honey, you're all alone in this world now. I know you were raised to be a proper young lady and your parents probably hoped to marry you off to some gentlemen of like means but that is all over with now. Take it from me; this world is very hard on a single woman. Make the best of it, honey."

One hour later dressed in the black satin dress that Madam Renee had so thoughtfully laid out for her and carrying her mother's old tattered carpet bag, Beth slipped out of the back door of Madam Renee's Chateau Pleasure. The night was cool and the moon was hidden behind a layer of dense gray clouds that threatened a storm at any minute. Beth looked up at the sky and considered the folly in choosing this night to run away. She pulled her shawl tighter around her shoulders and began to walk with no particular destination in mind. She only knew that she wanted to be away from Madam Renee's Chateau and Mr. Vance. She was tired of the waterfront and all of its decadence. She wanted to be as far away as possible from whores, drunkards and gamblers that had made that section of Philadelphia their own. But she didn't have any place to go. She couldn't go home, she had no home. The house had been sold months ago, along with everything else. She briefly considered going back to Mrs. Lena's boarding house, but she knew that if Mrs. Lena knew that she had taken employment at The Chateau, she would hardly be welcomed back. She considered a hotel. What little money she had was wrapped in a lace handkerchief and tucked into the elastic of her stockings. At best, she could only afford to pay for a couple of nights, and then what would she do.

Beth didn't know how long she had been walking but she suddenly realized that she was on the outskirts of town. A hard drenching rain began to pour. The rain made puddles in the road and the wind made the trees sway back and forth ominously. Her shoes began to stick in the mud of the road and the hem of the thin dress was muddied to the knee. Wet hair stuck to her face and neck, causing her to continuously push the wet strands from her eyes as she walked.

After another ten minutes of walking Beth was soaked right down to her undergarments. In the distance she could hear the creaking and snapping of carriage wheels as they rumbled down the gutted road. Her first thought was to wave the rider down and ask for a ride but the possibility of meeting some unsavory character from the waterfront quickly changed her mind. Soon the carriage wheels slowly creaked to a halt beside her.

"Miss Gable," the rider yelled as the door swung open. "Is the thought of spending an evening with me so repulsive that you've chosen to run away?"

Beth was too shocked to speak as Mr. Vance descended the carriage steps. He swung the hood of his cape over his head but it did little in the pouring rain. "I'm not running away, Mr. Vance. I have decided that my position at the Chateau is no longer one in which I am satisfied. It has nothing at all to do with you, sir."

"That sounds a little haughty for a chamber maid."

"I was not a chamber maid. If you must know I was a house-keeper but I no longer wish to be employed by Madam Renee." Beth tried to step around Mr. Vance, but one step to the right, and her path was once again blocked.

"It is a rather strange time to re-evaluate one's employment situation, don't you agree?"

Now Beth was angry. Just who does he think he is, she thought. "Why is it any of your concern Mr. Vance?"

"It isn't, really." He seemed startled by her frankness. "It's just that I feel somewhat responsible for your leaving the Chateau."

"Well that is easily remedied. I relieve you of any responsibility, real or imagined. Now go away!"

"Excuse me?"

"I said, go away. You are not responsible for me in any way sir and I do not wish to spend an evening with you. In fact, Mr. Vance I hope never to see you again." This time he made no move to stop her as she stepped around him and continued to walk. A few minutes later she heard the carriage wheels as they struggled to move over the muddied road. Again the carriage caught up to her and Mr. Vance yelled from the window. "At least let me take you to wherever it is you're going. My sense of responsibility would be somewhat as-suaged if I could assist you in some small way."

Beth stopped. "That would be agreeable sir, if you could tell me where I could rent a room at this late hour?"

"You are welcome to spend the night in my room." At that remark Beth turned and began to walk away again. "That's not what I meant. I apologize Miss Gable," Mr. Vance yelled after her. "I really didn't mean it the way it sounded. It's just that it is very unlikely that you will find lodging at this hour. My room is just a short distance away. As I said, you are welcome to spend the night and I give my word as a gentleman that I will make no unwanted advances Miss Gable. If you would just say yes we could both get out of this freezing rain. A good night's sleep and some warm dry clothes would do much to help in your decision making, I'm sure."

Cold, wet and tired, Beth stopped to consider Mr. Vance's offer. He swung open the carriage door and leaned out with an out-stretched arm to assist her in climbing into the carriage. Finally, she reached for his hand and he helped her into the carriage.

They rode in silence for several minutes before Beth asked, "Where are we going?"

"I have a room at the Pennsylvania," he said as he glanced at the young woman across from him. He wanted to tell her that even in her muddied clothes with wet hair matted over her head and face, she was still a very beautiful woman but instead he said, "I knew that you weren't one of Madam Renee's girls." Beth didn't answer. "I could tell the moment I opened the door. It's the eyes, you know. The eyes tell a great deal about a person. You have innocent eyes."

"Then why did you request to have me for the evening."

"I'm not sure. I opened the door and there you were with your innocent eyes, your face flushed in embarrassment. I just wanted another chance to talk with you. To tell you the truth, I really expected Madam Renee to deny my request. I had no idea that it would cause you any trouble."

The remainder of the ride was silent. Within minutes the carriage came to a stop in front of the Pennsylvania. David put his jacket around Beth's shoulders and she welcomed its warmth. As he helped her down from the carriage Beth caught a glimpse of his smil-ing face. It was a very handsome face and Beth smiled back at him.

David's room turned out to be a suite of elegant rooms occu-pying the entire top floor of the Pennsylvania. Once inside the room he motioned toward the dressing screen that stood in a corner of the room. "You had better get out of those wet clothes before you catch cold."

Beth went behind the screen and undressed quickly. She threw her wet clothes over the screen. David took the wet clothes almost as soon as she hung them. He fished in his pocket for a coin to give the maid who waited to take Beth's wet clothes. As Beth stood shivering behind the screen in nothing but her chemise, the room seemed a bustle of activity on the other side of the screen. David gave orders to the young maid to launder the clothes and return them to the room. Then he ordered a young man to light the fire and several lamps around the room.

Suddenly the room was very quiet as if he'd forgotten that Beth was even there. She peered around the screen looking for David but he had apparently left the suite. She hurried over to the bed, carefully folded down the satin quilt and removed the sheet to cover herself. She made herself comfortable on a short sofa in front of the fire and waited for David to return.

Minutes later he came in carrying two steaming cups of milk and honey. "Here. I thought you could use something to warm you," he said as he handed Beth a cup.

This was all so sweet and cozy Beth had begun to think that she had judged Mr. Vance too harshly. Knowing that he was a frequent patron of the Chateau, she automatically put him in a category as the other drunken gamblers that frequented the Chateau Pleasure. Many of Madam's customers were wealthy and prominent people but with an obvious dark side which Beth assumed would be quite evident. She saw no such darkness in Mr. Vance. In fact, he was a very charming and likable sort of fellow.

David shed his wet cape and hat and sat across from Beth. There was no conversation between them for several minutes. Finally he said, "So, tell me. How did you come to work for Madam Renee?"

"It's a long story. I wouldn't want to bore you."

"Why don't you let me be the judge?"

Beth didn't know why but she suddenly had the urge to unburden herself to Mr. Vance. Maybe it was the stress of the day, the warmth of the fire or the honey and milk that had soothed the rumbling in her soul. She couldn't explain it but reluctantly, she told David about her parent's deaths, her father's squandering the family money, her short employment at the confectionary shop and her pleas for employment at the Chateau Pleasure. David listened with rapt attention. Occasionally their eyes would meet, his narrowed in scrutiny, Beth's wet with emotion. The last thing Beth wanted from David Vance was sympathy.

"That's quite a story, Miss Gable."

"It's not a story, Mr. Vance. It's my life and I am not looking for your pity."

"I didn't mean to sound contrite. It's just that no one could have imagined that life had been so hard for you. You give the appearance of a very secure young woman."

"Do I? Secure is one thing that I don't think I'll ever be again. Believe me a year ago I couldn't even have imagined that my life would take such a turn."

Suddenly David was on his feet, his hands thrust deep into his pockets as he began to pace the floor. Something Beth said had struck a cord and he was now deep in thought. Beth felt invisible. It was almost as if he'd forgotten she was even in the room.

"Is something wrong Mr. Vance?"

"No," he said stopping to face her. "It just occurred to me that I might have a solution to your problem," he whispered.

"That's very kind of you Mr. Vance but I don't think you can help me unless you can offer me some sort of employment."

"No, but I can offer something much better than employment Miss Gable." Beth sat up and David leaned forward. "I can offer you a permanent position with a generous monthly allowance, room and board at one of the wealthiest plantations in the state of Virginia and respect and privilege greater than that to which you were born."

Beth glanced over at him. He couldn't possibly be serious, she thought. "Mr. Vance, although I appreciate your kindness, I've already told you that I am not for sale. I will not be a kept woman."

David smiled. "That's not exactly what I mean."

"What did you mean?"

"Miss Gable, I am offering my hand in marriage. The position I'm offering you is that of Mrs. David Vance."

Beth laughed. He was obviously joking, she thought, but his eyes told a different story. As soon as their eyes met she could see the sincerity in his green eyes. "You can't be serious?"

"I've never been more serious in my life." Beth could not hide her shock but before she could answer David went on, "I don't expect you to make a decision this minute and I know you must have many questions. I promise that I will answer all of your questions or concerns. Why don't we both get a good night's sleep? We can talk about it in the morning."

"Talk in the morning?" Beth repeated. "You don't really expect me to sleep after such a proposal do you?"

"I apologize. Maybe a bit of explanation is in order."

"I should think so."

He hesitated only briefly before he sat opposite her again. "I am the eldest son of William and Gloria Vance. My family owns one of the largest tobacco plantations in the state of Virginia. Gloria is a sprawling plantation with a beautiful Georgian Mansion surrounded by picturesque rose gardens. I know that you will fall in love with it the moment you see it."

Beth couldn't help noticing how he beamed with pride as he spoke of his home. "Gloria, Gloria," she repeated the name as if testing the feel of it on her tongue. "It sounds wonderful Mr. Vance. What a peculiar name for a plantation though."

"Gloria was my mother's name. My father named the plantation for Gloria after her death."

"I'm sorry."

"Don't be. My mother died a long time ago. I was just a boy when she died. I hardly remember her."

"How long have you been away from home?" At that question David began to move uncomfortably and Beth knew that she had touched another emotional nerve. He didn't bother to answer but moved quickly to another subject.

"You are a very beautiful woman, Miss Gable. Had we met under different circumstances I'm sure that I would be obliged to court you in a proper fashion. You must admit that our meeting was under somewhat extraordinary circumstances. Even so," he said as he moved his head around to look into Beth's eyes. "Your beauty and breeding was not the least diminished by the peculiar state of affairs."

"That's very kind of you to say but if memory serves me right, your earlier remarks were less than admirable."

"Forgive me. I was merely caught up in the ambience of The Chateau Pleasure."

"I do not forgive easily Mr. Vance."

"I don't expect you to understand this but I had a curiosity about you ever since Madam Renee told me that you had left the Chateau. It is somewhat odd that a woman of your background would accept a position at Madam Renee's Chateau and continue to keep her dignity in tact. You would rather be homeless and jobless than to sell your self-respect."

"Is that really so odd Mr. Vance?"

"Yes, I think it is. I thought that by finding you I could somehow pacify my curiosity but you continue to astound me."

"Could it be that your curiosity has been stimulated because I'm not willing to sleep with you?"

"Maybe or maybe it's because you are the most exquisite woman that I have ever met, even in a maid's uniform."

"That's hardly enough to justify a proposal of marriage."

"Haven't you ever heard of a marriage of convenience?"

"Is that your proposal Mr. Vance, a marriage of convenience?"

"Look," he moved closer taking both of Beth's trembling hands in his own. "I am obviously attracted to you and you find yourself in unpleasant circumstances. We could help each other."

"It is more than obvious that marriage to a wealthy planter would certainly improve my situation Mr. Vance, but I'm curious to know how you would benefit from such a marriage."

"I'd rather not go into the details at this point. Let us just say that it would be better for everyone concerned if I were to return home with a wife."

Beth pulled her hands away and got to her feet pulling the sheet tighter around her thin frame. "This doesn't make much sense to me Mr. Vance. Is there some clandestine motive for this proposal? I could be making the biggest mistake of my life, Mr. Vance."

"I promise you, I have no other motive. I know that I should explain more but there really isn't much more to explain. I want a wife and you need a husband. Marriages of convenience have been successful for many years. Sometimes the convenience is wealth or position and sometimes it's just to join two families just for the sake of business. It truly is a common thing."

"What if after a year we can't bear each other?"

"If we find that we are completely wrong for each other I will continue to provide for you for as long as you live or until you marry again."

"Well you are persuasive if nothing else."

"Does that mean you accept?"

"It only means that I promise to think about it."

David stood and moved closer to Beth. Before she knew it she was enveloped in his strong arms. She had spent the last few months of her life warding off the advances of men but this time she relaxed into the warmth of David's arms feeling comfort and security in his embrace. "I don't want to pressure you," he whispered against her head. "Take all the time you need. You are welcome to stay here for as long as you need to or until you've made a decision. I'm in no hurry."

"Thank you," Beth said. Her face nuzzled into the curve of his chest as his cologne tickled her nostrils. She was so close she could feel his chest heave up and then down with each breath. How wonderful it would be to always feel as safe as she felt at that moment.

Chapter 2

🍁

February 1832
Philadelphia, Pennsylvania

I must be dreaming, Beth thought. This can't be happening. She snuggled deeper into the warmth of David's bed. The sweet scent of his cologne still filled her nostrils as her head rested against his pillow. He was certainly right about one thing, she needed time to think. So much had happened over the past couple of months and especially the last couple of days that she hadn't had time to stop and figure it all out. Just when she had begun to settle into her new way of life everything was turned up side down again. She had been so angry when she realized that Madam Renee meant to hold her to their agreement and even angrier when she thought that Mr. Vance was intent on taking advantage of her misfortune. And now, completely out of nowhere came Mr. Vance's impromptu marriage proposal. Maybe I'm being too emotional about all of this, she thought. He did say that it would be a marriage of convenience. He doesn't even know me and I certainly don't know him. How could he even consider marrying a woman he hardly knows?

She glanced across the room at Mr. Vance, his long legs hanging over the edge of the lounge chair as he slept. His breathing was soft and even, peaceful. How long had it been since she had slept so peacefully, she wondered. It was so long ago that now she could hardly even remember.

When Beth finally did fall asleep her rest was far from peaceful. It was a fitful night and she woke several times during the night. Finally she just laid awake listening to the sounds of the winter morning. Falling temperatures had transformed the previous night's rain into snow, its crystals gently tapping at the window as it blanketed the city in white. Bare branches swayed back and forth as the wind lightly blew through the naked trees. She heard the occasional neighing of horses as they struggled to pull carriage wheels through the snow. At some point in the pre-dawn hours she fell asleep again. Every unpleasant event played out again and again in her dreams. She dreamed of Mr. Briscoe with his roaming hands that she'd had to slap away on more than one occasion. His wife's shrill voice yelling her demands as if Beth were deft and dumb, played in her mind like a tune that one just could not forget. She saw Madam Renee, her red lip rouge smeared above her lip line and the over powering perfume she used to cover the smell of stale cigars that seemed to cling to her.

Beth finally opened her eyes and stared at the ceiling. She smelled fresh coffee and realized that she was famished. She sat up and looked toward the lounge for Mr. Vance but he was nowhere to be found. She was alone and the room was very still and quiet. He must have gotten up and slipped away while she was still asleep.

A table had been set up in the middle of the room. Aware that he could return at any minute, Beth wrapped herself in the sheet again before she ventured to the table. A sumptuous breakfast of scrambled eggs, crisp bacon, flapjacks and maple syrup, strawberry preserves and coffee had been set on a white linen tablecloth on the small table in the middle of the suite. How very thoughtful of Mr. Vance, Beth thought as she sat down to eat.

After she had sufficiently satisfied her ravenous appetite, Beth went to the dressing screen to see if her clothes had been returned. Instead of the black gown that she had worn in her hasty escape from the Chateau, a very conservative gray wool suit hung from the top of the screen. On the chair she found new under garments, stockings and a pair of gray leather boots. Mr. Vance really means to take me to Virginia, she thought.

This was just too much. Her life had taken so many changes lately the thought of another made her wary. But maybe what Mr. Vance was offering was a final and lasting change, and why not? What have I to lose? I have no family, no money and no employment and I certainly could not hope to marry any better in my position, she thought. I have nothing to offer, no dowry, no family, nothing.

She was so deep in thought that she didn't hear Mr. Vance when he returned to the room. "Miss Gable," he called out.

"Yes Mr. Vance, I'm here behind the dressing screen. Am I to assume that this suit is a gift from you, sir?"

"Yes, but unfortunately it was not my plan that you should wear it today. It is a traveling suit. Until then I thought that you would be more comfortable in this." He handed a white gift box around the screen.

Beth took the box and opened it to find a velvet gown of emerald green with matching slippers and hair combs. "Mr. Vance, you are much too generous, especially since I have not decided if I should accept your proposal."

"My proposal has nothing to do with this gift. Need I remind you that the gown you wore last evening, even if it had not been ruined by the rain, was not exactly your style, wouldn't you agree?"

"You're very perceptive."

"I thought you would be more comfortable in something less revealing."

"Thank you. You are a very thoughtful man," she said as she

dressed quickly.

"I hope you slept well?"

"I did," Beth lied.

"Were you able to give my proposal any thought?"

"I could think of little else."

"Would you say that a celebration is in order?"

"Not just yet."

"We should talk."

"I agree." Beth appeared from around the dressing screen and David was momentarily stunned by her beauty. The green velvet gown was a perfect contrast to her shocking red hair which tumbled in huge spiral curls down her back. "I commend your taste in female attire, Mr. Vance. I can't imagine how you managed to get just the right size."

David could hardly take his eyes away from her. Even as a maid at Madam Renee's David could see that Beth was an attractive young woman but now she stood before him as a stunningly beautiful woman; a woman who could possibly be the remedy for the broken heart that had destroyed his life and drove him away from his home.

"More coffee, Miss Gable?"

"Thank you." Beth sat at the table across from David. "Tell me Mr. Vance, why would such an attractive gentleman need to hire a wife?"

He laughed out loud and his voice was a deep rumble. "I wouldn't exactly call it hiring a wife. It would be more accurate to say that I am proposing a marriage of convenience, your convenience as well as my own."

"Alright, why does a man like you not want a marriage born of love?"

"Love, Miss Gable, is an over-rated emotion. It is much like a drug. It can be helpful, sometimes even fulfilling, however, it has been my experience that those who are led by this emotion are eventually torn asunder by the addiction. The marriage I am seeking will be a mutually beneficial arrangement."

"That is a very cynical attitude I must say. Every young woman, including myself, hopes to one day experience an all consuming love that will sweep her off of her feet. Are you proposing that I forgo that dream for the security of an arranged marriage?"

"I never said that love was not a possibility. I am only saying that this marriage would have rewards for both of us. I am not opposed to love Miss Gable. I am just not so naïve as to think that it comes more than once in a life time."

"Oh I see. So you have been in love?"

"Yes."

"Is that why you want to return home with a wife?"

"Yes. I know that it may seem strange to you but I have certain obligations that must be fulfilled. I must go back to Virginia. I prefer to return with a wife."

"I don't mean to probe Mr. Vance but if I am to consent to this unorthodox proposal I must consider just what I'm getting myself into."

"Of course, I wouldn't have it any other way."

"So you are willing to be candid with me?"

"Yes, but this is a long and unpleasant story. Are you sure you want to hear it?"

"Quite."

David took a sip from his coffee cup and eyed Beth suspiciously. "As I've already told you, Gloria is one of the largest plantations in the state of Virginia."

"How long have you been away?" Beth noticed that David began to move uncomfortably and she knew that just talking about his home touched on something that was very painful for him.

"Almost ten years," he said as he rose from the table.

"That's quite a long time."

"Yes. It is. I left because I did not get on very well with my father."

"That doesn't seem so complicated."

"There is more. I understood from a very young age that I was not my father's favorite son and I had learned to live with that knowledge. My younger brother James always held a special place in the old man's heart. Maybe because James loved the plantation almost as much as my father did. I, on the other hand, had very little love and even less of a stomach for the inner workings of the plantation. That, of course, put a strain on an already tense relationship. The last straw was yet to come. I fell in love with a woman who did not meet with father's approval. Needless to say, he destroyed that relationship. There was a scandal and I thought it best to leave." He stopped and thought for a minute. "Let me correct that. I was ordered off the plantation by my father."

"Why go back now?"

"I vowed that I would not return as long as the old man lived. Six months ago my brother wrote that my father had passed. Gloria belongs to me now. My brother has been running the place but I think that it is time to go home."

"That doesn't explain why you feel that you must return with a wife."

"If I return as a single man there is the possibility that the scandal would surface all over again. I must be honest with you, Miss Gable. I don't think that I will ever fall in love again."

"So, you're offering me a loveless marriage?"

"Not exactly, the way I see it, you have already lost everything. I am offering to give you everything that you have lost and more. In return, you will bear my children and be my wife in every sense of the word."

"That is except love."

"It would be a marriage of convenience that does not preclude the possibility of love. It simply means that at the time of our uniting we are not in love. There is always the possibility that we may begin to love one another."

"But you just said that you doubted if you would ever fall in love again."

"And I believe that but sometimes two people who begin as friends will grow to love one another. It's a love born of friendship and thus it is uncomplicated by the emotional constrains that can turn love into something hurtful."

Beth was silent for several minutes as she considered his words. What did she have to lose? "And what of the other woman? If you are still in love with her how can I ever hope to make you happy?"

"That is a difficult question. It is hard for me to understand so I don't suppose I can ever make anyone else understand. I will always love her but I can never love her openly. You will make me happy just being my wife."

"Mr. Vance, I am not nearly as naïve as you presume. How can I ever hope to make you happy when you have quite honestly told me that you will always love another?"

"Yes, but why should it matter to you? I will be your husband and you will be my wife and as such you will acquire a very generous fortune. You will be mistress of a grand mansion with hundreds of servants that will cater to your every wish and you will be well cared for the remainder of your life. What more could you want?"

"It's just not what I expected, certainly not the love of fairytales. Most women dream of falling in love from the time they are just young girls."

"Life holds many surprises for us Miss Gable. Let's not forget that you are a beautiful woman. Any man would be proud to call you his wife. If there had not been some attraction from the very beginning I would not have spoken of you to Madam Renee."

"I suppose you're right of course. I have nothing to lose."

"Shall we plan a wedding?"

"Yes," Beth whispered slowly. "Yes!" she said louder and with more conviction, her own voice drowning any trepidation she felt.

He quickly rounded the table sweeping Beth into his arms. "Splendid!" he said before smothering her in a deep and passionate kiss.

"What's next?" she asked.

"Shopping!"

"You're not serious."

"I am. You will need an entire wardrobe befitting a woman about to marry into the Vance family and of course, you will need a set of luggage and a trunk to transport it all to Virginia. Oh, and let us not forget your trousseau and an appropriate ring. I will begin to make the appropriate arrangements right away. We should arrive in about two weeks and we will be married the first Saturday in March. Any objections?"

"Would it matter? You seem to have everything already planned. What would you have done had I rejected your proposal?"

"I never contemplated a rejection. I apologize. I promise that you will have complete control of the shopping."

"Thank you."

"I want our wedding to be the most exciting day of your life," he said as he pulled her to him again. Beth leaned into his embrace. With a finger beneath her chin, David tilted her head up to see her face. "You look tired."

"I must admit, Mr. Vance I am feeling a bit woozy. Things are moving so fast. Last night I escaped from a waterfront brothel in order to keep my self-respect, not to speak of my virginity, and twelve hours later I am betrothed to a wealthy plantation owner. My head is reeling from it all."

He leaned down and kissed Beth lightly on the lips. "First, I am no longer Mr. Vance to you. I am your fiancé David."

"You're quite right, David. I'll try to remember that."

"Why don't you lie down for a while? Would you like another cup of coffee?"

"I prefer tea, if it's no trouble."

"Tea it is. I'll have a fresh pot brewed right away."

As Beth went to lie down David walked to the window. In just a couple of hours the snow had begun to accumulate. The winds had increased and blew the light snow into drifts of 15 inches in some places. Travel by foot would be very difficult and by carriage almost impossible. He turned to Beth. "Unfortunately the weather will not permit a shopping trip today. Why don't you go back to bed? I'll order a pot of tea. You get some rest during the afternoon and we'll have dinner in the dining room this evening. Our shopping trip will begin first thing in the morning I promise."

The snow did not let up for the next five days and they were both confined to the hotel. David bought a few books to help past the time and they ate most of their meals in the dinning room. During his stay at the Pennsylvania David had become acquainted with most of the guest and many would stop by his table to greet him and the young woman in his company. David introduced Beth as his fiancé to each of the guests who greeted him and no one seemed to think it odd. She was received respectfully and wished well by everyone she met. She was quickly getting use to the idea of being David's fiancé.

Just as David promised, as soon as the weather permitted the shopping trip was underway. It took three full days of shopping but they returned to the hotel with more clothes than Beth had ever owned in her life and a set of engraved luggage to carry it all.

The shopping trip had exhausted them both. They decided to spend a quiet evening relaxing in front of the fire instead of the hustle and bustle of the hotel dinning room. Beth was happier than she had been in months. After spending an entire week in David's company she had begun to relax. She felt comfortable in his presence. She was, in fact, so comfortable that she didn't so much as flinch when he finally took her in his arms, covering her neck with sweet little kisses and finally finding her mouth he kissed her long and passionately. Beth welcomed him. She surrendered herself for the first time willingly and completely. David made gentle sweet love to her until she exploded with erotic passion that she hadn't known she possessed.

When it was over she lay in his arms free of guilt or shame but with a sense of finally being wanted. Maybe David would never love her as he had warned but she couldn't deny that he had made her feel more loved than ever in her life.

With a satin sheet wrapped around his waist with its end thrown over one shoulder, David looked the part of an ancient Greek god as he playfully fell to one knee at Beth's feet. "May I have the honor of your hand in marriage, Miss Gable?" he said.

Beth giggled. "You most certainly can, Mr. Vance," she said as she placed her hand in his.

David slid a ring on Beth's finger and when she looked down she lost her breath in a gasp. A one and a half carat round diamond ring set in white gold graced her tiny hand. She started to speak but David placed a finger to her lips.

"Don't say anything, Beth. This ring is a symbol of my promise that you will never regret your decision to become Mrs. David Vance." He kissed her lightly on the back of her hand and Beth swooned.

At that moment Beth knew that she was falling in love with David. She didn't know if that would spoil their arrangement but how could she stop herself. He was everything she had ever dreamed of in a man.

Chapter 3

*

February 1832
Pennsylvania to Virginia

The journey was long and tiresome but pleasant, none the less. Beth was full of questions. She wanted to know everything there was to know about the family that would become her own. David was usually eager to answer her questions but at times he seemed distracted. He often fell silent for long periods of time. Beth didn't mind those silent moments much. It gave her time to imagine the wedding that she would soon plan and the family of which she longed to be a part.

The buggy rocked back and forth over the frozen earth as David and Beth traveled through most of the day. Although warmly dressed and wrapped in heavy blankets Beth felt as if she were frozen right down to her bones. She was tired and hungry but kept her complaints to herself. She didn't want to do anything that might make David think twice about his proposal. Beth was relieved when David told her that they would reach the Maryland border before sunset.

They stopped at a small tavern in Hagerstown, Maryland where they dined and rented a room for the night. Beth watched her future husband as he downed several mugs of ale while he talked about his home. He told her about Gloria's vast lands, its holdings in the sale of tobacco and the people he remembered most. He reminisced about his brother James and their childhood and all the people that he had missed over the years. David seemed anxious to return home. Beth couldn't help wondering what would happen when the two brothers were finally reunited.

David said that they should reach the Chesapeake Bay ferry by mid-morning and Gloria before sunset. Beth was too excited to sleep and David hadn't seemed at all tired but he was asleep almost as soon as his head touched the pillow.

The journey continued at dawn. As they traveled south, once they had crossed the ferry, the icy roads slowly changed to gritty dirt that was kicked up by the horse's hooves and seemed to fly everywhere. The ride to the plantation was bumpy and dusty and by now Beth felt grimy. As they neared the plantation they turned down a long dirt road that was lined on both sides by large trees. Beth could see huge iron gates surrounding the property. Once inside the gates the dirt road ran into a red bricked path that led right up to the front door.

The mansion was beautiful. Huge white columns lined the portico and the forty room Georgian mansion sat atop a hill overlooking the beautiful James River. Although it was still winter the mansion was surrounded by gardens and orchards that in warmer weather would be beautifully tended. Flowering dogwood trees lined the brick road on each side for a couple of miles.

Just as the buggy came to a stop at the front door, a muscularly built young man galloped up on horseback. His skin was dark and his straight black hair hung over his brow. He had large almond shaped blue eyes and a square handsomely set chin. Beth knew that this must be James, David's younger brother. He skillfully swung his long legs over the saddle and rushed to open the door of the buggy.

"David, you old dog, I sure as hell hope you came home a damn sight smarter than you were when you left," James playfully greeted his older brother.

"Why look at you!" David said as he stepped down from the high step of the buggy. You look like an old Quaker with that beard. You even got a little taller." The two brothers embraced.

"Taller and a bit wiser, I hope. I was only eighteen years old when you decided you'd had enough of Gloria. I can't believe you're back!"

"Well, believe it, little brother. I'm back and I hope I never have to leave again."

David seemed to have forgotten Beth but she didn't mind. She was happy just watching the brothers' reacquaint themselves. But a moment later James noticed her. He stared in wonder. "I see my big brother has thoughtfully brought me a lovely gift," James said playfully as he tipped his hat and bowed deeply.

"Not this one," David said. "James, I would like to introduce you to Miss Elizabeth Gable, soon to become Mrs. David Vance. Beth, this handsome rogue is my brother, James."

James couldn't hide his surprise as his thick eyebrows arched in question. "Vance?" he whispered. "You mean to say that this beautiful young woman has agreed to marry you?"

"Brilliant! I always knew that you were a smart lad," David jested."

"I don't believe it."

"It's true," Beth said as she extended her hand. "I'm very happy to make your acquaintance James. David has told me so much about you that I feel as if we've known each other all of our lives." She didn't bother to tell him that most of what she knew of him was learned only in the past week.

"I don't wish to appear rude but my brother has told me nothing about you." Turning his attention to his brother he said, "You haven't written in quite a while Dave. I'm sure I would have remembered this bit of information."

"You're right, of course, but you know how compulsive I can be." David offered no other explanation.

"Welcome to your new home, Miss Gable. Gloria has been waiting for a mistress as lovely as you."

"Thank you. That's very kind of you James." He took Beth's hand and helped her from the buggy. With her hand tucked beneath his strong arm, he led the way into the house with David following behind.

The beauty of the outside of the mansion was nothing compared to the splendor that was found just beyond the large oak doors. The floor of the foyer was marble and double stained glass doors opened into a large parlor. Along the walls of the entry hall were several doors and between each hung a portrait of a deceased member of the Vance family. Beth immediately noticed the resemblance between William Vance and David. Both men were strong with sharp features and square chins. David had also inherited his father's emerald eyes. Although the two men were identical in features their coloring was different and their characters were somehow reflected in the lines of their faces. William Vance appeared hard and unyielding. His jaw was set, his mouth unsmiling and his eyes stared sternly. He had the look of an angry man. He showed nothing of the gentleness of the man to which Beth would soon be married.

David pointed out the portrait of his mother. There was no doubt that Gloria Vance had been a lovely woman. Her skin was very fair and her white neck stretched upward as she held her head high and proud but her face was strained. She had large almond shaped innocent blue eyes much like her younger son James. However, in Gloria's eyes Beth saw something very different. Her smile was void of warmth and her eyes appeared fearful. As Beth stared at the portraits of the Vance family she was suddenly chilled as if a cold wind had blown through the mansion. She shivered slightly. "My mother was a very proud and beautiful woman," David said.

"Yes. I can see that she was very lovely," Beth agreed. "I think your brother favors your mother."

"Lillian! Edward!" James yelled. "You must both be very tired from your trip," He said. "I'll have your trunks brought up to your rooms right away. You can rest up a bit before dinner."

A short balding black man with a round belly came running through one of the doors at the end of the entry hall. "Yes sa, massa James."

"Edward, this is my brother David and his fiancée Miss Gable."

"Yes sa, massa James. I remember massa David."

The thought of slaves on the Vance plantation had never occurred to Beth. Of course she knew that slave holding was popular in the south but in Philadelphia, Africans were more often free men and women. Of course there were some Philadelphia families who owned slaves but it was never looked upon favorably. Beth couldn't remember how many times she'd heard the minister of the First Presbyterian Church speak about how sinful he thought the entire idea of owning people no matter what their race. Now here she was, standing in the entry hall of the most beautiful house she'd ever seen and it occurred to her that she would now be a willing participant in the practice of slavery and she shuttered at the thought.

Beth noticed that Edward never looked directly at James or David when he spoke. He kept his eyes averted, often staring at the floor.

"How are you, Edward?" David asked.

"Just fine sa. I's doing just fine." Edward said as he bowed once and then hung his head as if in shame.

"Edward, please have these trunks taken up to the rooms on

the west side of the house."

"Yes sa," Edward said before he hurried off to do his master's bidding.

"Lillian!" James yelled again.

The same door opened at the end of the corridor behind the main staircase. The most beautiful black woman Beth had ever seen emerged. She was tall and slender; her bronze skin was unblemished and perfectly accentuated by large brown eyes and full lips. Her cheek bones were high and her dark eyes were shaded by long thick dark lashes. The woman couldn't have been more than twenty-five, Beth guessed. "Yes, massa James."

Unlike Edward, Lillian looked directly at James as she spoke. Her manner and tone were almost defiant.

"Lillian, this is Miss Elizabeth Gable, David's fiancée. I would like you to help her get settled in. Miss Gable comes without her own lady's maid so I leave it up to you to choose someone as soon as possible." Beth wondered why James felt the need to emphasize the word fiancée but, of course she said nothing.

Lillian nodded her head first to David and then to Beth. Her face was expressionless. "Yes sa," she answered evenly. Then turning to Beth she said, "This way, Ma'am."

As Beth followed Lillian up the grand staircase she could hear David's voice as it echoed from the entry hall, "James, have Edward put my trunks in my old room."

"Are you sure about that, David?" James whispered.

"Yes. Don't worry James. It'll be alright."

Beth's heart pounded as a flood of questions whirled in her head but she continued to follow Lillian up the stairs as if she had not heard David's strange request. Of course he would want his own room, at least until they were married, she reasoned. But why had he told her that he'd wired James about their arrival when James seemed not to have expected them at all?

Beth was directed to a large suite of rooms on the second floor. Lillian unlocked the door and handed Beth the key. The first room was a small parlor which was beautifully decorated with high back chairs with dark green velvet cushions and drapes. One of the chairs sat beside a small table and another at a small desk. There was a small sofa and two other chairs. Beyond the parlor door was an enormous bedroom with a four poster canopy bed, draped with sheer curtains. There was a matching vanity, chest and wardrobe.

When Beth returned to the small parlor where Lillian stood waiting, she noticed a small ornamented brass bell on the reading table. She picked up the bell and looked to Lillian.

"The bell is for calling your girl, Ma'am."

"My girl?"

"Yes Ma'am. The master says that you should have a lady's maid. She will sleep in the small room at the other side of your bedroom so as to be near when you need her. All you need do is ring the bell, Ma'am."

"I see," Beth said.

"Your trunks will be up soon along with fresh water for your bath. I will return shortly with your lady's maid. Is there anything else I can do for you Ma'am?"

"No thank you Lillian."

When Lillian finally left Beth alone she stood in the middle of the room not believing that this beautiful room was her very own. She could hardly believe her good fortune. She was to be married to a very rich man and become mistress of one of the largest plantations in the south. Why would a man with so much to offer seek a marriage of convenience? It was a thought that ran through her mine a hundred times since she agreed to the marriage. There must be plenty of eligible southern bells scheming to make just such a match. David could probably have any woman he wanted, why had he chosen her, she wondered. Would he have even considered her if she had complied with the arrangement she'd made with Madam Renee'? Probably not, she decided.

She slowly walked through the rooms of her suite, lightly running her fingers along the polished wood of the furniture as she wondered again why David had chosen her. The answer to that question would remain a mystery and Beth would never stop questioning David's motive.

A soft knock at the door startled her. Beth opened the door to find a skinny little black girl who stood looking at her bare feet. She did a quick clumsy curtsey. "I'm Denny, Ma'am, your lady's maid."

Beth smiled, surprised that the girl was so small. "How old are you Denny?"

"Don't really know Ma'am. Bell, she 's the cook, she says I'm almost eleven."

"Why you're just a baby."

"Beg your pardon Ma'am, I am not a baby. I helps with the cooking and sometimes the laundry and Bell says I gets bigger every day."

"Alright," Beth said slowly. "If you say so, I guess you're old enough."

"I came to tell you that your bath water is being brought up now, Ma'am. I be right back. I'm going to get some clean towels for you right away." She curtsied again and hurried off down the corridor.

*D*avid followed his brother into the library. "How about a drink?" James asked. David nodded in agreement. James poured two glasses of brandy and handed one to his older brother. David stared at the golden liquid for several seconds before he took one gingerly sip. It was the first drink of brandy he'd taken since he met Beth back at Madam Renee's.

"I'm glad you decided to come home. It's been a long time."

"Didn't you know that I would eventually come back?"

"Yes, of course, but you didn't come back when I wrote you that Big Bill was ill and probably on his death bed. You couldn't even pull yourself together to come home for the funeral." James words were forced through clenched teeth as he struggled to keep his anger at bay. "And now, almost six months to the day of our father's burial, I get a telegram saying that you're coming home. Then you show up here with a fiancé that you didn't even bother to mention in your telegram."

David watched his brother vent his anger as he stood rigid with his hands balled into fists at his side. James looked as if he would strike his brother at any moment. "I'm sorry if you were hurt by my absence," David finally said. "You know that the old man told me not to come within twenty miles of Gloria as long as he was alive. I just couldn't bring myself to come home and mourn the man who had made my life so miserable."

"He was an old man David and all that happened years ago." James moved away from the mantle where he'd been leaning and sat behind the desk. "The years had changed him, David. He wasn't the same man. He'd been sick for such a long time that he had time to reflect on his life. He was too stubborn to ever admit it but I know that he was sorry for so many things he'd done over the years. But you, I'm learning, are as stubborn as the old man was. You couldn't even give him the chance to make amends. You were so busy with your own damaged ego that you couldn't even give your father a chance to redeem himself."

"Oh stop it James," David said as he took a step toward his brother. "This magnanimous air is unbecoming. Why are you still defending that man? Yes, he was our father but he was also the most evil and vile man that I've ever known. Mine wasn't the only life that he destroyed and you stand here and chastise me for depriving him the opportunity of repentance? That's nonsense and you know it. He was an evil man, James. When are you going to face that truth?"

David took several steps toward his brother and James pushed his chair behind him and stood up, his fist still clenched.

"I had to face the truth," David went on. "Ten years ago when I left here I faced the truth. Our father was an evil man who was drunk with his own power. His money gave him power and he used it for the sheer demented pleasure of destroying people. After the things he did to me, did you really expect me mourn him? I'm glad the bastard is dead! How's that little brother? Is it a bit too harsh on our father?"

James sank down onto the leather sofa. He drained his glass of brandy and poured another. "You've been away so long Dave," James said. His rage was suddenly gone. "I guess that I had forgotten everything that happened before you left." He looked up at his brother. "You're right of course. Father was an evil man, but David, he hadn't been that man in a very long time before he died. Sure he was cantankerous and set in his ways but it took him years and the loss of everyone he had ever loved to realize that he'd made some terrible mistakes in his life."

"It's not at all surprising to me that he would think of repentance when he found himself so close to death."

"He loved you David."

"He had ten years to tell me himself and he chose not to write one single word to me."

"Where would he have written you? We rarely knew where you were."

"That's a little naïve, even for you brother. Believe me, Big Bill Vance always knew where and how to find me." David poured another drink. "You know James, the first couple of years I really did expect him to ask me to come home. When he didn't, I became determined not to be the one to come crawling back. It would have given him great pleasure to have me begging for his forgiveness. Now, if he was such a changed man, why didn't he ask me to come home?"

"I can't answer that."

"Of course you can't. He's always had you fooled. You looked up to the bastard, didn't you?" David didn't wait for James to answer. "Sure you did. You still do."

"No David. You're wrong. I'm ashamed of most of the things father did, especially to you, but he was still our father. I will always respect him as my father."

"Look James, I don't want to argue with you, especially about Big Bill. You know how I feel now let us just leave it at that."

"Why do you keep saying Big Bill? You can't even call him father."

"I don't remember him ever treating me like a father should treat his son. Why should I call him father?"

"Alright! You've made your point," James conceded. Both men were quiet for a few moments. James still grieved for the father that he had loved and respected while David tried to bury his hatred along with the man. Finally James said, "Elizabeth Gable? Why did you bring her here?"

"I've already told you she's my fiancée. We intend to be married."

"I know it's been ten years David but do you really think you have overcome your past?"

"I'm not sure," David said. "The only thing that I am sure of is that if I came home alone I knew that I would be vulnerable."

"So you think that this girl is going to keep you safe?"

"I guess you could say that."

"Does she know?"

"In a manner of speaking, we agreed that marriage was the best thing for both of us but she doesn't really know why it's best for me."

"I really hope you know what you're doing."

A short time later Beth's trunks were delivered to her room. After taking a long soothing bath, Denny helped her to dress. Denny told her that Massa James and David were in the library so Beth hurried down to meet with them. On the ground floor she heard the angry voices of James and David coming from the library.

"She is a very beautiful girl David, but I just don't understand how you could bring her here."

"She's my fiancée for God's sake."

"Yes, you've made that clear but if you really cared for the girl you would have never brought her here."

"I know what you're saying James, but it's all over now. Please let it rest."

"I have no problem letting it rest David but what about you? I knew the moment you looked at Lillian that it wasn't over. Don't lie to yourself David."

Beth stood in the hall outside of the library. She didn't want to eavesdrop but since their argument seemed to be about her she was rooted where she stood. She wanted to know why she was the subject of such a heated discussion between the two brothers. Suddenly there was silence. She opened the door. James sat on the sofa and David stood by the mantle with a glass of brandy in his hand. By the look on his face Beth could tell that the drink he held had not been his first. Both men looked up when she entered the room. Tension hung in the air like a cloud of smoke and Beth was sorry that she'd come in when she did. "The house is so lovely, James. Do you think that I might see the rest of the house?" Beth stammered awkwardly.

"Why of course you can," he cut his eyes toward his brother. "This is your new home now. I'd be happy to show you around." James led Beth from the library and David's eyes never met Beth's.

James' tour began with the bed rooms, all furnished in rich cherry wood and upholstered in silk damask and brocade. Heavy damask drapes covered the windows and were tied back with gold braiding. There were four suites of rooms on the second floor including Beth's and six individual bedrooms on the third floor. There was also a fourth floor but James said that there wasn't much to see because it was an attic room used only for storage and the slaves of their guests.

The first floor parlor was richly paneled with two white silk sofas and an impressively decorated stone fireplace. Beth was in awe. Her own family home, Gable Manor, just outside of Philadelphia was considered well to do by most standards. But this was something entirely different. Beth had never seen a house so luxurious in her life.

"This is the most beautiful house I've ever seen," Beth said as she and James stood in the entry hall after their brief tour of the house.

"This is only the beginning," James said. "There is much more to Gloria than this house. I'd be happy to show you around the grounds tomorrow. Do you ride?"

"I haven't been on horseback since I was a child."

"Don't worry, you'll do fine. In fact, I think I have the perfect horse for you."

"Really?"

"Yes. Her name is Smoke and I guarantee that you'll fall madly in love with her the moment you see her."

Beth was surprised to hear the sound of a child's laughter coming from somewhere in the house. "I didn't know you had children, James?"

"I don't. That's Becka, Lillian's daughter. She plays in the house a lot. The house slave quarters are just at the end of this corridor." James pointed to one end of the hall and Beth's eyes followed. Both she and James watched as David slowly closed the door to the servant's quarters.

"David?" Beth's question was plainly written in her eyes. She looked from one brother to the other not really knowing why she should be suspicious. James turned and slowly walked into the parlor leaving Beth and David alone in the hall.

"I was just speaking to one of the slaves. I've been away so long, you know. I thought they may have forgotten me." He smiled.

"You were playing with that child. I heard you."

"You heard a child. So what. Gloria has many children. I don't quite understand what has upset you?"

"I'm not sure I know either. I just know that something feels very uncomfortable." Beth couldn't explain what she was feeling but she knew that something was terribly wrong. Something was being kept from her by the brothers but she had no clue what was really going on. Then she had the strangest feeling that she was being watched. She turned slowly looking around the entry hall. The faces of the deceased members of the Vance family stared down at her as if they also knew the secret. She told herself that she was being silly and then she smiled up at David. He bent and kissed her lightly on the forehead slipping his arm around her slender waist. She wanted so much to please him that she forced the uneasiness she was feeling to the back of her mind. She needed to believe that everything was just fine. Whatever it was, she would not let it interfere with their arrangement.

David had successfully silenced Beth's questions for the moment but as he stared down into her sweet face he was suddenly filled with guilt. James was right; he should never have brought her here. How could he have believed that he had gotten over Lillian? How foolish he was to believe that bringing a wife home could somehow dull the fire that burned in him every time he was even near Lillian. Beth didn't deserve this; she didn't deserve the life he knew she would have here at Gloria. In a matter of hours he had already aroused her suspicion. How sweet of her to put up such a brave front for his benefit. Feeling ashamed and guilty he took Beth's hand and led her into the dinning room.

A lovely dinner had been prepared. The two brothers talked of financial matters and the changes that had taken place on the plantation in David's absence. "What do you think of Jackson and his controversial tariff? It's been steadily escalating year after year. If it continues at this pace some of the smaller planters certainly won't survive," James said as he sipped his wine.

"I think its robbery, plain and simple. President Jackson has this affinity for what he calls the 'common man.' These tariffs of his were specifically designed to harm the affluent of our society. But, not to worry little brother, I don't really think it will affect Gloria directly. At this point the tariffs only apply to imported goods."

"Certainly you can't believe that, Dave. If this thing is accepted lightly it won't be long before tariffs are placed on exports as well and that will cripple the southern economy. South Carolina has declared the tariffs "null and void" and has threatened to secede from the Union if the government tires to collect from them. This could be the beginning of a trend, as I'm sure other southern states will follow suit."

"I agree. It's certainly a situation that bears watching over the next couple of years."

The brothers debated back and forth about business, economics and politics as if Beth weren't even in the same room. She ate quietly as she watched the two of them. A sudden eeriness crept up her spine and she had the feeling that she was being watched again.

"How's the newspaper business?" James wanted to know.

"I wouldn't know. I'd planned to buy a piece of land in Collins County Pennsylvania and set up another press but the deal fell through and I quickly lost interest."

"That's too bad."

"Not really. I've still got four active presses around the country and I'm sure as soon as I've settled in here, I'll get back to actively running them."

Lillian came in to refill the wine glasses and Beth accepted a third glass of sherry. She watched Lillian pour the wine with her slender hands and long fingers. The heat from the fire and all the candles made the air heavy and the room became hot and stuffy. Beth dabbed at the beads of perspiration that dotted her forehead and neck. When she looked up at Lillian she was surprised to see that the heat seemed to have had absolutely no effect on Lillian. She looked as fresh as if she'd just awakened. Her full round breasts protruded from the top of her dress as she bent from the waist to fill each glass.

Lillian didn't look anything like the slaves pictured in the newspapers and some of the books Beth had read. In fact, Lillian's smooth, unblemished dark skin glowed in the candle light and her full lips were puckered as if she would pout at any moment. Her hair was wrapped in a cloth but silky charcoal ringlets escaped its wrapping and hung around her face. Beth watched as Lillian seemed to glide around the room with an elegant sway to her ample hips. Beth stared and when their eyes finally met, Lillian stared back boldly.

"Is there something you be needin', Ma'am?"

"No," Beth said uncomfortably.

"You look a little tired," David said.

Beth had sat quietly and patiently waiting for the men's conversation to end but after several hours and a fourth glass of wine, she decided that David was right. She was indeed tired. "I hate to interrupt you," she said. "But if you'll excuse me I think I'd like to turn in for the night. It's been a very tiring day."

"Yes, of course," James said.

Both men rose from their seats to bid Beth a good night. She mistakenly assumed that David would follow her. When she realized that he had returned to his seat at the table she turned to look at him, her eyes questioning him until the moment became awkward. David understood the silent question.

"I'll be along shortly, dear. Sleep well," was all he said.

Beth nodded her head in affirmation and then hurried along to her room. She wasn't angry or even hurt, but she *was* confused. She had the feeling that it all had something to do with Lillian. From the moment she had entered the entry hall David seemed to withdraw. Was he having second thoughts about their convenient marriage, Beth wondered.

Almost as soon as she unlocked her door Denny came forward with her nightgown. Once in her nightgown and robe Beth sat at the dressing table to brush her long auburn hair. Denny immediately took the brush from her hand and began to happily brush her mistresses' hair.

"You has such beautifully hair Miss Beth," Denny said. "I never did see any body with hair the color of fire."

Beth was so deep in thought that she hadn't heard a word the girl said. She would soon to be mistress of this house and as such she would have the right to know the family secrets. Maybe she had-n't asked enough questions of David and his family before consenting to this ridiculous situation. Why was David keeping something from her? All these and many other questions ran through her mind as she sat at her vanity blankly staring at her reflection. Suddenly David's face appeared in the mirror above her reflection.

"Oh, David! I didn't hear you come in."

"That's because you were lost in thought. Pleasant thoughts, I hope."

"I was thinking about you."

"About me? Then they should have been very pleasant thoughts."

"Not exactly," she admitted. "Would you leave us alone, Denny?"

"Yes Ma'am," the girl curtsied and hurried from the room.

Beth swung around to face David. "I feel like we are all play-ing some kind of game David, though I'm not exactly sure where I fit into all of this play acting and secrets."

"What on earth are you talking about?"

"Why does that woman keep staring at me? Why were you and James arguing when I came into the library and why were you in the slave quarters earlier?"

"I told you that my brother and I did not get on well. He's still angry with me for leaving. You can understand that, can't you?"

"I know what you've told me David but I have a feeling that there is more, much more."

"Don't shout! If someone hears you we'll be the talk of the shacks before morning. I'm sure word has already gotten around that a new Mistress has come to Gloria. They'll all be waiting to get a look at you tomorrow." He put his hands on Beth's shoulders. "I think you've gotten yourself all worked up over nothing. First of all, let us not forget that we aren't the happy engaged couple that you have imagined. We have a deal, nothing more."

"Still, we are engaged to be married. Under the circumstances I'm not sure that you are conducting yourself properly."

"I apologize."

"I agreed to this arrangement because you said that love was possible. Well, I haven't forgotten my dreams of love. In fact, David the only reason I agreed at all to this outrageous arrangement was that I knew that I was foolishly falling in love with you and I was sure that I could make you love me just the same. Are you now telling me that love is impossible?"

David turned away and walked toward the window. "Don't be ridiculous Beth. I haven't lied to you. Yes, it's true. I did say that love was possible but I also told you that I didn't think I could ever love again."

"What are you trying to tell me David?" Beth rose and turned to face David. "Are you trying to tell me that you will never be able to love me, that I am doomed to live a loveless life?"

"No, I'm saying the same thing I told you back in Philadelphia. I cannot predict the future any more than you can Beth but at this moment I don't think that I will ever love anyone completely."

"If that is true and I have accepted that truth, then why must you keep things from me?"

"I'm not keeping anything from you. Remember Beth, love must grow. Let's just take one day at a time, give our feelings a chance to grow. Don't push. Besides, you know nothing of plantation life. There is a great deal of work to be done on a working plantation and I am still the owner of several newspapers. That means that I will more than likely keep very late hours. I took a separate suite of rooms first, because we are not yet married and second, because I would not want to disturb you even after we've married."

Everything David said was reasonable but Beth couldn't

shake the feeling that he was keeping something from her. Maybe she was over reacting but she would have to be satisfied with his explanations for now.

"You've had a pretty chaotic few days. I think its best that you rest. You have nothing to worry about now except settling into your new life. Don't rush things, Beth. There is a great deal to learn about a plantation but you've got plenty of time. Good night, sweetheart. Sleep well. James has a full day planned for you tomorrow."

After David left, Beth laid awake for hours. She was angry with herself for agreeing to this arrangement which she now thought was not such a good idea. She was also angry with David because he had somehow deceived her. She wasn't sure how but she knew that there was more to this family than David was willing to share with her. She had been foolish enough to believe that she could make him love her, but not here, not in this house. This house seemed to have a strange effect on David. She sensed a difference in him from the moment they arrived. His demeanor was not only different he seemed to have lessened in stature. Beth admitted to herself that the notion was just a little ridiculous but David did seem smaller.

Beth tossed and turned for hours before she decided that she needed another glass of wine to help her to sleep. Instead of ringing the little bell, she peeped into the small bedroom behind her own and found Denny fast asleep. She would just have to fetch her own wine she decided. The house was pitched in darkness and the only sound was her own feet as they paddled softly down the steps.

Suddenly the quiet was pierced by the squeaking hinge of a door being opened. A soft yellow light from a single candle streamed across the entry hall and Beth peeped over the banister to see David once again leaving the servants' quarters. He lingered in the door as he and Lillian stood close and spoke in whispered tones. Just as Beth was about to make her presence known she saw David slip his arm around Lillian's waist and pull her to him. Beth felt as if she had been struck and she fell back on the stairs as if the wind had been knocked from her lungs. Tears quickly filled her eyes and she had to cover her mouth to stop her sobs from being heard. David and Lillian locked in a passionate embrace did not notice Beth as she turned and climbed the steps back to her room.

Chapter 4

❦

March 1832
Richmond, Virginia

The entire household was whispering about the pretty lady with hair the color of fire. Everyone knew that Master David would come home once Big Bill passed on. He would surely come to claim his birthright. Although Master James was a far cry from the iron authority of Big Bill and was a welcome change for the slaves, most knew that James lacked the strength of will needed to run a plantation such as Gloria. The slaves prayed for the return of the young compassionate Master David. Many assumed that his return would restore some sense of order to the way things had been running since Big Bill had become ill. The two brothers would, of course, rule together. One with a mind for business and the other a mind of kindness for the people; or at least that was what they all hoped.

The time came when no one could have expected Master David. Even Master James, who knew his brother would return soon, was as surprised as everyone when his brother came home. But the greatest shock of all was the young beautiful woman who returned to Gloria with David.

Lillian had prayed night and day for David's return. Earlier that day when massa James called for her, she could hear the glee in his voice and knew that it could only mean that her David had returned. The sight of David standing in the entry hall, just as handsome as she remembered, took her breath away. She wanted to run right into his arms and smother him with kisses. Everything around her seemed to have come to a complete stop. The whole world seemed to have frozen for one moment. The faces of everyone around her seem to fade into the shadows as she gazed up at David. The moment she'd prayed for year after year had finally come and the only thing her mind would allow her to see was the return of her first love, David.

Yet, in only a second the moment dissolved as she caught sight of the woman. Her first thought was that this must be a distant relative or an old friend of the family but when massa James introduced the woman as David's fiancée, Lillian felt as if she would faint. She had been so happy to see David that she hadn't at first even noticed the woman. She stared at massa James hoping that she hadn't heard him right, but she had heard exactly what he'd said. David had brought home a woman that he intended to marry. How could he do this to me, she thought. Her head began to spin while a throbbing pain banged at her temples. Lillian felt as if she would die right there on the spot. How could he do this to me, she thought again as tears welled in her eyes.

I will not let them see me cry she told herself and as she had done so many times before, she immediately blinked back her tears and assumed an expression void of all emotion. With her back straight and her head held high she led Beth to her room.

As head housekeeper Lillian was often able to innocently overhear bits and pieces of the Vance's conversations. By the end of the day she knew that the lady's name was Elizabeth Gable and that she had come from the northern city of Philadelphia. Lillian also knew that the lady and massa David were planning to marry in a month's time. She knew that some of the other slaves that worked in the big house wanted to ask her how she felt about massa David taking a wife right under her nose but Bell was the only one who had the courage to actually voice the question.

Lillian and Bell sat on the steps outside the kitchen house as they often did in the evening. The house was quiet and most everyone else was already asleep. Lillian looked forward to the peaceful evenings that she and Bell and sometimes Nan would spend at the back of the kitchen house.

The evening was cool and the two women sipped warm milk as they talked. "Guess God done finally answered your prayers, ah?" Bell asked.

"Yeah," Lillian answered half-heartedly. "At least he's home."

"Sho is. Guess you done already met that woman he done brought back with him? Massa James says theys planning a wedding. That tells you something, don't it?

"You don't know what you're talking about old woman," Lillian said.

"What I know is that you had ten years to rid that white man from your heart but you still dreamin' bout something that ain't gone ever be."

"Bell, you don't understand."

"I don't, huh? Why you think he done brought that woman back with him?" Bell didn't wait for Lillian to answer. "I'll tell you why. Cause he ain't no boy no more girl. He ain't bout to make the same mistakes he made when he was a boy."

"What are you talking about?"

"You know exactly what I'm talking bout. I'm saying that he don't want no more trouble. He needs that white woman sos folks tongues won't start to wag all over again. He's a grown man now Lil. He can't afford to be so foolish."

"Even if that's so, it don't really make no difference."

Bell chuckled deep in her throat, a sound that said she really didn't find anything funny. "You really think that white man loves you, don't you?" Bell mocked.

"Why is that so hard to believe Bell?"

Bell laughed again. "I can hardly believe you is so stupid. He ain't got to love you girl, he owns you."

Lillian sprang to her feet to go into the house but Bell stopped her with a firm hand on her arm. She gently guided Lillian back down onto the step. "I'm gonna tell you something that I promised I would never speak of to any living soul." She took a sip of her milk and cleared her throat. "More than thirty some years ago I had this same talk with your Mama."

"You're lying Bell."

"Think so, huh? I told your Mama the same things when Big Bill came a buzzin round the slave quarters like a bee buzzin' round nectar. He was a young man then. He had broad shoulders and them green eyes that seemed to look right through to your soul. Your Ma and me was just kids then but it didn't make him no never mind. All that man saw was a pretty little black gal that belonged to him. He was massa and he could do whatever he fancied, and he fancied your Mama. He took her one day, kickin' and screamin' about a month after he brought her here. Took her up to the big house and kept her there for a while.

After a time Mamie got to thinking that she was better than the rest of us. She started prancing around with her nose stuck up in the air. Every now and again he'd bring some little trinket or a new dress and it all made Mamie just full of herself. She start to thinking that she'd won the old man's heart. She even thought she was better than his own wife cause, after all she was the one keeping him satisfied. Just like you, Mamie thought he loved her. His wife didn't like Mamie so she had to move from the house into one of the shacks. It didn't matter to Mamie though. She thought he loved her so much that he was gonna give her freedom papers. Huh!" Bell chuckled again. "Big Bill ain't never set nobody free. Mamie wasn't no more than a slave to him and as soon as he tired of her, he sent her right back to them tobacco fields."

"You're making this up as you go along," Lillian accused. "I know that you're lying because my mother hated Big Bill."

"Sure, by the time you came along she did hate him."

"Then why did she send me to him when I was just a girl?"

"Lillian, it ain't like she had a choice in the matter, but she knew about his lust. Mamie knew better than anybody that if you pleased him, it would keep you away from those tobacco fields at least until he tired of you."

"I don't believe you."

"Why would I lie?"

"I don't know." Lillian was thoughtful for a moment. "Do you think that Big Bill was my father?"

"No! Truth be told, he passed your Ma around so much there ain't no telling who your daddy is. Your Ma always thought your daddy was old Walker from the Cambridge plantation. If you didn't know better you'd think Walker was a white man himself."

Both women were silent for a few minutes. "I'm telling you these things for your own good, Lillian. You right about one thing. Your Ma hated Big Bill but when she was a girl she thought all that attention was love. Took some time but she learned that a white man's lust ain't got nothing to do with love. It'll do you good to learn that yourself."

Lillian got to her feet. She could no longer stand to hear another word of this nonsense. "Even if everything you say is true David is not Big Bill. He loves me now, he always has and he always will."

"Maybe he does. You wouldn't be the first slave a white man

has loved and you sure as hell won't be the last. But one thing is certain. You ain't gone ever be no more than a slave to him. You ain't gone ever be his woman and the sooner you realize that the better off you'll be."

Lillian brushed the dust from her faded dress and turned to go inside. "One of these days someone is gonna rip that tongue right out of your lying mouth old woman."

Bell chuckled again as she rose to follow Lillian into the house. On her feet and facing Lillian again she pinned her with a hateful stare. "That day is likely to be the same day that massa David takes a nigger for his wife." With that she pushed her heavy body pass Lillian and went into the house.

In her small room at the back of the house Lillian undressed in the dark and slipped into her nightgown. The sting of Bell's words still lingered like a dull ache at the back of her throat and her head ached from holding back her tears for most of the day. She wanted to strike back at Bell. After all, David had already proved his love for her when he abandoned his family for ten years so that no harm would come to her or Becka. Would he have sacrificed so much if he were not truly in love with her?

She had to admit, she was as surprised as everyone else when she heard that David intended to marry the fire headed white woman. Lillian was sure he had good reasons. In the end no one wanted another scandal. As she had tried to explain to Bell, none of it really mattered. She and David would go on loving each other just as they always had, even if he did take a wife. Why couldn't Bell see that? Why couldn't she understand that David would never stop loving her?"

Bell was just bitter, Lillian reasoned. After losing her own husband and son it pained Bell to see anyone else happy. Lillian remembered it well.

Bell's son Willie couldn't have been more than sixteen when

it happened. A young girl had run off from the Cambridge plantation after her Master sold off her Mama. Word spread from one plantation to the next like wild fire. No one on Gloria knew the young girl but everyone felt her pain. Most of them knew the pain of having a loved one just sold away and the grieving that was worst than losing someone to death. They understood the pain she felt at losing her Mama, the fear of being caught and the hatred she felt for those who without regard would tear our families apart, but they also knew what their own fate would be if anyone tried to help the girl. Little Willie was the only one who had the courage to help the girl.

Willie had come across the girl hiding in the woods. She was ragged and scared near out of her mind. Willie took pity on the girl and hid her in the barn on Gloria. For almost six days Willie stole food from the kitchen house to feed the girl. No one knew or even guessed where the girl hid until the day a posse of angry white men stopped at the Vance plantation to inquire if anyone had seen the girl. It seemed like every man in the country was searching for that girl.

Big Bill joined the posse. He even got the hounds out. Six hound dogs bought and raised for the sole purpose of catching runaway slaves. Once those hounds got your sent, you'd surely be caught before long.

The Overseer from the Cambridge plantation let the hounds sniff an old dress belonging to the runaway girl. As soon as the men mounted their horses the dogs started barking and pulling away from the men holding their leashes. When they were let go, the dogs headed straight for the barn. Willie heard the dogs barking and the men screaming but it was too late. He and the girl tried to slide around the backside of the barn and back into the woods but with the hounds on their heels, they didn't get far.

The girl was hauled off by the Cambridge's overseer but not before Big Bill had Willie strapped to the whipping tree in front of the big house and whipped him until his back looked like raw meat. Bell screamed and pleaded with Massa to stop but he pushed her away. His whip whistled through the air in forceful lashes that struck Willie's raw back over and over again. Bell screamed with every lash of the whip until every ounce of energy was sucked from her lungs and she fell to her knees in the dirt. Bell continued to plead but she had no more tears to cry and her voice was only an agonizing moan.

When word finally got to Henry, Bell's man and Willie's father, he came running all the way from the tobacco fields. Almost every slave on Gloria watched in horror as Willie was taken down from the whipping tree. His legs were too weak to hold him and he fell.

Henry couldn't believe what he saw. "What did he do?" he shouted. "What did he do to deserve this?" No one answered so Henry walked straight up to Massa. "What makes a man who has everything in the world be as mean as the devil himself?"

Big Bill just turned and walked away but Henry wouldn't let it rest. He followed behind Big Bill. "There ain't nothing that boy could of done to deserve this!" he shouted after Big Bill.

Everyone gasped. No one had ever spoken to Big Bill that way before. The old man stood on the front steps of the big house and scratched at his straggly beard. Henry turned to help the others carry his son to their shack. Big Bill didn't say a word. He just lifted his shotgun and shot Henry in the back of the head.

Willie never recovered from his injuries. In some places the lash of the whipped had torn the skin and flesh away right down to the bone. His wounds became infected and he died in his sleep about two weeks after the beating. Bell was never the same. She never took another husband or even accepted the advances of any other man. From that day forward Bell said that we weren't meant to be happy. "If God had wanted happiness for the black man, He wouldn't have let the white devil own us."

Looking back Lillian decided that Bell had good reason to be bitter and even more reason to distrust whites. But she knew that David was not like other white men. David was different.

Later that night David came to her as she knew he would "I missed you so much," she whispered. David slid his arm around her waist and pulled her to him. Lillian threw her arms around his neck and buried her face into his strong embrace. "I knew you would come to me." David kissed her hungrily. The lovers undressed each other as they stumbled to the small cot in the corner of the room. As she stood before him in the dim light of the single candle, her caramel colored skin glowing, David marveled at her beauty. She lay down and opened herself to him and David gave in to the call. Lillian welcomed him and he ravished her, losing himself in the reverie of the past. The spell was cast once again and David found himself intoxicated by her touch.

As soon as their lovemaking was over David began to dress. "You're not leaving?" Lillian questioned.

"I can't stay here all night, Lillian."

"Why not, why must you go?' Lillian got to her feet. "It's her, isn't it? You can't stay with me because of her?"

"She's my fiancée, Lillian. Do you have any idea what that means?"

"Of course I know but it don't really mean nothing. There ain't nothin that's gone ever stop me from loving you and you from loving me. Don't you know that?"

"No! It means that Miss Beth will soon be my wife and your mistress. I knew that I shouldn't have come here. She doesn't deserve this."

"What are you saying, David? You ain't gone come to me no more? Is that what you're saying?"

"God knows I shouldn't."

"But you will, just like always. You can't stay away from me.

any more that I could live if I didn't know that you would come back to me."

He opened the door to leave but Lillian was once again in his arms. God how he wished he could resist her. She kissed him again and he held her for a moment knowing that he would hate himself in the morning.

Part Two

Chains

"... Lord, thy God hath delivered them into thy hands,
and thou hast taken them captive ..."

Deuteronomy 21:10

G L O R I A
The Vance Plantation
Richmond, Virginia

*T*he plantation was alive with activity. Footsteps moved up and down the corridor outside Beth's room and she could hear the voices of the house staff as they went about their daily chores. The alluring aroma of country sausage, buttermilk biscuits and freshly brewed coffee filled the house. Had the family already gathered for breakfast while she slept the morning away? It was no wonder, seeing that she had laid awake most of the night and had only fallen off to sleep just before dawn. How could she have let such foolishness keep her awake? She had planned to rise early and meet with James for their tour of the plantation. Beth looked around the room, squinting against the sunlight that streamed through the windows.

She was grateful to find that Denny had taken care to leave fresh water for washing and clean towels on the wash stand. Without ringing for assistance, Beth dressed quickly hoping that the family was still gathered in the dining room for breakfast. When she reached the bottom of the stairs she heard the door to the servant's quarters open and she turned just in time to see it quickly shut again. The scene was an unwelcome reminder of what she had witnessed the night before. Could David have spent the night with Lillian, she wondered. Suddenly overwhelmed with suspicion she cautiously approached the door. Every muscle in her body throbbed with tension as she reached for the door handle.

"Ain't nobody there," a tiny voice said.

Startled, Beth whirled around to see a tiny little girl who couldn't have been more than nine or ten years old. Large hazel eyes filled her small round face. The girl huddled in a corner under the steps as she clutched a one arm rag doll. "Hello," Beth said trying to sound cheerful. "What's your name?"

"I'm Becka," the girl whispered. "Mama says that's short for Rebecca. But everyone just calls me Becka."

"Glad to meet you Becka."

"You the new mistress?"

"I will be. My name is Miss Beth."

The girl stood and did a clumsy curtsey. "I glad to meet you Miss Beth," she said with a pretend air of sophistication. "If you're lookin' for Mama, she's in the kitchen house with Bell."

"Oh, I see. Thank you Becka." Beth was again struck by the child's eyes. If she didn't know better she would have thought her a white child, especially with those eyes. But of course, she couldn't be a white child. Without warning the child scampered across the foyer and out the front door.

Unlike any house Beth had ever seen, Gloria's kitchen was separated for the main house. It was a small building just behind the main house. Beth opened the door at the back of the house and stepped out onto a small path that led directly to the kitchen door. As Beth approached she could hear the slaves inside talking and laughing as they worked. But as soon as she stepped over the threshold their conversation stopped. Three wide-eyed black faces stared blankly at each other but not one ventured to look directly at Beth. "Hello." Again Beth tried to sound cheerful but there was no re-

sponse. "My name is Miss Beth. I'm to be married to Master David."
Again the women just stared at each other.

At first Beth foolishly thought that the women didn't understand her. She had seen many Africans in Philadelphia but most were not slaves and she had never encountered anything remotely similar to these blank stares. The Africans in Philadelphia mostly lived north of the city. The only slaves Beth had ever seen were in picture books. In fact, Beth realized she hadn't ever really been this close to an African or a slave in her entire life.

Maybe she shouldn't be here. She was, after all, unfamiliar with the customs of the south and it could be that seeing a white woman where she didn't belong was the reason for the women's silence. Several nervous seconds passed and Beth decided that it might be better if she left the kitchen altogether. Then the largest of the three women came forward. "Morning ma'am. I'm Bell and this here is Nan. That gal over there is Rose. We're glad to meet ya, Ma'am." Each of the women nodded their heads in turn.

Beth sighed with relief. "Thank you, Bell. I'm happy to meet all of you." Beth said. "Are you the cook, Bell?"

"Yes Ma'am. Nan helps me and Rose just fills in anywhere in the house where there's a need."

"Then I guess that I'm to give you the day's menu each morning?"

"Oh, no ma'am! Beg your pardon ma'am but Lillian handles most everything in the big house." Bell seemed excited.

"Not any more Bell. But don't worry. I'll speak with Lillian."

"Yes Ma'am," Bell said.

"Right now I'd like to have a cup of that rich coffee you're brewing."

"Yes Ma'am, right away Ma'am."

Beth left the kitchen wondering why the mere mention of Lillian had agitated Bell so. Outside the kitchen house she saw that

James was riding up and as she stood waiting for him to dismount she noticed that the kitchen was once again buzzing with conversation. The voices of the three women filtered through the screened door.

"Lil ain't gone take kindly to Miss Beth taken charge around here," Bell said.

"Oh you right bout that, Bell. Lil done made herself think that she is mistress of that big old house," one of the other women said.

A third voice said, "I say it serves her right. Guess she can climb down off that high horse of hers now. It's time she learned that she ain't no better than the rest of us. No matter how many white men take her to their bed, she still just a slave."

"Hush your mouth child. You know we don't talk bout that. If Massa James hears what you say, you be whipped for sure," Bell scolded.

"Bell, you know as well as me that ain't nobody round here seen a whipping since Big Bill took sick. Massa James ain't got the stomach for such cruelty."

"I know that's right."

"Hush now, I said. Don't neither one of you know what's in that man's mind. Ain't nobody been whipped caused ain't nobody give him reason. But don't fool yourself, if Massa James sees fit, he'll whip you quick as look at you. He ain't as weak as you all think."

Beth was shocked but she said nothing.

"Good morning, Beth," James said as he swung down from the saddle. "I hope you slept well."

"I did, thank you. Maybe I slept a little too well. Seems I've gotten off to rather a late start. David tells me that you have quite a day planned for me."

"I certainly do. I thought you might like to see the grounds from horseback. If there is still time before supper, I'd like to introduce to you our neighbors, the Burtons."

"I'd be delighted. When do we start?"

"Right after you've had your breakfast."

The dining room was large and the table was long enough to comfortably accommodate twenty people or more. Lillian served the wonderful breakfast Bell had prepared. Beth couldn't take her eye away from this very regal black woman. There she was in her faded calico dress, her hair wrapped in a rag as she gracefully fluttered about the room as if she were a queen. Beth remembered the kiss she saw David and Lillian shared the night before. She also remembered the words of the other women in the kitchen house. It was apparent that this haughty black woman was David's unnamed lover and the reason for the family scandal. Maybe that was enough to explain the woman's coolness but Beth knew that there was more. David said that he'd been away from Gloria for ten years. Beth prayed that whatever intimacy David and Lillian shared by now it was no more than a sweet boyhood memory for David. Even as she prayed she knew that it was much more than a memory to Lillian.

The two woman's eyes rarely met and Beth felt rather than saw the woman's eyes as they bore into her very soul. What was it about this woman that was so intimidating, Beth wondered. She reminded herself that in a couple of weeks, after she and David were married she would actually own this person. The thought was so unnerving that she shivered a little. Better to draw the line of authority early rather than be mistaken for a mistress of little fortitude, she thought.

"Lillian," Beth said as Lillian poured her a second cup of coffee. "I spoke with Bell this morning." Lillian sat the coffee pot down and turned her icy gaze on Beth. "From now on I will give Bell the day's menu each morning. You need not worry yourself with that duty from now on."

"I beg you pardon, ma'am. I've been planning the meals for this family for quite a long time. There is no need for you to concern yourself with planning the meals."

"Oh, Lillian you misunderstand me. Planning meals is not something that worries me. It's not a chore, dear. As Master David's wife it will be my responsibility to plan the meals for my family. You see, I plan to be a very good wife to David and a good mistress of this grand house. I will take my wifely responsibilities very seriously." Beth stared back at the woman but Lillian did not speak nor drop her gaze. "I'm sure that additional changes in the running of this house will be forthcoming. However, that is the only change I have chosen to make at this time."

At that moment James entered the dining room and both women turned in his direction. A look of marked surprise creased James' face and Beth knew that he'd overheard her last words. "Beth, I didn't realized that you were so eager to assume the duties of mistress of Gloria."

Realizing that James was not about to dispute Beth, Lillian quietly left the room. "Oh yes. Gloria is the most beautifully house I've ever seen and I know that I'm going to love being its mistress."

"I'm sure that David will be please with your enthusiasm."

"I've dreamed of living in a house as grand as this my entire life. I can hardly believe my good fortune." James frowned. "Oh, I'm sure that you're not interested in my girlhood dreams," Beth went on. "I'm sorry. I didn't mean to go on."

"Don't apologize, I find your eagerness refreshing." James smiled. "David says that you're from Philadelphia?"

"Yes, actually I'm from a small town just outside of Philadelphia. Narberth, have you heard of it?"

"No, can't say that I have."

"I'm not surprised. It is a very small but lovely little town. I guess you could say that Philadelphia is as much my home as Narberth. My father owned a lumber company in the city."

"I'm afraid Virginia is a far cry from Pennsylvania. We southerners have our own unique way of living down here. There is much to learn about living on a plantation and I'm sure that the adjustments will sometimes seem overwhelming." James spoke with an air of nonchalance; his eyes were always stern and very serious. Beth felt as if he were giving her a warning of some sort. "I've taken the liberty of having one of the mares saddled and ready for you. We can begin our tour whenever you are ready Madam."

Beth excused herself and went to her room to change into an outfit more suited for riding. She hurried back to meet James at the back of the house.

They rode slowly, conversing in light conversation. "I admit to not knowing southern customs or having ever set foot on a plantation, however, I learn quickly and since my parent's death I've gotten use to making adjustments," Beth said.

James smiled as he wondered yet again how this innocent young woman came to be associated with his rogue of a brother.

Gloria was larger than Beth could have imagined. Behind the kitchen house was another small cabin which served as a pantry. The cabin was stocked with can goods, bags of flour and sugar, crates of candles, bolts of fabric, animal feed, nails and a variety of tools. To the left of the house was a small garden. The ground was paved in red brick with white wrought iron furniture; two chairs and a table and a larger table with four chairs. The garden was surrounded by rose bushes which James said would bloom into red, yellow and white roses in just a couple of months. The entire garden was surrounded by five foot high shrubbery. Beyond the garden, about four miles away from the main house, was a row of one room shacks made of white-washed flanked wood. "This is where Gloria's field slaves are housed," James explained. At the end of the row of shacks was a small white house which was occupied by the Overseer.

Gloria's land extended for miles. A long row of stables housed some of the finest horses in Virginia. In the other direction they came upon the fields which were bordered by three crudely built small enclosures which had only three walls and a roof. James said these were tobacco barns were the stalks were hung for drying. He went on to explain why, unlike most of the plantations in Virginia who grew cotton; The Vance's made their fortunate in tobacco. "Gloria didn't start out to be a tobacco plantation," James said. "My Great Grand Dad won the land in a poker game in Richmond. He had no idea how much land he'd won until the surveyors came out and marked the boundaries. He didn't even give the place a name. Of course it was little more than a farm then. The main house was a two story farm house and the only other structure was dilapidated barn."

"When did he decide to plant tobacco?"

"He didn't. He spent his life drinking and gambling until he finally drank himself to death. After my Grandfather starting running the place he planted the first tobacco crop and was impressed by the size of the harvest and the amount of profit the tobacco crop brought in at auctions. After that first year he planted a new crop every spring. When my Daddy brought my mother here we already owned a few slaves but as the crops got bigger he had to buy more slaves to work the land. Before long there were acres of tobacco crops and hundreds of slaves to keep them. My father had the original farm house torn down and replaced with the mansion. After my mother died my father named the place for her."

"Your father must have loved your mother very much?"

"I never knew my mother. She died when I was born."

"Oh, I'm sorry. It must have been difficult to grow up without ever knowing your mother."

"No, not especially, I had Bell. She used to be my mammy. It was much more difficult for David. He knew our mother and he missed her much more than I ever could."

"David told me that he and his father were estranged. Were you and your father very close?"

"No one has ever been close to my father." James suddenly wished to end the conversation and he dug his heels into the stallion's flesh spurring the horse into a gallop. Beth followed suit and galloped only a few paces behind James until they came to the top of a hill.

As they looked out over the tobacco field Beth could see hundreds of slaves. Even in the cool weather their backs glistened with sweat as they worked methodically in time with some unheard rhythm. None of the men spoke. Their picks went up and down mechanically. Most of the men wore rags tied around their heads to keep the sweat from running into their eyes. Beth was surprised to see that there was also a number of women who worked along side the men. Some of them had babies tied to their backs with large pieces of fabric. A large white man in a tattered old straw hat was the only white face among the hundreds of black faces. He was a broad man with an angry face and one jaw bulged with a wad of tobacco stuffed into it. He frequently spat a stream of brown liquid through a gap in the front of his yellow teeth. With a whip in one hand and a rifle in the other, he slowly paced the fields on horseback.

Beth watched as one of the slaves stuck his pick into the ground and stood. He pulled a dirty rag from his britches and began to mop the streams of sweat from his brow. He shook the rag, folded it neatly and began to tie it round his head. The Overseer yelled for him to get back to work.

"Yes sir," the man said as he continued to tie the rag around his head.

Just then Beth heard before she saw the Overseer's whip slice through the air snapping the man across the back. "I said get back to work you lazy nigger," he yelled.

The black man stood rigid, his arms down at his sides as he glared at the overseer with marked hatred. "I been swiggin' this here pick since before dawn," he turned his attention to James. "Mister TJ ain't even let no body stop for water, massa."

Before James could speak the overseer's whip whistled through the air a second time and came down across the man's back, slicing through the thin fabric of his shirt and leaving a blood stained stripe. "That's enough!" James yelled. "Is what this man says the truth?" he asked TJ.

"The nigger's lying. They're all liars. Ain't that right boy?" TJ snapped his whip again as a warning if the man did not answer correctly. "Now you tell Master James here the truth boy. You hear me?" TJ's voice was threatening but the black man would not be intimidated.

"Massa James, every man in this field can tell you sir, just how long we been working in this field this morning. We ain't stopped once sir."

"What's your name boy?" James asked.

"Moses, sir. Folks just call me Big Moe."

"How long have you been at Gloria, Moses?"

"Going on four years now, sir."

"Anyone here ever beat you Moses?"

"No sir."

"Then I guess I can't call you a trouble maker can I?"

"No sir."

James looked out over the fields. One by one each of the men stopped working, dropping their picks to the ground in wordless affirmation. James returned his attention to the Overseer. "Mr. TJ, you came to Gloria highly recommended, sir. However, I can't say that I approve of your methods. Did you know that Gloria hasn't had a run-away in almost fifteen years?"

"No I didn't."

"Why do you think that is, Mr. TJ?"

TJ spat a stream of brown liquid through his teeth and wiped at his mouth with the sleeve of his soiled shirt. "Don't know," he said.

"Well, one reason is that the whip is a last resort. Do you understand sir?"

"He's lying I tell you! They're all lying. You gone take a nigger's word over mine?" TJ yelled as he brought the whip down over the black man's back again. "You lying son of a bitch! I'll teach you." His whip sliced through the air again striking the man's back again and again, tearing the flesh in gleaming red stripes.

"Oh, my God," Beth whispered as she turned away from the ghastly sight. "Stop him James! He'll kill that man."

"TJ!" James yelled. "That is enough sir."

TJ ignored James and continued to whip Moses until he fell to the ground and rolled out of the way of the whip. James jumped down from his horse and ran toward TJ. In one swift move he grabbed TJ's foot from the stirrup, yanking him to the ground.

"You don't hear so well do you? I ordered you to stop that beating and you ignored me. If you ever willfully disobey my orders again you'll be off of Gloria land so fast you won't know what happened. Do you understand me?"

"Beg you pardon Mr. James but I've been dealing with niggers for over thirty years. I know how to get a full days work out of them. You just leave everything to old TJ."

"An injured slave can't work, TJ. It seems to me that you should have learned that at some point in your thirty years." James instructed two of the other slaves to help Mosses back to his cabin. "If that man is too hurt to work tomorrow you'll take his place in the fields."

"No offense, Mr. Vance but you're a young man with not too much experience. I know that if you let these niggers do as they please and you mark my words, one day you'll have real trouble on your hands. If your daddy were here he'd tell you that I'm right. Niggers have got to be trained."

James eyed the man thoughtfully. "Is that so, TJ? Well maybe you should pick-up your pay from the house in about an hour. When you were hired I assumed you to be a highly recommended Overseer. However, Gloria has no need of a trainer Mr. TJ. Your wages will be calculated promptly."

James and Beth rode back to the main house in silence. Beth had never seen a man beaten before. She had not wanted to look but something inside her would not let her keep her head turned away. The image of Moses sprawled on the ground with his flesh being torn from his body would be forever seared into her conscious. Beth wanted to speak with James about the incident but she didn't know where to begin or what words could adequately express her outrage. She was not only horrified by what she saw but she could not understand why James had not intervened sooner. He seemed hesitant and more willing to hear TJ's explanations than the pleas of the man being beaten. She had glanced at James several times and saw that his face was void of expression as if the entire incident was a part of the normal way of things. He seemed not be affected by the incident one way or the other. He had appeared to be a gentle man but how could anyone be witness to such cruelty without so much as a flinch?

As they neared the house Edward came out to take the horses to their stables. "James," Beth said. "Did you fire that man because of me?"

"No," he said a bit surprised. "As I said, Gloria doesn't need the likes of TJ. I'm sorry you had to witness that but try not to let it bother you too much. You'll get use to the way we do things down here soon enough."

"I don't think I will. I'm not sure I will ever be use to seeing people treated so cruelly. I really had no idea." Beth vowed that she would never go anywhere near the tobacco fields again.

James was right when he said that there was much to learn. It was almost like being a visitor to a foreign country. The news papers and books that Beth read as a child in Philadelphia portrayed slaves as happy little pick-a-ninnies. In school and church she was taught that the Africans were savages. The good Christian people of the Americas and Europe brought them out of their primitive tribes and jungles to a land of hope and prosperity. The work was for their idle minds and in return for their labor they were clothed, housed and fed and most of all they were given the true Christian God to worship and obey. Beth never had reason to question the things that were commonly believed until now. What she saw on Gloria was something very different.

Every human need and desire was provided by the slaves. The entire house was run by ten house slaves. Lillian was the head housekeeper. Besides Denny, who was Beth's private maid, there was Edna, Winnie and Polly. Each of the women was assigned a section of the house that they were responsible for cleaning daily. Edward was James' valet and an older black man named Jeremiah was David's valet. Bell and Nan were responsible for cooking and serving and Rose did the laundry. There was even a small boy used to warm the feet of Big Bill before he passed on. Since neither James nor David required a foot warmer the boy was used to run errands and help out wherever he was needed.

Most of the salves were allowed off-time on Fridays after supper was served. Only two of the women would remain in the house to see to the family's needs while the others were allowed to go to what they called the valley.

The valley was a clearing about a half a mile from the slave quarters. The women who worked in the house were allowed to take any left-over food from the kitchen house. Some of the women who worked in the fields would also cook and bring food. The sounds of their laughter and singing floated up to the house. They sang to God and of God. Loud, mournful spirituals that sometimes brought tears to your eyes could be heard for miles. Their laughter was without inhibitions, raucous and infectious as if they were somehow able to pass on a spirit of joy from one to another. Beth wondered how, in their lives of cruelty and servitude, could they find anything to laugh and sing about.

Beth spent the rest of the afternoon reading in her room until Denny came to announce the evening meal. Dinner was pleasant even though James and David once again talked of only business. Beth was anxious to see David alone. She wanted to tell him of the incident with the overseer in the fields, but when dinner was over, the men retired to the study for more business talk and cigar smoking. Feeling a little rejected by the brothers Beth went to her room to wait for David. It was near dawn and Beth had already gone to bed when David finally came to her room. He reeked of brandy and cigar smoke and Beth smelled him even before she opened her eyes. "David, you're drunk!" she said.

"So, I'm drunk. So what!" He stumbled over to the bed and dropped to his knees. "I'm a grown man Beth. I'll drink if I damn well please. Don't you start telling me what to do. You're not my wife yet!" Those were the last word he said before he passed out at the foot of Beth's bed.

She thought about calling for James or sending Denny for help but finally decided that it would be better if no one saw David in such a drunken state. She knew that David took a drink now and again but she never dreamed that he would ever consume enough liquor to become completely inebriated.

Beth climbed out of bed and undressed David before she struggled to push his heavy body onto her bed. She climbed in next to him but slept very little. David's breathing was heavy and labored and the sound of his loud snore echoed off from the walls. The room became suffocating and dank as the smell of brandy and old cigars filled the air. Beth didn't know what time she finally fell asleep or when David had left her bed. As soon as she opened her eyes she caught sight of a note on the bedside table.

"My Dearest Beth: I humbly apologize for my intoxication last evening and I sincerely hope that I was not in any way a burden to you. Do not fear, my love. The state of drunkenness in which I found myself last evening, is not one in which I indulge frequently. Again, I do apologize. Fondly, David."

David was sick with guilt. After the first night that he'd spent with Lillian he was grateful that he had thoughtfully had his trunks taken to his old room. He had gone to his own room that first night, but tossed and turned most of the night. No matter how hard he tried he just couldn't stop thinking about Lillian so he went to her. As he held her warm body close to his own she had awaken those old passions and desires that he'd kept hidden in the recesses of his heart and mind for the ten years he'd been away from Gloria.

The night he went to Beth's room he had wanted to go to Lillian again. Instead he chose to cool the all too familiar fires of lust with brandy. He told himself that he needed one drink to clear his head and then he would go to Beth as he knew he should. But one drink was hardly enough. He just couldn't seem to shake the image of Lillian. Her face haunted him both day and night. The feel of her slim body in his arms also haunted him and he took another drink hoping to push her from his mind. Still, his loins ached for Lillian. Finally, he sank to the floor of the study and snuggled close to his bottle of brandy for another drink, all the while hating himself for his own weakness; hating himself because once he and Lillian were under the same roof, he knew that this was the only way he could go to Beth.

It was just before dawn when he finally awoke and Beth still slept. He glanced down at Beth and was struck by how innocent she looked as she slept. Her dark eyelashes lay as perfect fans across her high cheek bones while her pink lips were pursed as if she expected to be kissed. She deserves much more than me, David thought as he lifted himself from the bed. He pulled the covers up over Beth before he hastily scrawled a note of apology then quietly leaving the room.

The rest of the house slept while David made his way to the stables. He chose a gray stallion and headed south toward the river. He found a spot where the river could not be easily seen from the road. The area was thick with foliage. David tied his horse to a tree then picked his way through the thicket to the river bank. He sat down with his back against a boulder and pitched pebbles into the river. He needed to get away from Gloria and this was a place all his own. He had come here as a boy when things at the plantation had become unbearable. He had come here ten years ago when he'd made his decision to leave Gloria.

David wanted to go to Beth and explain his feelings. But he knew that she would never understand just as his father had not understood. His father had said, "Listen David. I'm not telling you that you can't take the woman. On the contrary, take her whenever you please. Just be discreet, son. Lord knows I've had my share of nigger ass."

David had sat across form Big Bill in his study. "But it's not like that Father. I love Lillian. I want to be with her always."

"You can't love a nigger boy. It just ain't done."

"I know what you're saying Father but it's not the same with Lillian. She's different and I can't help how I feel about her."

"She's just a nigger boy. Now you just get rid of this sissy romantic nonsense. You can't ever be with a black woman <u>always</u>. That's the most ridiculous thing I've ever heard. No decent white woman will have you if you don't stop all this fuss over that nigger witch."

"Father, I'm going to be with Lillian whether you approve or not. I'm going to marry her even if we have to leave Gloria."

Big Bill roared with laughter. "There ain't a preacher in this world that would marry you to a nigger. Besides, it ain't legal. I think that nigger must be a witch. She sure as hell got you spooked. Maybe she put some kind of spell on you. You ain't thinking right boy. You just can't marry a nigger and that's all there is to it. Now I don't want to hear any more of this nonsense."

"Then I'll just have to be with her without marriage. We'll go somewhere else to live if we have to." No one had ever stood up to Big Bill but at that time David thought that he was in love with Lillian. He would do anything to be with her, even stand up to his father.

Big Bill stood up and walked around the desk to face his son. "Now I've had just about enough of this foolishness David. That woman is my property and you'll take her nowhere, do you understand? You had better understand or I swear I'll sell her off this land so fast you won't know what happened."

David remembered the conversation as if it had happened just moments ago. He knew that Big Bill met every word of what he said. He also knew that it would destroy him not to know where Lillian was or if she was safe. He forced himself into silence. But no matter how hard he tried he could not stay away from Lillian.

When Big Bill began to treat Lillian more harshly then the other house slaves, David felt responsible and was consumed with guilt and remorse but he could do no more than stand by and watch as his beloved Lillian was humiliated.

A tobacco buyer, Mr. J.P. Boroughs, had come from Boston to discuss business with Big Bill. Mr. Boroughs was a fat and balding man who had the nasty habit of spitting when he spoke. David was often included in his father's business meetings as Big Bill assumed that David would one day run the plantation. He wanted to prepare him for that time. David remembered the night Mr. Boroughs came to Gloria. After the evening meal had been served and the men retired to the study to talk business, Mr. Boroughs made it clear that although he was interested in a large portion of the Vance's tobacco harvest, he had other interests and desires that he expected to sweeten the deal.

After accepting Big Bill's offer to spend the night at the plantation Mr. Boroughs said, "I'm told that the nights in this part of Virginia can be quite chilling."

"And so they can Mr. Boroughs, and so they can," Big Bill agreed. David had no doubts about Mr. Boroughs other interest and he knew that his father would be more than willing to accommodate Mr. Boroughs other interest in order to seal their very profitable deal. "Might you be interested in someone to warm your bed on this cool evening, sir?"

"You are a very perceptive man Mr. Vance. Men such as ourselves should take some time away from business to enjoy some of the pleasures our world has to offer. Wouldn't you agree sir?"

"I do indeed, Mr. Boroughs." Big Bill rang his little silver bell and a few moments later one of the house slaves appeared at the door. Big bill spoke to the young girl in hushed tones and the girl quickly left the study. A few moments later Lillian appeared at the door. David nearly choked at seeing her and Mr. Boroughs could hardly contain himself.

"My, my, my," Mr. Boroughs spat.

"I trust you will feel no chill this evening sir," Big Bill said as he quickly stole a glance at his son. David was red faced and seething with anger.

"No. I'm sure I will be quite warmed," the fat man said smiling and licking his huge wet lips as he drooled at the sight of Lillian. Turning his attention to Big Bill again he said, "You know, Mr. Vance this has been quite a tiring day for me. A good deal does tend to tire one." Another glance at Lillian who waited in the doorway dressed in a long white dress. The collar of the dress had been torn away causing the dress to hang loosely from Lillian's shoulders revealing her smooth brown neck and stopping just short of her cleavage. Her hair was pulled back from her face, but streamed over one bare shoulder. "Although this evening has been most delightful, I beg you to forgive me if I retire early."

"Oh I do understand Mr. Boroughs and there is no forgiveness necessary. Lillian will show you to your room."

When Lillian left the room with Mr. Boroughs in tow David turned to face his father. "I won't ask you why or even how you could do this to me. I know now that you are an evil vile man. You'd stop at nothing to humiliate and destroy the lives of everyone around you."

"I'm not destroying you David. It's your infatuation for that nigger that's destroying you boy. I've told you before son, she's just a nigger and I own her. I'll do with her as I wish."

"Was she just a nigger when you took her to warm your own bed?"

"Why that is just the point, son," David watched as his father drained his glass of whiskey. His hatred rose in his throat like bile and David wanted more than anything to strike the old man. He took several steps toward his father, quickly closing the distance between them. As he came face to face with the father that he hated, he was suddenly engulfed with all the feelings of inadequacy that had been so much a part of his young life.

"You hate me, don't you father? You've always hated me. It's the part of me that is a reflection of yourself that you hate, isn't it?

Once again I've not been able to live up to the Vance name. I've shamed you again and you are determined to make me pay for not being the cold heartless brute that you are."

"You're talking nonsense boy. You're not quite the man that you think you are but one day you'll understand that I'm the one that knows what's best for you. This infatuation you have for Lillian can only hurt you in the long run, so stop it. Stop it now."

"No! You've hurt me and you've done it all of my life. Well no more! I'm leaving Gloria and I'm taking Lillian with me."

In an instant Big Bill grabbed his son by the throat. "Now you listen to me boy. You leave if that's your wish but that girl is my property. You try to take her away from here and I swear you won't make five miles and when I catch the two of you, you won't ever have to worry about seeing that little witch again."

Two days later David left Gloria without Lillian. Even after ten years he still wanted her more than he could have imagined. The first couple of years after he left Gloria he had desperately tried to erase her image from his memory. Lillian had haunted him day and night. He tried to lose her in his lust for other women but no woman could ever fill the void left by Lillian's absence. It took years before he finally felt that he could live a life without Lillian. And finally he had almost forgotten what she looked like. But seeing her again had brought back a flood of memories and a burning lust for the only woman he had ever loved.

And then there was Beth. He knew he had given Beth the impression that he was, at the very least, attracted to her and he even dangled the possibility of a future love like some precious trinket. He knew now that he could never love Beth as he loved Lillian. Although it was hardly his intention, he had deceived Beth. He realized now that he should never have brought Beth to Gloria.

Chapter 6

GLORIA
The Vance Plantation
Richmond, Virginia

The wedding celebration was set for May 10, 1832. Beth rejected the idea of a large celebration with hundreds of guests. After all, she knew absolutely no one. She preferred a smaller, more intimate gathering of family, close friends and a few neighbors. The event would not only celebrate her marriage but also introduce her to the families of neighboring plantations. Beth spent countless hours with fabric swatches and seamstresses who came from as far away as New York. She went over her plans with both Lillian and Bell making sure that every detail was understood.

She and David took a trip to Richmond to meet and talk with the Reverend Fitzgerald Langston of the First Baptist Church of Richmond. The Reverend, a portly man with a rich baritone voice, seemed overjoyed that the Vance's eldest son was ready to take a bride. "I'm so glad to finally meet with you Miss Gable," he said as he led them into his office at the back of the church. "The first Sunday you attended our services I saw a long needed ray of sunshine glowing from the Vance pew. Right then I said to my wife, that young woman will bring happiness back to the Vance family. I could see it in your eyes. God sent, I said to Mrs. Langston. Only one of God's chosen could help that family rise out of the despair caused by such scandal. I've known young David here since the day he was born," the Reverend said. He hardly took a breath before going on, "Strong willed young man I must say, been that way his entire life. Oh, but I am delighted that he's chosen to take a bride, especially such a beautiful young woman."

Mrs. Langston, although not as enthusiastic as her husband, nodded her head several times in agreement. "Marriage is a wonderful gift from God dear. We must not take such gifts lightly."

"Yes, yes," the Reverend went on. "Marriage is just the thing to smooth out the ruff edges of a high spirited young man."

The meeting took longer than either Beth or David anticipated as the good Reverend went on and on about David and James as young boys. In the end, Reverend Langston agreed to perform the ceremony and Beth and David were on their way back to Gloria by sundown.

The next couple of months passed peaceably. David made every effort to be more attentive toward Beth. In fact, Beth thought him even more charming than before they'd come to Virginia. He spent his days working on the plantation accounts or other business matters. Once supper was served he and James would spend an hour or so discussing business but David rarely took a drink. Beth was disappointed that David had insisted on keeping his own suite of rooms on the upper floor but he came to Beth most every evening. She had begun to think that she had worried needlessly.

When their wedding day finally arrived the entire house was in an uproar for several hours before the actually ceremony was to begin. The Reverend and Mrs. Langston arrived promptly at eleven in the morning but most of the other guests had already arrived.

Beth nervously paced back and forth in her small sitting room while frantically fanning herself. The room was stifling as the French doors that opened onto her balcony had been closed so that the breeze would not destroy her perfectly coifed hair. She'd been dressed and waiting for the ceremony to begin for over an hour. She had no idea what was taking so long and she couldn't help but wonder if David changed his mind and decided against making her his wife. Finally there was a frantic knock at the door. "It's time Miss Beth," Denny whispered in her small voice." Beth was so relieved that she bent down and placed a kiss on the girl's forehead. Denny smiled. "Come on," she pleaded taking Beth's gloved hand and pulling her from the room. "Everyone is waiting."

They had planned a very small wedding but as Beth entered the ballroom she was stunned by the amount of people in attendance. She was so happy that she could hardly concentrate on the words Reverend Langston spoke. She only knew that the ceremony was over when David removed her veil, swept her up into his arms and kissed her. The guests applauded in approval.

"I didn't realize that there would be so many people here. I know we didn't send as many invitations," she whispered to David.

With his lips close to Beth's ear David swung Beth into the center of the ballroom for the first waltz of the evening. "Not having an invitation would hardly stop people from coming to see for themselves if Big Bill's wayward son would actually take a wife," he whispered. "Smile, Darling. Let them see that I have made you the happiest woman in the world."

Beth didn't know what to make of David's comments. Was this all just a performance for the planters of Richmond? Of course it was. Hadn't he made that plain enough even before they left Philadelphia? What a fool I am, Beth thought.

As the reception progressed Beth was introduced to so many of Richmond's wealthiest planters and their families that she doubted if she would remember all of the names and faces. When the evening was over and the last carriage left Gloria, Beth was grateful to be alone with her new husband.

James kissed his new sister-in-law on her cheek and welcomed her to the family before he retired for the evening. David took his new wife into his arms and carried her up the grand staircase to Beth's room. For the first time since leaving Philadelphia David made love to Beth and she fell in love all over again. The dream had finally

The peace that had reigned over Gloria for the past couple of months would begin to slowly erode. James continued to run the plantation alone but not without great difficulty. There was much concern about an article that appeared in the Norfolk Herald on June 25, 1832. It was reported that the leader of a band of Desperadoes, a black man by the name of Bob Ferebee and a six year fugitive were captured along with several others. The band was known for their opposition to slavery and it was believed that they would help runaway slaves in their escape to freedom. Many of the outlaws were killed or captured. The news spread quickly among the slave population and the peace that had been taken for granted by the Virginia planters would begin to slowly change.

In light of this new tense atmosphere James was confident that his decision to fire TJ was a prudent one. It was just TJ's type of discipline that might provoke the slaves. James wasted no time in hiring a new overseer. The man was an Irishman named Thomas McCauley. He was a large man with square shoulders and a reddish face hidden behind a full beard. His face was hard and stern and his beard made him look like he was incapable of smiling. Still, Mr. McCauley came highly recommended and both David and James had approved his hiring.

Beth found plantation life difficult. She was amazed to learn that the violent injustice that she often witnessed on Gloria was commonplace in the south. Young boys were sometimes stripped of their ragged clothing and whipped by the new overseer or their own parents if they were caught neglecting their chores. Bell explained to Beth that the parents would sometimes whip their own children because they knew that the overseer's whipping would be far more violent.

Beth was sickened even more the first time she witnessed a family's separation. James decided that the eldest of three brothers was to be sold. He was a fifteen year old boy named Jesse, and a known trouble maker. He'd been caught hiding to get out of working on many occasions. Now it was also rumored that he'd been talking of rebellion, something that would not be tolerated on any plantation. Jesse's younger brothers were seven and five. Jesse's mother, Mary, with her younger sons at her skirt begged James not to sell her son. "Please massa James. Jesse maybe lazy but he's a good boy, sir. He's gone grow into a fine healthy man for you sir. Please don't sell my boy."

James ignored the woman and Jesse was loaded on the back of a wagon with his hands and ankles shackled. His mother wailed as she and her younger sons ran after the wagon. Finally, strangling on her own tears and the dirt that sputtered from the wagon's wheels she fell to the ground smothering her sobs in the dry earth. Beth turned away in disgust.

As the months moved into summer and the afternoon heat rose to sweltering, the slaves became despondent and sluggish in their service and both James and David seemed to have little patience. Everyone seemed to be on edge and there was to be no relief in sight. Occasionally, a slave would try to run away hoping to reach freedom in the northern states. In most cases before they could get more than a few miles away from Gloria they were caught and brought back shackled to the back of a wagon like animals.

There was a big tree in the front of the main house. The slaves called it the whipping tree. Any indiscretion meant being tied to the tree and whipped until their backs were raw and their spirits broken. Everyone on the plantation was forced to witness these atrocities. The beatings not only punished the run-away slave but were also vivid warnings against disobedience of any kind.

Each time Beth was forced to witness some injustice she had come away feeling that her own hands had been soiled with blood. She was told by both James and David that the running of the plantation was not her concern and she had tried not to interfere.

Her promise not to interfere would be broken late one evening when she decided to take a walk around the garden. The sun was just beginning to descend behind the hills. A cool breeze rustled through the trees as Beth stood at the edge of the garden. Her gaze traveled down the line of slave shacks that housed the field slaves. Suddenly the peace was shattered by a loud scream that came from the direction of the slave shacks. Beth stood frozen. She expected to hear James or David leave the house to investigate. Surely, James must have heard that scream, she thought. When Beth left the house he was working in his study with the terrace doors wide open. One scream after another came but no one came to investigate. Where was James? Beth ran into the house. First she went to the study. James wasn't there but her attention was drawn to the gun cabinet with its display of fire arms. She tried the door but it was locked. A key, she thought. There must be a key around her somewhere. Then there was another long and piercing scream. Beth ran to the desk and search in each of the drawers but there was no key. She considered breaking the glass but when she turned back to the gun cabinet she noticed a tiny gold key hanging from a string on the wall. Beth quickly opened the cabinet and took out a rifle. In her entire life she had never handled a gun before and she didn't even know if it was loaded. She lifted her skirts with one hand and clutched the rifle in the other as she ran toward McCauley's cabin where it seemed the screams were coming from.

As she reached the clearing outside of the garden she could see that McCauley was caring one of the female slaves under his arm. The girl kicked and screamed, frantically pulling at the strong arms that held her captive. McCauley kicked open his cabin door and after going inside he kicked it shut again. Beth ran to the cabin and pushed the door open. Standing very still in the doorway she took in every detail of the inside of the cabin. Little Maggie, not more than ten years old Beth guessed, was laying on the bed with her clothing torn from her small body. Her hands were tied together and looped over one of the bed post. The hairless body of a child lay exposed while McCauley was perched on one knee ready to mount her. He swung around at the sound of the door opening. Beth was standing in the open doorway with a rifle aimed at his head.

"Get away from her," Beth whispered in an unusually deep voice. "You get away from that child or I swear I'll drop you right where you are."

"No call for alarm Miss Beth," McCauley said with a smirk. "I'm just doing me duty Miss."

"Your duty? I won't pretend to know what you're talking about and I don't care. Just move away from her now."

McCauley stood his britches still down around his knees exposing himself shamelessly. "Didn't your husband tell you how things is down here? These here nigger bitches got to be broken in by a white man first. It's our duty."

"I won't say it again McCauley," Beth said while keeping her eyes on his red face. All the shock, abhorrence and disgust that she'd

F. HAYWOOD GLENN

felt at the treatment of the slaves seemed to impregnate her barley audible voice. "You're fired McCauley. I want you off of Gloria land now."

"I'm fired?" McCauley seemed stunned as he reached down and pulled his trousers up. "For fuckin' a nigger? Your husband and Mister James ain't gone like that ma'am. It ain't no harm in this. Even your own husband's been fuckin' a nigger for years and it ain't no secret."

McCauley's words hurt as if her heart had been pierced, but Beth was so angry and appalled at the scene before her, that she chose to ignore those biting words. She moved closer to McCauley, hoping that he would realize that his life was now in danger. "Mr. McCauley," she whispered as she leveled the barrel of the shotgun between his eyes. "I don't want to kill you but I will blow you straight to hell if you don't get out of here this minute." McCauley seemed to suddenly realize that Beth was not simply trying to scare him. She actually wanted a reason to shoot him. He took a step back and adjusted his clothing before he grabbed a bag and pushed passed Beth out of the cabin. As soon as he left, Beth dropped the gun and went to Maggie who was huddled up against the headboard of the bed with her hands still attached to the post. Beth untied her hands and the girl fell into her arms in sobs. Beth cradled the girl in her arms trying to sooth her.

She took Maggie back to her own cabin where her tearful mother waited. Then she headed for the big house. She wanted to find out why no one cared enough about the screaming child to even see what was happening.

James was back at his desk in the study going over the accounts. He lifted his head to see Beth standing in the doorway. She was as white as a sheet with a rifle tucked under her arm. "Beth," James said in surprise. "What on earth . . .?"

"You heard those screams James," she cut in. "I know you

heard. Why didn't you come?"

James closed the distance between them with a few long strides. He took the rifle from Beth's hands and led her to the sofa. "What in God's name are you doing with this rifle?"

"Why didn't you come, James?"

"Because I knew that it was just McCauley having his way with one of the women."

"She wasn't a woman James. She was a child and McCauley wasn't just having his way. He was going to rape that child."

"Rape?"

"Yes, James. McCauley was going to rape the child."

"Beth, I've tried to explain to you that things are just different here. I'm sure McCauley had no intention of hurting the girl. Besides, they have to learn sooner or later don't they?"

"I can't believe what you're saying. Do you really believe that?"

"Sure. Why wouldn't I believe?"

"Because I thought you were an educated man James. These people have reproduced for generations before they were brought to these shores. It's absurd to believe that any people have to be taught to procreate."

"Alright, alright! Just calm down. I know that you're right of course but that's just the way things are done down here. It's been this way for years."

"James, that child couldn't have been more than ten years old. Doesn't that mean anything to you?" Beth was sobbing now. "What kind of people are you?"

"Beth you are butting in where you don't belong again. As I've already told you these things do not concern you. Pull yourself together and just forget whatever it was that you saw. You shouldn't get so worked up over nothing. Just forget about it."

"I can't do that James and neither can you." Beth backed

away from James as if she had seen an apparition. "I fired McCauley."

"You did what? You can't do that." James was angry now. "You have no right!"

"Maybe I don't but James, I've tried to pretend that I don't see the horrible things that go on here but I just can't do that anymore. I can't go through life with my eyes closed. I'm almost afraid to close my eyes because when I do I can still see the brutality in my nightmares. I just don't understand how you can have such little regard for the very people whose sweat and hard work have made you and every other southern gentleman rich and comfortable. I simply cannot understand it."

"Your understanding of the southern way of life is of little concern to me Beth. You have no right to fire anyone. Gloria belongs to me and my brother and I will not have you interfering in our affairs." James saw the tears well in Beth's eyes and she began to tremble as she cringed and moved away from him. James turned and slowly walked back to his desk. In a more composed and softer tone he said, "This is not Philadelphia Beth. You don't know these people. You haven't lived with them. What you see as cruelty is merely discipline and structure. Sometimes they can even be like animals."

"First TJ and then McCauley and sometimes even you act more like animals than any of the slaves I've seen. If you think that these people are like animals it's because you treat them as animals. Beast of burden, isn't that right James? How can you expect them to behave otherwise?" Beth turned and ran up the steps to her room.

The next day Beth breakfasted alone and early. She didn't want to have to face James after their disagreement the night before. After giving Lillian the day's menu she took a basket and a pair of shears and went into the garden to cut fresh flowers for the house. Midway across the front yard she saw Lottie, Maggie's mother. Lottie was screaming and crying as she ran toward the front of the house.

'Miss Beth, my Maggie is gone. She done run off in the night,"

Lottie screamed hysterically.

"Alright, Lottie. Don't worry. We'll find her. She couldn't have gotten very far. We'll find her, I promised," Beth said as she tried to calm Lottie.

"You don't understand Ma'am. If they find her they gonna whip her for sure."

Hearing the commotion, Nan and Bell came running from the kitchen house. Beth handed Lottie over to Bell and ran into the house. "James! David!" Beth screamed. She went to the study first and then to the library but she could not find neither James, David nor Lillian. She could still hear Lottie's screams from the front of the house. Beth stood in the foyer not knowing what she should do next. Then she heard voices coming from the servant's quarters. Surely Lillian would know where James and David had gone. Without another thought she ran to the door and flung it open. The room was dim, the only light coming from a small window near the ceiling. She tried to adjust her eyes to the darkness as she peered around the room. "David," the name was spoken softly but it was more of an affirmation than a question. Somehow she knew that her husband would be in this room as she was sure he had been here many times before. There was an odd odor in the room and Beth could hear someone breathing heavily. Her heart pounded as she moved further into the room. "David," she said again more loudly. The room was suddenly very still. Finally Beth was able to focus on the two bodies entangled on a corner cot. She took a step closer but the two bodies made no attempt to separate. "David!" she said again. This time she screamed his name as if a dagger had sliced through her heart. The two bodies slowly untangled themselves and David rolled away from Lillian and reached for his trousers. Lillian sat up unashamed and hugged her knees to her chest. A look of triumphant flashed across her pretty face. Beth wanted to run away but something kept her rooted where she stood.

Finally David said, "What are you doing here Beth?"

"How dare you ask me what I'm doing here? I certainly don't need to ask you the same question." She starred at him hoping to see some sign of remorse or apology or even a pitiful explanation. Whatever he said Beth knew that it would be a lie but he wouldn't even offer that much. "I knew that you would be here. I've known for months."

Lillian made no attempt to cover her body as she swung her bronze legs to the floor and stood to dress.

"I'm sure there's nothing I could say that would change what's happened," David said.

"You disgust me David." Beth turned and left the room leaving the door open behind her. She was numb, too angry to cry and to hurt to fight. As she reached the foyer she saw James coming down the main staircase. As soon as she looked up at him all of her resolve crumbled and the tears came in torrents. "Oh, James!"

"What is it? What's happened?"

"She couldn't bring herself to tell James that she had just caught her husband in the throws of loving making with another woman. Instead she said, "It's Maggie. She has run away and Lottie is frantic. You've got to do something James. You've got to find her."

"Tell Edward to round up some men and saddle my horse. Don't worry, we'll find her. Where is Lottie now?"

"She's with Bell."

"Good. Tell Bell to stay with her until we're back. Where is my brother?" Beth didn't answer. "Have you seen my brother this morning?" James asked.

"Yes, he's with Lillian."

James starred with knowing eyes. I'm sorry Beth."

"Why should you be sorry? I don't need your sympathy James. I'm the one who is sorry. But don't worry about me. I'm stronger than I look. We don't have time to deal with my problems.

Just find that little girl."

Beth left James standing in the foyer and went to find Edward. The men were ready to leave in less than five minutes. There were five slaves, David and James. As the men mounted their horses her eyes met David's. She wondered if he felt any regret. For a moment she thought she saw something in his eyes but she couldn't be sure. Suddenly he turned away and following his gaze she was not surprised to see Lillian standing on the porch. A cloud of dust rose as the men road off in search of little Maggie.

The men were gone for over six hours and Lottie had just about given up hope. "My baby is dead, I just know it. She's gone forever." Beth tried to reassure Lottie but she had her own doubts and didn't know quite what she could say to make Lottie feel any better.

"Miss Beth, I know you tried to help by running McCauley off and making him leave my baby alone but if you'd just let him take her she'd still be with me today."

Beth was horrified. She hadn't considered that anything would happen to Maggie because she'd interfered. There was nothing she could say now that would change how Lottie felt.

The men had searched for hours and found nothing. James was just about to turn back when he noticed a piece of cloth caught in the thicket. He dismounted to inspect further. One of the men confirmed that the fabric matched the dress that Maggie wore. David instructed the men to spread out and inspect the entire area. It wasn't long before one of the men called out. "Massa James, I think we found her." James and David hurried down an embankment to a shallow creek only a couple of miles from Gloria. Maggie had been raped and beaten. Her hands and feet were tied to wooden stakes in the ground and her small budding breasts were spotted with blood. The child had apparently clawed at her attacker and pieces of his shirt were caught under her finger nails. There was no doubt that McCauley had been her attacker. David turned away, sickness welling up from his stomach. "I was afraid that something like this would happen," James said.

"Why?" David wanted to know.

"It's your wife's meddling that has caused this tragedy."

"What are you talking about?"

"McCauley was having his way with the girl last night. Beth heard the girl scream. She burst into McCauley's cabin with a rifle."

"Beth?"

"Yeah, she threatened to blow his head off if he didn't leave the girl alone. McCauley tried to tell her that the girl would not be harmed but Beth fired him. She held a gun on him until he cleared out." David was stunned. "It might be wise if you keep your wife from interfering in our affairs," James said angrily.

When Beth heard the gallop of horses she knew that the men had returned and she ran to the front of the house, Lottie and Bell at her heels. As soon as the women reached the porch they saw Maggie's limp body hanging over the back of one of the horses and realized that the child was dead.

Lottie screamed hysterically and Bell wrapped her arms around her and tried to console her.

David said nothing as he walked past Beth into the house. All James would say was that there was no doubt that McCauley had attacked the girl.

Beth spent the next couple of days in her room. She blamed herself for Maggie's death as did most everyone at Gloria. If only she hadn't interfered, McCauley would have had no reason to kill the girl. James was right, she decided. She didn't belong here. Everyday she felt more and more estranged from her new family.

Sleep became almost impossible for Beth. Her nightmares were filled with the brutal killing of the little girl and when she was awake she couldn't shake the image of David and Lillian, their naked bodies intertwined in carnal abandon.

Everything was so clear now. The reason David wouldn't come to her at night, Lillian's attitude toward her, all of it made sense now. And there was the child, Becca, who was different from all the other children of Gloria. Her complexion, the texture of her hair and her eyes made it all clear that the child had been sired by a white man. Becca was nine years old and it was no secret that David had left Gloria exactly ten years ago. Beth now knew that Becca was David's child.

Why did he bring me here, Beth asked herself over and over again. Did David really think that a marriage built on nothing would keep him from Lillian? If that was his plan he was as foolish as Beth now believed she'd been for agreeing to this marriage.

It had been three days since Maggie's death and no one had come to see her. At first she didn't want to see anyone but after a few days she thought that at least her husband should have come.

When Denny told her that Lottie had not left her bed in the three days since Maggie's death, Beth thought the least she could do was to visit with Lottie. Had she known that Lillian would be the first person she would encounter upon leaving her room she might have chosen to spend another day in seclusion. As she descended the steps she saw Lillian standing at the bottom. Their eyes met and Beth continued to move slowly down the steps not taking her eyes from Lillian's face. I am the mistress of Gloria, Beth thought. I will not be intimidated. In a few steps the two women were face to face. Beth was close enough to reach out and touch Lillian's face and still, the woman did not move aside. "You are a foolish girl, Lillian," Beth finally said.

"No Ma'am. I am just a slave. I was raised from a babe to serve my master," Lillian said with her usual defiance. "The fool is the woman who could marry any man in the world but chooses to marry a man that don't even love her. That seems pretty foolish to me, Ma'am."

"How dare you speak to me like this? I could have you whipped for that." Beth could hardly believe the woman's insolence. Every muscle in her body went rigid as she struggled to maintain her control. "You're right Lillian. You are just a slave and as such you must obey your mistress as well as your master and I, your MIS-TRESS, want you out of this house. Beginning tomorrow you will no longer live under this roof. I want you to have yours and your daughter's things moved into one of the shacks. You will begin work in the fields tomorrow. Is that understood?"

"Oh yes, Miss. I do understand, but you don't. Massa will never permit this. You see, I am his weakness and he is my salvation and that ain't gone ever change." Beth couldn't answer. She was so shocked at Lillian's words that she just stared at the woman. "You see Miss Beth, you the white woman, the white wife he gotta have sos people will respect him. But me," Lillian swayed her hips and skirt in a sweeping dance motion. "I can't ever be his wife but I'll al-ways be his slave. I'll always be his lover and there ain't nothing you or me can do to change that."

Finally finding her tongue Beth said, "If you think that I am willing to accept that you are sadly mistaken. I will not rest until you are away from Gloria."

"Away? You think Massa gone sell me? No Ma'am, he ain't gone sell me cause I am what he needs. He will leave himself before he'd sell me, just like he did before."

Beth had heard enough. "Get out! Get out of my sight this minute." Lillian let her stare linger for a moment before she slowly sashayed away.

Even though David had not come to Lillian since the day Beth had found them together, Lillian made no attempt to move out of the mansion. She waited for David until late that evening. Miss Beth would look the part of a fool when David came and set things right again, she thought. As she dozed in and out of sleep Lillian now wondered just how long David would try to stay away from her.

It was near dawn when David finally came to her room. As the door creaked open a warm breeze blew through the room making one of the burning candles flicker. "I knew you would come," Lillian whispered. She opened her arms to him and David buried himself in the familiar scent of her bosom. "Your Missus has sent me and Rebecca to work in the fields. She don't want me in the house no more. She says I gotta move into one of them shacks. But I know you ain't gone let me work in them fields."

David was silent for a few minutes. Finally he said, "Lillian, she's my wife."

"I know but I'm who you really love, the one you've always loved. That is what you said ain't it?"

"Yes, you're right. That is exactly what I told you but now I'm telling you that Beth is my wife."

Lillian couldn't believe what she was hearing. What spell had this woman cast on her sweet David? "You mean you won't stop this? You want me and your daughter smelling like tobacco and living in one of them run down old shacks?"

"No. That's not what I want, but if my wife doesn't want you in the house what can I do? I'm sorry Lillian, but you'll have to move out of the house. That's the least I can do for her."

Lillian pushed him away. "What about me?"

"Look Lillian, I don't want to hurt you either but Beth is my wife. I have an obligation to her. Do you understand?"

"No! What about me?" Lillian asked again.

"Try to understand. When Beth saw us together it hurt her very much. She doesn't deserve this. I wasn't completely honest with her about why I wanted to get married. Finding us together was not something that should have happened but it did and now I've got to make it up to her somehow. Beth doesn't deserve to be hurt anymore than I have already hurt her. Do you understand?"

Lillian jumped to her feet. "No! What do I deserve, massa? I've given you all of me. That's all I got so what do I deserve?"

David didn't answer. He stood up and slowly walked to the door. "I'll make the arrangements for you and the child to be moved in the morning. You will continue your duties in the house. You can stop worrying about working in the tobacco fields but you will no longer live here in the house."

"Does this mean that you won't come to me?"

David didn't answer. He quickly left the room leaving Lillian alone and bewildered.

Lillian and Rebecca were moved into a small dusty shack behind the kitchen house that was no better than the shack where she'd grown up. She sat on the straw mattress and looked around the one room shack. The dirt floor was covered with hovels made by the rats that scurried from the kitchen house and pantry. The wind whistled through the rotting wood planked walls. Lillian was humiliated. Her room in the big house was a palace compared to this hovel. She hadn't slept in a place like this since she was fourteen years old, not since she learned how to please old man Vance.

Being with David was very different then when she was with his father. She loved David more than anything in the world and she knew that no matter what he said, he loved her just as much. When they were both very young they had begun to meet in the wooded area behind the big house. In the beginning their meetings were innocent, each fascinated by the differences between them. To Lillian, David's emerald green eyes were seductive in their opaqueness and she would stare at him in loving awe. David was likewise struck by the softness of Lillian's smooth unblemished bonze skin. Lillian had wanted to give David the same pleasure that she'd learned to give his father, not because of what he could give her in return but because she loved him. She had no way of knowing that the pleasure she gave David would become as addictive to him as the most potent of drugs. Their roles seemed to change before her eyes. He was the master's son but when they were alone, David became the slave and she commanded his every action. It took time but soon Lillian learned that she was the one who possessed power over David.

David was ignorant of the relationship between his father and Lillian and she was always afraid that if he found out he would no longer love her. She had not anticipated that David would ever confess their relationship to anyone, let alone Big Bill. Lillian was horrified when David told her that he had confessed to his father. She was sure that Big Bill would have her sold away from her family but Big Bill had a much more sinister punishment in mind. He chose to make her the sexual entertainment for every white man who visited Gloria. The old man took great pleasure in presenting her to his associates as slightly used and soiled merchandise that could be of some use.

Now Lillian was back in a one room shack just like the one where her humiliation had begun. She remembered the night Emma had come to tell her Mama that Big Bill wanted her at the big house. She had said good-bye to her mother and promised to return to the shack whenever she could get away. At first she thought that the old man wanted her for himself as usual but she soon found out that this would be the beginning of the retribution Big Bill had planned for her for loving his son. She remembered the evening when Big Bill had given her to a business man right in front of David. She also remembered the shock on David's face when she entered the room and the hatred in his eyes when she left with the fat white man. Lillian was sure that she would never see David again.

Now she sat with her head in her hands, her bravado crumbling around her, she wept. "Don't cry Mama," Rebecca said. Lillian looked at her child, David's child and realized that Rebecca could one day suffer the same humiliation. Bell was right. When it was all said and done, she was just a slave.

"Rebecca," Lillian said as she wiped at her tear stained face. "Mama wants you to remember something."

The child starred at her distraught mother not knowing what could have happened to make her mother so sad. "White people control everything," Lillian said. "They can even control your own body if that be what they want, but they can't ever control your mind. You gone always be a slave but don't you let no body control your mind. Once they can get you thinking like them there ain't nothing you can do, you be theirs body and soul, forever and ever. Promise me you ain't gone ever let that happen."

"Yes, Mama," Rebecca muttered but the child really didn't understand.

Part Three

Torments

"For what is evil but good tortured by its own hunger and thirst?
Verily when good is hungry it seeks food even in dark caves,
and when it thirsts, it drinks even of dead waters."

The Prophet, Kahill Gibran, 1923

Chapter 7

GLORIA
The Vance Plantation
Richmond, Virginia

The day that Lillian and Rebecca were moved out of the mansion Beth went to speak with James. She found him in the study. "Are you busy?" she asked.

"Not terribly, why?"

"I wanted to speak with you for a moment, if I may?" Beth asked hesitantly.

"Sure. What's on your mind?" James put down his pencil.

"You knew, James," she softly accused.

"Knew what?"

"You knew about Lillian and David."

"Yes," James stood and briefly turned his back to Beth. He thrust both his hands into his pockets as he rounded the desk. "but I couldn't be the one to tell you. I didn't know how much or even what David had already told you." Beth suddenly felt as if she were too weak to stand. She blinked back hot tears that seemed to burn behind her eyes. "I also knew that it was only a matter of time before you would find out on your own," James continued. Suddenly he turned to face Beth. He took a few steps toward her. "Apparently, I was right."

At that moment Beth felt her legs turn to water and she collapsed into James' arms. She held him close and let the tears come while James smoothed his hands over her back as he tried to comfort her. "Come on Beth, it's not as bad as it seems. David loves you or he wouldn't have married you."

"That isn't true," she sobbed.

"Of course it is."

"No, you don't understand. I know that David does not love me. He told me so himself."

"Then why on earth did you marry him?"

"I guess I thought I had no other options. He said that it would be a marriage of convenience and at first I thought that I could live with that. I hadn't planned on falling in love with him. Once I realized that I was falling for him I stupidly thought that I could make him love me too. I guess I was wrong about that too."

"A marriage of convenience," James asked. He released her and took a step back to look at Beth. He couldn't believe what he was hearing.

"You see, your brother and I met at a time when my whole life was falling apart. He convinced me that this marriage would somehow serve both of us. He said he needed to return home with a wife and I had no hope of marrying any better so I agreed to marry him. I didn't love him and I knew that he didn't love me and maybe that was the reason why I thought it could work. The problem is I've fallen in love with David. I didn't mean for this to happen, it just did. I can't help it."

"I see," James said.

"Now I know why he thought he needed a wife before he came home. I also know that he's in love with Lillian. He expects me to keep up this charade while the whole world knows he sleeps with Lillian and all the while my heart aches for him."

"Listen to me Beth," James led her to the sofa and sat down beside her. "Lillian has caused scandal in this family since the day she was born. David left Gloria because of Lillian and he knew nothing about the child until he returned here with you."

"Are you telling me that Rebecca is David and Lillian's daughter?"

"You didn't know?" James was surprised but seeing the look in Beth's eyes let him know that she'd had no idea. "I'm sorry," he said.

"Don't be sorry. I suspected but to hear you actually say it suddenly makes it real to me. Does the child know that David is her father?"

"No. There are many children like Rebecca among the slaves. David isn't the first white man to sire a child with one of his slaves. It goes on all the time we just don't talk about it."

"The child makes me nervous. She's always sneaking around the house, peering around corners and hiding. Sometimes I feel like she's watching me."

"Don't worry about her. I know that this must be very difficult for you but it will all work out eventually. Even though David would never let me sell Lillian and Rebecca I'm sure he'll soon realize that his infatuation with Lillian can only cause him pain. He'll come back to you begging for your forgiveness. Just give it a little time."

"I'm not sure I want him back," Beth said as she stood and began to pace.

"You don't mean that."

"Yes I do. Why would I want a man that doesn't love me? If David wants me to keep up this charade that is exactly what I'll do."

"I hope you're not blaming yourself for all of this? If you are, don't! This whole thing started when David was just a boy. She's had him under some sort of spell. Did you know that David actually wanted to marry her? He couldn't have been more than a boy of fifteen when he came to our father and actually told him that he planned to marry Lillian. Big Bill laughed at him."

"James, I don't think you understand. You think that this is just some infatuation David has with Lillian, forbidden fruit, as it were. That may have also been what your father thought but I'm telling you that David actually loves Lillian. The fact that she is a black woman and his slave has nothing to do with it and Lillian knows that better than anyone."

"No. He's infatuated with her. We can't deny that Lillian is a very beautiful woman and any man would be tempted by her beauty. I refuse to believe that David is in love with her as you say."

"Then why does he go to her every night while I lie awake waiting for him to remember that I am his wife?"

"I don't know, Beth."

"I do. He couldn't marry a slave. Besides being illegal, for him to openly declare his love for Lillian would bring shame on this family. That is exactly what sent him running away ten years ago. So he marries me to keep his dignity while he sleeps with her and what's worst, everyone knows, including Lillian; she's even said as much."

"She wouldn't dare."

"Oh, yes. She is well aware of the power she has over David. She uses his weakness for her like a weapon," Beth said as she dropped into a chair as if the weight of all that had happened was suddenly too much for her to bear. "I've been such a fool," she whispered.

"Maybe there is some truth to what you say Beth but you are not the fool in this. If there is a fool it's David. Now, I can see that the stress of all of this nonsense has worn on you my dear. You look very tired."

"I am."

"Why don't you go on up to your room and I'll have a cup of tea sent up to you."

"No. I don't want Denny to see me this way. There's no sense in giving the slaves more to gossip about."

"You're right, of course. I'll bring the tea up to you myself."

Shortly after Beth undressed and climbed into bed James knocked softly on her door before he came in. "Feeling any better Beth?"

"A little."

James sat the tea on the bedside table and sat on the edge of the bed. "I put a little brandy in your tea to help you sleep."

"Thank you. You are so kind to me James." Beth looked up at James as if she had never laid eyes on him before that moment. Not only could he be charming, he was every bit as handsome as his older brother. Beth remembered just how secure she had felt moments ago when he had wrapped his arms around her and tried to comfort her. She watched him closely as he stirred her tea and she felt her body go rigid, tightening with the ache of longing. She closed her eyes and leaned back on the pillows trying not to think of James in the way that she knew she shouldn't.

"Beth," he said softly. "Are you sure you're alright?"

"Yes. I'm fine. Thank you, James. You seem to be my only friend. I'm lucky to have you."

"You don't have to thank me Beth. I think that you're a very special lady who deserves much more than by brother has given you. Now, stop worrying and get some sleep. I still think that this will all work out for the best." He leaned forward to kiss her forehead but Beth swung her arms around his neck and held him close for a moment too long. James raised himself and looked down at Beth as she pushed against him. He knew that he should leave but at that moment he wanted nothing more than to have Beth for himself. He kissed her hungrily and Beth returned the kiss with the same intensity. In the next moment he was on top of her, his weight pressing her body down and Beth could feel his manhood rise against her. A chill went through her body and she shivered but in the next moment the warmth of desire spread through her like a sudden fever and she knew that she wanted James as much as he wanted her. Beth caressed his back and shoulders as he frantically fumbled with the tiny ribbons closing the front of her gown. "Beth, this is wrong his whispered against her ear."

"I don't care," she said as she struggled to remove the bed covers between them. James finally opened her gown and buried his face between her soft breasts. A small moan escaped from Beth's lips as she breathlessly waited for James to enter her.

Suddenly the weight of his body was lifted as James stood up and adjusted his clothing. "Beth, I can't do this. I'm sorry but this is wrong and we both know that we'll regret it later."

"Speak for yourself, James. I don't think that I will regret it for one moment. What am I to do? Please don't reject me James. I couldn't bear another rejection."

"I'm sorry Beth. I'm not rejecting you but I just can't do this. David may be many things but he is still my brother and I just couldn't do this to him." Then he left Beth alone, quickly closing the door behind him.

Beth buried her face in her pillows and cried. She had managed to make a fool of herself all over again. How could she bare to face any of them again?

illian was furious with David for having her moved from the main house. As she had done many times in the past, she withheld her sexual favors as a sort of punishment. She refused him time and time again and with each refusal David would sink deeper into despair. Not even brandy could extinguish the flames of his burning desire. He spent many nights drinking alone in the study until his brain and body refused to lend itself to his desire. He often passed out before reaching his own bed. He would awake to find that his desires had only been disguised and his spirits would sink to their depths, leaving him numb with only loathing for himself and Lillian. It was at these times that he would remind himself that Lillian was his slave. He was the master of her fate and she had no earthly right to refuse him.

One evening David stormed into Lillian's cabin startling both she and Rebecca. The cabin was cold and damp and Lillian wrapped her shawl around her as she hurried to light the kerosene lamp. "What is it?" she said with annoyance. As the dim light began to fill the one room cabin, the fire and fury that had spurred David on his mission to forcibly take what he considered to be his property faded. His face suddenly paled and his shoulders fell as he crumpled at the sight of Lillian. Their roles were once again reversed and this time Lillian took great pleasure in humbling the man that the entire world considered her master.

"Massa be needin something?" she asked using the language of the field slave, mocking her own people as well as David. The ragged nightgown she wore did little to diminish her beauty. The silhouette of her svelte bronze body was completely visible through the thin fabric that hung loosely from her shoulders. The sight of her heightened David's desire and he hung his head, hating her for being able to reduce him with only her presence. He walked slowly toward her. When he finally stood over her he dropped to his knees and let his head rest on her lap.

"Lillian please don't do this to me," he pleaded.

"What am I doing to you, massa?" Lillian fought with the only weapon available to her, the truth. "I am your property. You can do with me whatever suits your fancy, ain't that right?"

"Alright, you're angry with me for having you moved from the house. I know that but, don't you see, I had no choice? I had to do it."

"Oh no, massa. I'se very grateful to ya, sa. Cause ya give me somewheres to lay my lazy head," Lillian mocked again.

"Stop it!" David finally realized that Lillian mocked him. "Stop it," he shouted again as he slowly got to his feet. He suddenly noticed the child as she huddled on her small cot in the corner. Lillian followed his gaze.

"Oh, massa don't you be worrin' bout her. She got to learn some day, ain't that right. She got to learn that she ain't nothin' but a slave. She got to learn that whatever massa wants she got to give."

David didn't answer. Lillian continued her mocking as he slowly walked to the door. "There is gone be a white man to take her real soon. Ain't that right massa? I know because I was nothing but a girl when your daddy took me. Course, her being your daughter and all shouldn't make no never mind because she's still just a slave, a wench, a nigger slave. Ain't that what you see when you looks at her massa?"

Her words cut through him like the sharpest of blades but David did not turn around. He left quickly and quietly, closing the door behind him.

*I*t was late August and James had planned a gala to celebrate the end of harvest season. Everyone was busy preparing for the annual celebration. Even David was at home to help for most of the week. Beth had spent many pain staking hours supervising the cleaning and decorating of the house. The dinning area had been transformed into a festive ballroom. She also had to supervise the preparing of the food and had gone over the menus with Lillian and Bell several times.

Beth was almost grateful for the celebration. Besides taking her mind off of her own troubles, it gave her a chance to prove that she could be the kind of mistress Gloria needed. She would be expected to be a pleasant hostess, meeting and greeting the rest of the Vance family, friends and neighbors. Many had already become acquainted with her at the wedding but there were still many who were waiting to see just what kind of woman had tamed and brought home one of Virginia's most eligible bachelors. She was sure they all wondered if the naïve young woman from Philadelphia could quiet the scandalous gossip that had surrounded the Vance family for years. Beth wanted everything to be no less than perfect.

Even David was caught up in the festive atmosphere. He was content to play his part as the loving and attentive husband. Beth was sure that the success of this evening would seal her place as Gloria's mistress.

After Beth was satisfied that every detail had been scrupulously attended to, she retired to her room to dress for the ball. She sat at her vanity table staring at her reflection in the mirror. Deep, darkened creases surrounded her eyes and her once fiery colored red hair had even lost its luster. Her eyes were sullen and sad. How tragic it was that loving one man could reduce you so easily, she thought.

"Hello sweetheart." Beth was startled by David's husky voice. He had entered her room without knocking, which was unusual in itself. This was the first time he'd come to her room since the night he passed out from an overdose of brandy and Lillian. Beth did not move from her position at the vanity but stared at David's reflection in her mirror above her own. He was still the most handsome man she'd ever known and the only man who could be completely casual even though formally attired. David placed his hands on her bare shoulders and bent to kiss her cheek lightly. Beth pulled away but the heat that radiated from his touch lingered enticing her to accept whatever he came to offer but she rebuffed him.

"There's no one here but the two of us David. You can stop your play acting. You have no audience."

"What are you talking about?"

"Please David don't do this, not tonight?"

"What am I doing?"

"Don't come to me pretending that we have something that we both know is not so."

"Beth," he leaned closer. "I know that I've hurt you and I'm sorry but remember, love was never part of our bargain."

"How could I possibly forget? You remind me of that fact at every opportunity. In fact, you've gone out of your way to prove just that. Well, it may have taken a while but I believe I understand our agreement fully now. I'm not as naive as I was when you brought me here. Thanks to you, I've grown up more than you could have imagined. I no longer think that I can make you love me. What's more, the thought no longer appeals to me in the least. At this moment my only desire is that you go away and leave me alone as you have for the past four months."

"But I do love you Beth. It has just taken me a little longer to realize what a wonderful woman I've married."

"Oh stop it David. I knew that you were in love with Lillian even before I found you two together. Now I know why you left Gloria. The only thing that still puzzles me is why you came back and why on earth did you bring me here?"

David did not leave as Beth expected. He sat down on the opposite side of the room, his face partially hidden in the shadow of the drapes. "Beth," he said softly. "I'm ill. I just can't seem to stop doing the things that hurt people I love, that includes you."

Beth turned to look at him. Was this a new David or just another way to disguise his true identity, Beth wondered. The shadow of the drapes and the glow of the candles cast an eerie light on his face and Beth thought she saw a tear in the corner of his eye.

"I do love you Beth," he whispered. "Please believe me when I say I really don't want to hurt you. You're right of course, I do love Lillian but not in the way you think."

"What other way is there?

"I don't know. I can't explain it. I'm a different man with Lillian. Hell, even I don't like that man. He's weak and vulnerable and he's lead by is carnal desire instead of his wits. I guess what I'm trying to say Beth is that's not the man you married."

"David, I'm tiring of this game. Exactly what are you trying to tell me?"

"Lillian has some sort of perverted hold on me. It's almost supernatural and I am powerless to fight it."

"Don't be ridiculous. You sound as if the woman is a witch."

"It's not as ridiculous as it seems. I simply can't help myself when she's around. I truly don't mean to do the things I do but I can't stop myself."

"What's the matter David? Can't you even say the word? It's adultery, David."

"I know you're angry with me Beth and you have every right to be. All those years away from home had convinced me that the problem was under control. But as soon as I came back here I was under her spell again. Do you understand?"

"No David, I don't understand. I don't understand anything.

You have brought me nothing but grief since the day we met. I don't even know who I am anymore. You've taken my self-respect, my dignity; you've even taken away my ability to trust. How dare you ask me to understand?"

"Beth," he slowly moved out of the shadows to face his wife. "Everything that you say is right of course. I should have told you everything and I'm truly sorry that I've put you through so much anguish but things can change. I really do want to be a good husband to you and a father to the child that you will one day bare. But I know that I can't do it alone. If you care anything at all for me you'll help me. You're my wife Beth. You've got to help me."

"Help you? Help you to do what exactly? You're asking me to help you forget your adultery, your lies and your drunkenness?" Beth turned away from him and began to brush her hair again. "Don't be absurd David. It's not my help that you really want. You want absolution. You want me to tell you that it's alright. You want me to ease your conscious but I won't do it!"

"No, that's not what I want. I know that you don't believe me and I can't say that I blame you. I've hurt you so much but I realize now that there is no one on God's earth that loves me as you do." Now he was standing behind her chair again, his solemn face above her own in the vanity mirror. He placed both of his hands on Beth's trembling shoulders and Beth felt her resolve weaken at his touch. "God knows you don't deserve the pain I've caused you," he whispered.

"David, I really want to believe you but I just don't think that we can begin again, too much has happened."

"Of course we can. I know that it was you who ordered Lillian and Rebecca from the house."

"And I know that my orders mean absolutely nothing around here."

"You're wrong Beth. Lillian is out of the house just as you

ordered. Doesn't that tell you something?"

Neither spoke for a few moments. Beth continued to brush her hair and David continued to stare at her reflection. He wondered why he had not been able to see Beth as the strong woman she turned out to be.

Beth wanted desperately to believe all that David had said. He was, after all, the only man she had ever loved. Finally David said, "I really do want us to begin again. I understand that it will be difficult but you've got to give me a chance."

Beth hoped that David would finally say the words that she longed to hear all of these past months. She cringed inwardly, yearning to accept David at his word but knowing that with acceptance came vulnerability. Even now, after so much misery and longing, David still had the ability to make her blood race through her veins. "Maybe this will help you to realize that I am truly sincere about being the husband you deserve. I love you Beth," David said as he presented Beth with a small black velvet box.

He said it, Beth thought. Oh, he'd said it before but this time she really believed he was sincere. Maybe he really does love me. She opened the box to find a beautiful sapphire necklace and she gasped in awe. "David, it's beautiful. Will you help me to fasten it?"

As he bent to fasten the necklace around her slender neck, the nearness of him made Beth tremble with excitement. "I love you Beth, he said again as he placed a kiss on her cheek. " Maybe this isn't the right time but promise me that you will think about all that I have said. We really can't go on like this."

"Yes, you're right dear. We can't go on like this," she said as she stood to face her husband. Her tone was much softer now and she felt ashamed that her anger could be so easily appeased with a small gift. "Thank you David. This is a lovely gift." She leaned forward to kiss David on the cheek in a gesture of thanks. David's arm quickly encircled her waist and pulled her to him.

"I am so sorry that I've caused you so much pain," he whispered, his breath hot against Beth's face. He leaned into her, his mouth in search of her lips. As his lips finally found Beth's her heart began to pound. He kissed her hungrily and before Beth knew what was happening David swept her up into his arms and carried her to the bed.

"No, David. Too much has passed between us. There is so much that must be settled before we can come together in this way again."

"Beth," he whispered as he gently laid her on the bed. "I have denied you too long and in so doing, I have denied myself as well. I need you, Beth. I need you just as much as I needed you in the hotel back in Philadelphia. Please don't deny me Beth. If you turn me away now I don't know what I might do."

"But the guests will be arriving soon."

"I don't care about them. Right now I want to make love to my wife. The guests can wait."

The picture of David and Lillian entwined on the small cot in the servant's quarters quickly flashed in Beth's mind and she did not protest further. She willingly surrendered to her husband knowing that her body needed David as much as he wanted her. He undressed her slowly kissing, caressing and tantalized every inch of her body. Beth lost herself in the ecstasy of love making. It was a passionate hungry union and when it was over and all of their energy spent, they laid in each other's arms, neither wanting the moment to end.

Chapter 8

GLORIA
The Vance Plantation
Richmond, Virginia

The celebration had begun and Gloria was deluged with high stepping southern gentlemen and their ladies. Both David and James were gracious hosts and Beth was the consummate hostess. She gracefully moved through her guests, enchanting each with a warm smile and a pleasant greeting. She soon found herself with a small circle of ladies that gathered in a corner of the ballroom. She smiled brightly hoping to conceal her disinterest as the ladies chattered on about the new French fashions and Richmond's most salacious gossip. Beth's eyes scanned the room hoping for some reason to leave the group. James finally came to her rescue, sweeping her away from the circle of ladies. "Beth, there's someone I'd like for you to meet." As they made their way across the ballroom, James stopped to introduce Beth to so many people, that she knew she would never remember all of their names and faces after the evening had ended. James then led her to a handsome older gentleman who was amusing a group of ladies with tales of his adventures as a General in the Virginia Militia. "Beth, may I present General Kent Barnett. The General owns the plantation just south of Gloria."

The General was dressed in full army regalia, including a long silvery sword that hung at his side. I'm so very happy to meet you Mrs. Vance." He bowed deeply and Beth presented her gloved hand for the customary kiss.

"I am likewise delighted to make your acquaintance sir," Beth said. The General was a distinguished gentleman of about fifty, Beth guessed. He apparently knew the Vance's well because David greeted him as an old friend.

"I see you've met General Barnett," David said as he joined the group. "Kent, how are you?" The men shook hands.

"David? Why, look at you boy. The last time I saw you, you were just a skinny kid. You're a fine young man now with a pretty young wife. Your Pa would be real proud of you son."

David chose not to acknowledge the last remark. "The General is an accomplished horseman, as I remember. Do you still ride for sport, General?"

"Well, not as much as I'd like I'm sorry to say. However, I do still get out for a ride every now and again. I'm sure I don't have to tell you boys that running a plantation is hard work. Unfortunately, I don't have my boys around to help out anymore." The General spoke to David and James but his eyes spoke to Beth. As his dark eyes bore into her, Beth felt the flush of embarrassment and turned away from the General's stare.

The ballroom was becoming extremely hot, the air seemed heavy and humid, and Beth was beginning to feel ill. The men went on talking of plantations, crops, harvest, slaves and newspapers as if they'd forgotten that there were ladies present. Beth wanted nothing more than to escape to the privacy of her own room.

"Did you see the article in the Herald?" the General asked. "It's a bit of a crock don't you think?"

"Oh, yes. James and I were just discussing that article," David said. "But I must say General, I disagree with you. I don't think it's a crock at all. In fact, I think we all better think carefully about just how we're running things."

Beth turned to look at her husband. She knew that David rarely discussed his views on slavery with anyone but his brother but now seemed very adamant in his views.

"I think," David went on. "The south will soon be forced to take up arms in defense of the institution of slavery. There has been a barrage of recent slave revolts in the West Indies and many of the white settlers were killed. Even though there has been blood shed both black and white, the government is quickly losing control every day. My fear is that the planters of the southern states are rapidly heading for the same fate."

"Nonsense!" The General moved closer to David as if he meant to impart some secret knowledge. "My boy," he said. "We southerners did not invent slavery. It's an institution that has been in existence throughout the ages for one simple reason. It is extremely profitable. I expect it will continue for the same reason, despite those who stand in opposition. We are all businessmen after all. We would be remiss if we did not take full advantage of such an ancient and profitable practice."

"Ah, yes, but the number of those who are in opposition grows daily, sir. The entire country is moving toward a revolution that will tear this country apart. A war, General, a battle between north and south and I guarantee you the north will rally the slaves against their owners. They'll fight side by side with white men. It is an unavoidable conclusion to this barbaric practice."

"Have you gone soft in the head boy?" The General could not hide his shock at David's words. "Maybe you've been away from the south too long. I guess all that time in Philadelphia has made you forget your southern upbringing."

"No sir," David said seriously. "I haven't forgotten at all. I am simply relaying the situation as I see it."

General Barnett seemed to have reached his level of tolerance but with great effort he was able to keep his voice even as he scolded the younger man. "Do you realize son, that the south has become prosperous through slavery. To abolish slavery would virtually collapse the southern economy. Neither you nor I could afford to hire and pay the salaries of the number of free men it would take to work our fields. We'd be ruined in a matter of months. My suggestion to you, my boy, is to keep your idealistic views to yourself and if you enjoy being a rich man, you'll fight for slavery with every ounce of southern blood coursing through your pampered veins."

"You misunderstand me, sir. I take no stand against or for slavery as an institution. I merely wish to forewarn you and the other planters of the catastrophic climax to which we are speedily approaching."

"David seems to think that there could be trouble brewing in our own backyards," James added.

"Nonsense!" the General said. "I treat my niggers well. There ain't one of them that would turn against me. They ain't the smartest lot but they're smart enough to know that as long as they stay at the Barnett Plantation, they'll be fed, clothed and housed. Freedom is the very last thing a nigger needs." The General lifted another glass of champagne from the passing waiter's tray. In two gulps the glass was empty, leaving the General red faced and wet with perspiration. "You boys are young yet!" he went on. "You'll learn soon enough. Niggers are like children, all of them. When you got a disobedient child you paddle his bottom. Make sure he knows that the next time he'll get even worse. You might have to paddle him a few times but eventually he'll learn. Niggers ain't no different. If your niggers need a whipping, give it to them swift and hard."

Beth gasped. She couldn't believe what she heard from a respectable military man of wealth. She looked first at David; his brows pushed together, his face rigid with anger. When she gazed up at James she knew that the brothers did not agree with the General.

"Once again, General," James said. "My brother and I do not agree. History teaches us that violence begets violence. It is the violence against our slaves that will be the catalyst for revolution."

Again, Beth wondered how these people could speak so ill of the very people that saw to their comfort. Suddenly her head began to pound and she felt as if she needed air. The men were so engrossed in their conversation that no one noticed Beth as she slipped away and headed for the garden. She stood with her hands pressed against the railing taking in deep gulps of the crisp night air. A rustle came from the bushes. "Who's there?" Beth asked. She took a step toward the noise and knew that someone was hiding there. She decided that it might not be a good idea to investigate on her own so she turned to go back inside the house. Before she could reach the door there was another rustle in the bushes. Beth turned quickly toward the sound. There stood a young white boy who looked to be about fourteen years old. His clothes, although, apparently of good quality, were ragged and soiled. "Oh my God!" she said.

"I've come for the General Ma'am," The boy could hardly speak. It was obvious that he had just come through some awful calamity. Blood stained the sleeve of the boy's jacket and a long slash down the side of his soiled face glistened with fresh blood.

"You wait here. I'll get the General for you." Beth turned and ran into the ballroom. "David! David!" she called.

David was at her side in an instant. "What is it? What's happened?"

"There's a boy in the garden. A white boy and he's been hurt. He said that he came to get the General."

David, James and the General all followed Beth into the garden.

"Why, this is the Waller boy from the Hampton plantation,"

the General said. "Tell us what happened son."

"It's the niggers sir, they've revolted. Some nigger who calls himself a preacher named Nat Turner," the words seemed to flood from the boy's mouth as he rushed to tell all he could in only a moment. "He's been going from one plantation to the next, freeing the slaves as he goes. He's giving guns to the niggers and his group gets bigger with every plantation he hits. They're killing all of the white people, sir, and he's headed this way. They should be here by morning if they're not stopped."

"What about your family son?" David asked.

"Dead!" the boy said. "They're all dead, sir. They hit us before we knew what was happening."

"How is it that you managed to save yourself?" the General wanted to know.

"Nigger shot my Pa right in front of the house. As soon as I seen all them niggers with guns running and screaming, I didn't wait to see what they were going to do next. I ran straight for the woods and hid out there until I heard them ride out. When I went back to our house I saw that they shot my Ma too and both my older brothers."

"Beth, take the boy inside and tend to him," David said.

The party was over. The general told the men to escort their women home and lock them in the storm shelters. They were to return to Gloria within an hour, armed and ready for war.

James and David gathered the family's valuables and hid them in a safe in the Master bedroom, Beth's room. It was then that Beth learned of the secret room. In the front parlor James slide the mantle and fireplace to one side revealing a narrow stairway. Beth, Lillian, Bell, Denny and Rebecca were to descend the stairs to a hidden room under the house. They would stay there until the men returned.

The room had been carved out of the earth and its floor,

walls and ceiling were nothing more than tightly packed soil. The men made sure the woman had pillows, blankets, jugs of water and bread for provisions. Bell thoughtfully took some of the food left over from the party and packed it in towels in the bottom of three baskets.

The room was dank and the smell of wet earth made Beth feel as if she had been buried alive. At first there was little conversation among the women but as the days wore on the tension between them seemed to lessen. They ate and slept most of the time and Beth read aloud from the Bible to past the time easily. Bell, Nan and Rebecca were attentive listeners while Lillian pretended disinterest.

They had been in the room beneath the house for four days and three nights and Beth was beginning to feel more and more claustrophobic. No sound came from the house above. Beth finally reached the point when she could not stand being underground any longer. She decided to see if all was well in the house above. With Bell at her side she slowly climbed the stairs and slide away the hidden door. The two women stood at the top of the steps for several minutes as they listened for any sounds of movement in the house. Then with Bell's help Beth slid the mantle aside just the way she had watched James do it days earlier.

The house was exactly as they had left it and Beth decided that the danger had passed and they should get back to the business of running the plantation. She sent Bell to get Lillian and Rebecca while she searched the rest of the house. The house was completely empty.

Beth thought it best not to leave the house by the front door in case someone had been left to watch the house. She went through the back of the house and then through the kitchen house. As she stood there looking out over the land and down the row of slave shacks an eerie silenced seemed to settle over the entire plantation. Nothing moved. There was no sway of the trees by the wind, no work in fields, no children running and playing as usual. There was just complete silence.

The plantation remained shrouded in silence over the next couple of days. There was no work in the fields and the slaves that hadn't run away kept to their shacks. The house slaves served Beth well but their eyes held a resentment that Beth had not noticed before. No one spoke in her presence except the usual, "yes Ma'am," and their communication with each other was hushed and private.

Lillian no longer lived in the house but was still responsible for its keep which meant that she was frequently in the house. Her encounters with Beth were frequent and although Beth knew that having Lillian removed from the house was a small victory, she refused to let Beth know just how much she had been hurt by the move.

Lillian never expected David to agree to her moving out of the house. This was the first time that he had ever done anything to remind her that she was no more than a slave. Now she was reminded of this each time she saw Beth but she continued to hold her head high and walk with assured audacity.

Every evening after the sun went down, Beth could hear the slaves as they sang for deliverance in low, almost mournful tones. At first Beth thought their singing was beautiful and soul bearing, before she realized that the deliverance the slaves prayed for included their mistress. She was the enemy. With that realization she worried that there were close to a hundred slaves on Gloria and she was the only white woman. What would she do if there was trouble? What was there to stop them from killing her and running off to join up with the Reverend Nat Turner? For the first time since her arrival at Gloria, Beth was afraid.

The men had been away for almost seven days while Gloria remained still and silent. Nothing seemed to move; even the gentle breeze that usually blew across the James River in the evenings had suddenly stopped. It was as if God had removed all the blessings of nature, leaving them barren and alone like a wasteland.

Beth paced the floor of her sitting room restlessly. She not only feared for her husband and brother-in-law, she now feared the slaves. Her apprehension made it impossible to sleep. Near dawn Beth was finally overcome by sheer exhaustion and fell into a fitful sleep.

"Miss Beth! Miss Beth!" Denny's insistent voice called in alarm. Beth rose on one elbow, a bit annoyed at being disturbed after finally falling asleep.

"What is it Denny?" Beth had never spoken to the girl so sharply.

"They's comin!" Denny shook with fear. "They's almost here Ma'am."

"Who?" The girl seemed so frightened that Beth became anxious. "Who is coming, Denny?"

"The rebels ma'am, Walta sees them coming from the hill. He says they's bout four miles back but they's moving fast."

"Oh my God!"

"Bell says we need to hide you right away. She says to get everything we can carry and take it to that dirt room. Come on Ma'am! We ain't got a second to waste."

"Calm down Denny. We'll be alright," she tried to comfort the frantic girl. Beth was wearing only her night gown. She grabbed some clothes, stockings and her boots and stuffed them into her pillowcase.

"Ma'am, we best be going," Denny said from the door.

Beth took a candle from the mantel and lit it to light their way to the secret room.

"No!" Denny said as she blew out the candle. "That light be seen for miles on a night like this. We got to find our way in the dark." The girl took her mistress's hand and the two of them quietly crept, feeling rather than seeing their way through the darkened house. They could hear the thunder of many horses as they came closer to Gloria. Beth thought of her possible fate at the hands of the rebels and run-away slaves and she was suddenly stricken with a gripping fear. Her legs seemed suddenly unable to carry her and she stumbled and fell more than once. Denny was just as afraid as she pulled her mistress along. Again Beth stumbled and fell on the main staircase but before she could cry out a large and callused hand covered her mouth. She struggled to free herself but the arms were too strong and they held her tightly.

"It's me Miss Beth, Jacob." Jacob was Nan's man. He was a big muscular man whose shoulders were still broad and erect despite his advancing years. "Don't say nothin," he whispered. "You just hold tight to my arm." The three were joined by Nan at the bottom of the stairs.

"Miss Beth, you best be getting out of that fancy gown," Nan said as she motioned to the bundle of clothes Denny carried.

"I don't understand," Beth said. What's happening here?"

"It's the rebels Ma'am. They'll be here in a minute or two. We ain't got time to talk now," Nan said.

"Yes I know but why must I change my clothes?"

"Ma'am," Nan paused and looked into Beth's fearful eyes. "Ma'am, it ain't us they be wantin to harm. Denny and me just want to make you safe. Now you got to get out of that fancy gown and cover up that red hair."

"I brought some clothes," Beth said. "They're in the pillow-case."

"Not your clothes Ma'am. These here clothes," Nan said as she handed Beth a bundle of ragged clothes. Beth did not argue further but quickly removed her nightgown and dressed in the ragged clothes Nan held for her. When she was done Nan tied her hair up in another rag.

As they neared the parlor they could hear horses and the voices of the men as they entered the main house. They all knew that it was too late to go to the dirt room behind the mantle in the main parlor. Before Beth knew where she was going, Nan and Jacob, with Denny following behind, rushed Beth from the back of the big house and along a muddied, well worn path behind the slave shacks. Nan stopped behind one of the shacks and pushed its back door open. The four rushed inside.

The men's voices could be clearly heard now and they knew that the rebels had taken over the plantation. There was screaming and yelping, some in glee and some in agony as Gloria's slaves met the rebels. Some of the slaves ran from their shacks with their meager belongings already packed and ready for flight and their first taste of freedom. Still others screamed at the rebels, calling them murders and damning them to hell for their rebelliousness. They feared that the entire race would soon have to answer for the actions of the rebels.

Nan and Beth watched from the dusty window of the shack while Jacob guarded the back door. The women watched in horror as the big house was ransacked. Valuable furniture, clothes, paintings and books were tossed from the windows and balconies of the mansion. The Vance's most precious belongings were heaped into a large pile in the front of the house and set on fire.

Lillian and her daughter had joined the crowd of slaves that had gathered in the front of the big fire with the rebels. One of the rebels, a man who had obviously stolen the uniform of a soldier, walked up to Lillian and she faced him with outward contempt. "Leave her and her bastard here!" someone in the crowd yelled. "She ain't fit to be free."

"The massa's whore is what she is," another yelled.

"I bet she don't even want freedom," someone else yelled. "She's content to stay here and warm the massa's bed." The entire crowd yelled and screamed in affirmation. With Rebecca clinging to her skirt, Lillian swung around to face her accusers. She lifted one hand and stepped forward, ready to defend herself but someone threw a rock that struck Lillian on the side of her head. She swayed in pain but before she could recover her balance another rebel struck her in the back of the head with the butt of his gun sending her sprawling to the ground. The violent action seemed to invigorate the crowd and they began to chant, "FREEDOM! FREEDOM!" Someone had broken into the gun cabinet and rifles and ammunitions were being passed around to the rebels and the slaves that had just joined their group.

Beth had never felt anything but contempt for Lillian but now as Lillian laid helplessly on the ground while her daughter huddled over her mother praying that she would open her eyes, Beth felt pity for the woman. Even Lillian's own people did not embrace her.

"Ma'am," Nan said. "We best be hiding you. Theys sure to search the shacks before long.

Beth glanced over at Jacob who had begun to remove several large stones from around the fireplace which would widen the chimney a fraction. Beth was instructed to squeeze into the cramped space as best she could and Jacob gently replaced the stones. "Miss Beth, I promise you ain't gone be in here no longer than you has to," Jacob said.

Wedged between a damp mud wall and the sharp stones of the fireplace, Beth could hardly breathe. The slightest movement would send a stream of powdered soot over her face and shoulders. The stones seemed to stab at ever part of her body and the narrow space made it difficult to stand upright. After only a short while her knees began to ache while her head ached with fear. She had long ago stopped crying. She only prayed silently that she would not be found by the rebels.

After what seemed like hours she finally heard footsteps and voices just outside of the wall and she knew that the rebels had finally reached Nan and Jacob's shack. She heard yelling and what sounded like preaching.

A robust voice boomed through the small shack. "Praise God all mighty! It is His Hand that makes all men free. No longer will you serve the oppressor. Rise up children and take a breath. Inhale the sweet taste of freedom and Praise God for this great blessing."

"You mean we can go?" Nan asked in pretense of excitement.

"That is exactly what I mean. You can walk off this white man's land never to return again." The voice went on preaching and when Beth could hear no more she knew that they had left the shack.

At first there was just silence. It was so quiet that Beth thought she could hear her own heart beating. When she next heard voices they came from far away. Then she heard the thunder of horses' hooves as they galloped away from Gloria. Still afraid to leave her hiding place in the wall Beth waited and prayed.

Finally, after what seemed like hours Jacob came to help her out of the wall. "The rebels is all gone, Ma'am," Jacob said. "A good many slaves are gone too. Mostly field workers, Miss."

As Beth brushed the soot from her face and shoulders she smelled smoke and ran to the door of the shack. Several of Gloria's small buildings were ablaze, including the kitchen house and pantry. People ran in all directions as they tried to put the fires out.

Besides the fires that had been set, the main house had been ransacked. Gloria was in complete ruin. Still in her ragged clothes with her face darkened from soot and dirt and her eyes burning from the fire, Beth tried to help put out the fires but the slaves repeatedly refused her, saying that massa Vance would not approve.

Several days after the rebels had left Gloria, Beth stood in the study looking out over the vast lands of Gloria and her hand went instinctively to her throat and she fingered the sapphire and diamond necklace that David had given her the night he left Gloria. She remembered their last moments together when David had held her close with his strong arms and whispered that he wanted to be the husband that she deserved. "I really do love you Beth," he'd said. She heard him repeat those words over and over in her head and she wanted so desperately to believe him. His absence kept him constantly in her thoughts. Through all that had happened she realized that she still loved David and she prayed for his safe return.

Many of the slaves had left with the rebels. Some stayed because they were simply too old for the flight to freedom, while others stayed because they had no wish to leave other family members who were unable to travel. Some others, like Bell, Nan, Jacob and Denny stayed because they feared the unknown. And, of course, Lillian stayed, not because the rebels had refused her but because she could not bear to leave David.

"Why did you help me?" Beth had asked the four slaves after the rebels had gone.

"I ain't got no wish to help somebody to their death Ma'am," Bell answered.

"Why didn't you leave with the others? You could have all left Gloria while I was hidden in the wall. I just don't understand why you stayed. Don't you want to be free?"

"Don't know," Jacob said. "Ain't never been free. The way I sees it, to be free in this here land is to be hated and sometimes even hunted like an animal. Maybe if them rebels had come twenty years ago I would have been the first one to shout freedom. But now, I seen too many who went after freedom only to be brought back here to die on a tree."

"Besides," Denny said. "How we gone ever be free in merica. Everywhere you go folks gone see what you is and they ain't gone never let you really be free."

Beth felt more than just mere indebtedness toward the slaves that had saved her life but how would she ever repay their kindness?"

The men had been gone for two weeks and finally returned on a Thursday afternoon with the news that several white families, mostly women and children, had been massacred. The days that followed the massacre of the whites would be set down in history as slaves were killed at random. It didn't matter if they had been participants in the raids or not. If any slave was caught away from his master's land he would be slaughtered or hung. Many of Gloria's slaves that had run off with the rebels soon returned begging David and James for forgiveness even while they knew that at the very least they would be severely whipped. Nat Turner was the most wanted man in the country. Whites hated, hunted and feared him with the same ferocity. No white man could feel safe until the rebel was caught and swiftly put to death. But among the slaves Nat Turner, though feared, was a hero. After his massacre of the whites, many independent abolitionist groups sprang up all over the south. The slaves continued to talk, although in hushed tones, about the escape and revolt. Several weeks would pass before news began to spread that Nat Turner had been caught and executed.

James found that the running of the plantation became increasingly difficult. The slaves dared to show that they possessed stature and dignity that the whites had not thought them capable of. Though still in bondage, the slaves protested their bondage in other ways. Some complained of illness thereby reducing the number of slaves in the fields and slowing production. Those who did work moved with deliberate slothfulness, slowing the work as much as possible. Morale was low and production even lower.

Nat Turner's raids had given the slave the taste of freedom and Gloria was losing at least two slaves a month. Some of the runaways were never captured, never heard from again and presumed to have found freedom, while others were brought back and severely punished.

The circle in the front of the house became a place where

captured runaways were tied to the tree and thrashed as an example to the others of what would happen if they dared to run away. Though it was a barbaric practice it was also a useless effort. It was meant to deter future runaways but it only served to make freedom even more appealing.

Everyone had been affected in some way by Nat Turner's raids. For the first time in his life James felt almost afraid of the slaves. He'd seen entire white families butchered in the revolt. He had been taught to see the slaves as helpless children who needed direction and he'd never questioned that belief. Now he saw them as angry men and women. With great apprehension James realized that there were only four white people to more than fifty slaves left on Gloria and recent events had given James good reason to fear. At any given moment the slaves could rise up against the Vance family and they wouldn't stand a chance against them all. He knew that it was imperative that an overseer as well as several other white men be hired as soon as possible.

David had obviously shared James' fears because he began to spend more time on the plantation. He had never cared much for riding the fields to watch over the field hands but now he cared for it even less. But he knew that the job had become too dangerous for James to handle alone.

After the rebellion life on Gloria would never be the same. It was October, exactly two months since the slave rebellion and although Beth would never be totally at peace, she had found more peace in the last couple of months than she had since her arrival on Gloria. David had moved into her room and it seemed that he was making every effort to keep the promises he'd made the night of the ball.

Occasionally Beth would smell brandy on his breath but not once since he'd moved into her room had he come to her in a complete drunken stupor. They would often retire early and spend hours together in the rooms they now shared. David was kind and gentle and his lovemaking was passionate. Each time Beth would lie awake in his arms she was reminded of just why she had fallen in love with the gallant southern gentleman.

However, her happiness was short lived. Just when she was beginning to feel that she was truly David's wife he began to pull away again. She would sometimes catch him starring blankly into space. More and more he came to bed very late and was distant and sullen when they were alone together. Beth ignored his sullen moods attributing his distance to the difficulties he and James were now having in the running of the plantation. But somewhere deep inside Beth wondered if David were thinking of Lillian. She wondered if he were missing Lillian when he made love to her. Beth knew that she could make David happy but she didn't know if she could make him forget the woman who had almost destroyed them both.

One cool October day Beth and David had planned to ride into town after breakfast. David would, of course, take care of some family business while Beth, along with Denny, would be free to shop for fabrics and hats in Richmond. Beth came down to breakfast full of energy and excitement. "Good morning all," she said as she took her usual seat at the table.

'Good morning, Beth," James said. "Does my brother intend to join us for breakfast this morning?"

"He will be along shortly I'm sure."

"Good morning," David said as he took his place at the table. "Beth and I are going into Richmond today. I thought I'd look over those contracts at R.J. Reynolds today. Care to join us?"

"No. I've got business right here. It seems we've lost another overseer."

"We'll, I'm sure you'll find another in no time," David said as Lillian served him a plate of grits, eggs and hot biscuits.

Beth watched silently as Lillian sashayed around the table

smiling at no one except David while he did his best to ignore her flirtations. It was at that moment that Beth realized that she and David could never truly be happy as long as Lillian remained at Gloria.

Lillian was in the house day and night. Surely she and David had run into one another when no one else was around, Beth thought. How much longer could David resist her charms? Lillian's duties demanded that she be in the house and as Beth had learned, David would never agree to send her to the fields. All of these things ran through Beth's mind as she watched Lillian's prancing around the room. Suddenly their eyes met. Beth could feel the hatred that poured from the depths of Lillian's soul. As mistress and slave their stations in life had already placed them at odds with each other but both women knew that it was much more than that.

Beth now knew that the only way that she would ever truly be happy is to get Lillian away from Gloria permanently, but how? She really had no idea but she vowed to find a way to be rid of Lillian forever.

Chapter 9

Spring, 1836
GLORIA
The Vance Plantation
Richmond, Virginia

*I*t had been four years since David promised Beth he would be the husband she deserved. Unfortunately, it wasn't very long before David's resolve began to crumble and fall away. He assumed that as long as kept up the pretense of a happy marriage he would somehow have the strength to resist Lillian but he weakened more each time he saw her. His lust for Lillian was as addictive as it was intoxicating. Even he knew that it was slowly destroying him and he had no power to stop it.

Though he and Beth still shared a room as husband and wife he began to visit Lillian's shack every evening after Beth had fallen asleep. Lillian was smart enough to know that David's lust was the source of her control and she rarely turned him away. The last time she turned him away he went straight into the arms of his white wife and Lillian would never let that happen again. Instead she chose to feed his addiction whenever possible, finding some satisfaction in

David's inability to stay away from her. His weakness was evenly matched with his self loathing and he often stumbled back to Beth in the wee hours of the morning. On those rare occasions when he tried to be strong and not go to Lillian he would drown his sorrow in brandy. As he became more dependent on Lillian and brandy he came to accept that he was incapable of being the husband he'd promised Beth.

David agonized as he watched his daughter Rebecca grow from a shy child into a lonely, misplaced, but beautiful young woman. He wished that he could buy her the clothes and education that would do her beauty justice. Besides Bell and Lillian no one ever said anything to the girl. While there were plenty of other mixed race children on Gloria, Rebecca was set apart from them. She knew that she wasn't white but she didn't feel black. Some said that Lillian's superior attitude had inflated the child's impression of herself among the other slaves. She was the massa's bastard, a fact that others thought should bring her shame but a fact that she thought lifted her above her own people.

David once watched Rebecca from a window as she sat on the wooden steps of the kitchen house. A young slave named Warren brought wood for the kitchen stove. When he spotted Rebecca on the steps he looked quickly around him to see that no one saw him as he approach her.

"Becca," he said. "You sho is lookin good. Seem kind of lonely though. How about you and me jumpin the broom this Sunday? I can promise, you sho won't be lonely no more."

"Warren you talks real sweet but I ain't bout to jump no broom with no body and if I was, it sho wouldn't be with the likes of you and your kind."

"MY KIND? What you mean my kind?"

"You knows right well what I mean Warren."

"I hate to be the one to tell you Missy but you my kind. You may be a shade lighter but you just a slave like the rest of us, even if your daddy is a white man."

Rebecca had never heard anyone mention who her daddy was but folks took great pleasure in pointing out that her daddy, who ever he was, he was a white man. Warren talked on, "I hope you ain't thinking that massa David is gone marry you off to a white man cause that ain't gone happen. You better start looking some of our kind over, lessin' you want to be what your Ma is, a white man's whore."

With tears streaming down her soft cheeks Rebecca screamed at Warren. "You get way from me Warren. You get away from me this minute or I'll scream for Bell, I swear."

Warren didn't answer. He picked up his bundle of fire wood and took a couple of steps away from Rebecca. When he turned back Rebecca held her head in her hands and sobbed. "When you start thinking bout jumping the broom you remember, I'm about the best you gone find round these parts and you'll be lucky to have me."

With his heart heavy David turned away from the window and went to pour himself a drink. It seemed that his entire world was falling apart. Even Beth seemed to have become complacent. She no longer tried to comfort him in any way. When he came to her in the early morning after leaving Lillian she did not accuse him as he'd expected. She didn't even ask where he'd been or why he came to bed so late. She never said a word. She didn't pressure him to make love to her or to even spend time with her. David had begun to think that Beth no longer loved him at all but he was wrong. Beth still loved her husband very much and she never stopped thinking of what she could do to win her husband back from Lillian's addictive curse.

She and David still slept in the same bed, ate all of their meals together and spent weekends shopping in Richmond a couple of times a month. She knew that the loving couple that they portrayed was little more than a farce. Even so, people were beginning to talk. "Why hadn't she been able to give the Vance family an heir? Poor David had married a northern girl not knowing that she was barren. Unless the younger Vance brother married, the family name would end with the brothers."

Beth knew that there was little chance of reconciliation between her and David as long as Lillian remained on Gloria. She spent many nights praying for a way to get Lillian away from the plantation. The opportunity came in late September of 1837 when Bell became very ill. Beth was reading in the parlor when Nan came to tell her that Bell had fallen ill. Her first reaction was to immediately tell Lillian that she would be assigned to the kitchen but it occurred to her that such an order may appear vengeful to David and James and might, in fact, prompt one of them to rescind the order. She couldn't take that chance. She didn't want her authority to be undermined in front of Lillian. No, she would first discuss this with David, calmly pointing out the advantage of such a decision.

Visiting the sick had become Beth's custom and she prepared to visit with Bell and her family. She packed a basket of assorted jellies and biscuits and set out for the shacks behind the kitchen house. As she passed Lillian's shack, the glow of the flickering lamp blinked in the window and Beth briefly wondered if David were with Lillian. She resisted the temptation to peep into the window and continued on to Bell's shack.

Over the years Beth had made many visits to sick slaves, always bringing a small gift for the family. She had always been warmly received and her interest appreciated. But this time Beth was greeted with an unexpected cold indifference. She tapped lightly on the door and it was answered by Nan's man Jacob. He could not forbid Beth entry into the cabin but the look on his face could not hide his displeasure. Beth entered warily. "Good evening," she said. "I brought some sweet jellies for your girls," she said.

"Thank you, Ma'am," Jacob said as he took the basket and put in on the center of the only table in the shack.

"I've come to see Bell." Jacob did not answer but pointed to Bell who was laying on a cot in the corner of the drafty room, wheezing and gasping for breath. Beth knew that Bell was ill but she hadn't expected her to be quite that as sick as she appeared. She immediately took off her shawl and went to Bell's bedside.

"Bell, I had no idea that you were so ill. I'll send someone for the doctor right away."

"There ain't no need for a doctor Miss Beth. I've made my peace. Now all that's left is for me to do is to wait for my true Master to call me home. Then I will truly be free."

"No Bell! That's nonsense you are not going to die." Beth placed her hand on Bell's head. "She's burning up. Why didn't someone tell me she was ill before now?"

"I thought it would pass," Bell said.

"I'm going to send for a doctor right now."

"No doctor, Ma'am," Bell whispered.

"Bell, I'm sure you don't know what you're saying. The fever is probably making you irrational."

"She knows exactly what she's saying Miss Beth," Nan said as she came in and joined her husband. "Bell thinks this sickness is God's way of bringing her home to be free."

"It's the only thing a slave got to look forward to Miss Beth," Jacob said.

Beth looked from one face to the next. She couldn't believe what she was hearing. These people who had been so kind to her since her arrival actually preferred death to slavery.

Bell coughed and everyone's attention turned to that small cot. Bell's body was jarred by an eruption of violent coughing and she grabbed for a rag under her pillow. Beth watched as the woman brought up clots of blood and spat into the rag and she knew that

Bell was dying. She also knew that a doctor could only provide a small measure of comfort but she felt as if she owed Bell at least that much. Tears filled her eyes as she looked away from Bell to Jacob and Nan but they both only shook their heads.

"No need to shed them tears for old Bell, Miss Beth. I'm gone be just fine," Bell said.

"She gone be a damn sight better off than us who's got to stay here. Bell is gone be free."

Beth knew that her words would only fall on deft ears so she said no more about the doctor. She bent down and kissed Bell's moist forehead. "I'll look in on you again tomorrow Bell."

"Yes Ma'am," Bell whispered.

"Stay with her tonight, Nan."

"Oh, I will Miss Beth. Me and Jacob gone be right here."

Beth nodded and left the shack.

That evening after supper Beth told David and James that Bell was dying. It angered Beth that both men received the news with marked indifference. "Has it ever occurred to either of you that the people who serve you prefer the freedom of death to a life of servitude?"

James did not answer.

"Yes," David said after several minutes. "Yes Beth, it has occurred to me but I cannot be the one who takes responsibility for another's station in life."

"David," she screamed. "You actually own people! You own entire families. If you are not responsible, at least for the people you own, just whose responsibility is it?"

David was suddenly angry. He pushed his chair back with such force that Beth jumped at the gesture. "I am sick to death of all this talk about slavery, slave revolts and responsibility; and I'm sick of you with your misplaced compassion and your righteous indignation. The institution of slavery did not begin with the Vance family. If we did not own slaves, Elizabeth, we would not make the kind of money that allows you to live like a queen."

"That is exactly the point, isn't it David?" Beth stood up and walked to face her angry husband. "I am no more a queen than you are a king. We are all guilty of using people, black people David. And I fear that we will all one day pay dearly for the advantages we now enjoy at their expense."

"Beth, you just don't understand business and what's more, it is not your place to understand. I've told you more than once to stay out of plantation business."

"Is that what this is, a business? Is that what you call it, a business? If that is true, than you are right, I don't understand. Over these five years that I've lived here I've tried to understand or at least block it out of my mind. I even tried to believe all that nonsense about the Africans needing us like the southern gentleman was some knight from a different era. But when I see a woman who has served this family her entire life say that she prefers death, rather than to be in your service, I am hard pressed to find anything appealing in the buying and selling of human beings as beast of burden."

"Beth, this is not my doing. Why must you lay this at my feet? It is exactly that same Master that they long to serve in death that has made me Master over their lives."

"You are so wrong David. God does not make slaves. Only men can make slaves of other men."

"I refuse to stand here and listen to another word of this. Bell is not dying because she's a slave, Beth. She's dying because she's old and weak. She probably has pneumonia."

"She is going to die, David, probably before morning. Doesn't that mean anything to you?"

"Yes. It means that Gloria needs a new cook. Replace her immediately and in the future remember that you are the mistress of this house and I prefer not to be bothered by such trivia."

Bell died quietly in her sleep two nights later. Early the next day Beth was awaken by the low and mournful voices of the slaves as they sang their loved one into Glory. Beth lay awake for hours listening to the slaves as they sang spiritual songs of the Promised Land. They sang of a place where they would toil no more, where they would be free of sickness, heartache and bondage. Just as Jacob had tried to explain, the slaves did not mourn for Bell's death but rejoiced in her freedom. They mourned only for themselves who would be left here to toil the rest of their lives. Beth wondered why they had chosen this predawn hour for their ritual.

The voices of the slaves seemed to come closer and closer until finally it seemed as if they had surrounded the entire plantation. As they came even closer, Beth heard something menacing in their tone and she was suddenly alarmed. She left her bed to watch from the balcony outside her room. Her alarm faded as she watched in complete awe. Men, women and children, all clad in white from head to toe were marching in a single line with slow deliberate precision. Bell's body had also been dressed in white and was being carried on the shoulders of six men at the head of the line. Two men in the very front and each person in the line that followed those carrying Bell's body, carried a lighted torch. David came to stand beside his wife on the balcony and Beth leaned into him grateful for his strong support. "Where are they going?" she asked.

"To their graveyard," he answered.

"But I thought that the graveyard was on the other side of the house."

"No. It's against the law for blacks and withes to be buried in the same ground. The Vance graveyard is on the other side of the house. The slaves bury their dead about three miles west."

Even in death they are persecuted, Beth thought as she watched the slaves continue their march. Their white robes and the glow of their torches illuminated the sky to form a golden arch with a moon lit background as they walked slowly across the horizon. "I've never seen anything like this in my life," Beth said. "Do all slaves perform the same ritual for their dead?"

"I don't know but here at Gloria, it's been their tradition for as long as I can remember. By the time they reach the grave site the sun will be just beginning to dawn. They'll push their torches into the ground in a circle around the grave. Then they will pray and sing until the sun rises. After placing the body into the ground, they'll sing praises to God for taking his child home to live in the Promised Land. When I was a child I use to be very afraid of this ceremony."

"Why?"

"The entire ceremony is quite symbolic. Their torches mark the spot on this great earth to aid God in finding the child He has called home. Of course, they all know that God doesn't need their help. It has something to do with an ancient African practice but as a child I use to think that their torches would let God know where he could find all of us and we would somehow be punished for enslaving his children. I actually thought that the slaves were God's children and we were not."

"You see, David," Beth said. "Even as a child you knew that there was something very wrong in slavery. As an adult, do you still believe that God will punish you for their enslavement?"

"Don't be ridiculous." David went back to the bed. "I'm not even sure that we pray to the same god. What I'm more afraid of is that the bleeding hearts of the world, like yourself, will one day fight to end slavery and we will all be ruined."

Beth did not ask any more questions. Watching the slaves march to their graveyard had touched her in a way that she couldn't quite understand. She wasn't sure how but there was something in her that had not been there before. She was filled with remorse but not just because the woman who had helped to save her life had now lost her own, but because she felt that all those that Bell had left behind were headed for some sort of doom. Something spiritual and unexplained had taken hold of her entire being and Beth knew that even if everything remained the same, she had somehow been changed by Bell's death.

By the next day things on Gloria had returned to normal. Beth wasted no time in carrying out her mission to get Lillian out of the house and away from Gloria. Lillian was summoned and Beth waited in the library impatiently. After what seemed like hours, Lillian appeared at the door. "Miss Beth, you wanted to see me?"

Beth swung around to face her adversary. "Close the door," she commanded. Lillian stood perfectly still as Beth slowly advanced toward her. Lillian's face still held a smirk of defiance. "The last time we spoke I told you that I was prepared to fight. I also told you that I would not rest until you were permanently off of Gloria land. Well, fortunately for you, I have not, as yet, devised a way to rid Gloria of your presence. You were right, of course. David would not allow me to sell you or to send you to the fields. I have, however, found a way to rid the house of your presence. David has agreed that from this day forward you will work the kitchen house and your daughter will assist Denny as my personal maid. You will start in the kitchen house today. See to it that Rebecca begins to spend some time with Denny. There is much for her to learn. She will begin her complete duties in one week's time." Beth waited for a response and hearing none, she went on. "You are not allowed in this house from this day forward. If I find you in my house I will have you severely punished. Do you understand what I've said Lillian?"

Lillian chuckled. "Ma'am always wants to know if I understand," she said. "Yes. I understand but I'm not so sure you understand."

Beth was speechless for several seconds. She couldn't even have imagined such insolence. She watched Lillian as she began to slowly sashay around the library.

"You see, Miss Beth. None of this means anything. Do you know why?"

"Enlighten me."

"There ain't nothin you can do that's gone keep massa from me. You can keep me out of the house but you can't keep me out of his heart and you can't keep him away from me."

"I could have you whipped for that statement."

"You think I don't know that. Even a whipping ain't gone change the truth."

"Get out! I don't ever want to look at you face again, get out!" Beth screamed. She had come to the library with feelings of triumph and victory. She would finally be able to put that woman in her place but once again, Lillian had defeated her with only a few words. What was even worse, Beth knew that Lillian was right. She knew that David would continue to go to Lillian for as long as she remained at Gloria. The only solution was to rid Gloria of Lillian entirely.

Part Four

Retribution

"Nay, but for terror of His wrathful face,
I swear I will not call injustice grace."

The Rubiyat of Omar Khayyan
Translated by Edward Fitzgerald, 1992

Chapter 10

❦

GLORIA
The Vance Plantation
Richmond, Virginia

*I*t had become Beth's habit to ride over the countryside in the early morning before breakfast was served. In summer the mornings were the coolest part of the day and in the fall the air was cool and crisp. David and James rarely accompanied Beth and she was often grateful for the few hours alone.

It was the end of September and David had traveled to Richmond for supplies as he often did at the end of the month. James was continually busy with the family accounts. With both brothers busy with family business Beth saw the day as the perfect opportunity to get a few hours of riding before the sun brought on the heat of the day. After sending Denny to have her horse saddled she dismissed Denny and Rebecca until the afternoon meal. A few minutes later Jacob walked the horse around to the front of the house.

"Thank you Jacob. Isn't it a beautiful morning," Beth could hardly contain her excitement.

"Nice day," Jacob said as he wondered what could possibly make his mistress so happy this early in the morning.

With Jacob's help, Beth swung herself into the saddle and urged the horse forward. She rarely ran into anyone on the road in the early morning but lately she seemed to encounter Martin Stone quite regularly. Martin Stone was the owner of the plantation just north of Gloria and had been a guest at the Vance home on many occasions. He was a tall thin man with neatly cropped brown hair and dark eyes. His features were sharp, almost common but Beth thought that he was every bit as handsome as David was.

It sometimes occurred to her that these meetings were not altogether accidental. In fact, there were many mornings that she looked forward to bumping into Mr. Stone.

"Good morning," she yelled as Mr. Stone reined in his horse next to her.

"Morning," he replied as he tipped his hat.

"It seems we just keep running into one another," Beth said coyly.

"Maybe that's because I know exactly what time you ride."

"Have you been planning these meetings Mr. Stone?"

"What if I were?"

"You're not playing fair, Mr. Stone. You cannot answer a question with a question." Beth dug her heels into the horses flesh and the animal was spurred forward at a steady pace. Mr. Stone followed.

"You're right. Let's begin again and I'll ask the first question."

Beth nodded.

"Would you be offended if I told you that running into you in the morning has never been an accident?"

"No, I would take no offense. I would only want to ask why?"

"Alright, you've found me out," he said playfully.

Beth pulled the reins in and stopped. "Are you flirting with me Mr. Stone?"

"A hundred apologies if I have offended you in any way Mrs. Vance but I cannot lie, I enjoy running into you."

"You are flirting," Beth said.

"I admit it. I am quite taken with you Mrs. Vance. You are so beautiful yet you seem to be so sad whenever we meet."

"Believe me my sadness hasn't anything to do with you, Mr. Stone."

"I know that but I can't help wanting to see such a beautiful woman smile at least sometimes."

Beth frowned. She didn't know where this was going but she was beginning to feel uncomfortable.

"I've offended you again?" Martin asked.

"Mr. Stone, are you forgetting that I am a married woman?"

"That Madam is unfortunate for both of us."

Beth couldn't deny that she was flattered by Mr. Stone's advances but now she felt that he had gone too far. "What does that mean, if I may ask?"

"It's no secret that your marriage is not the steadiest of unions. Of course, gossips rarely have all the details but your unhappiness is written on your face for the whole world to see."

"So my marriage has become the topic of afternoon tea parties?"

"I thought you knew."

"No, I had no idea." They rode in silence for a few minutes. They probably all know about Lillian too, Beth thought. "What comes after the accidental meetings Mr. Stone?"

"Whatever you like, your wish is my command."

"You know David isn't the same man I met in Philadelphia. There is just something about this place that changes him."

"Beth, I want to make you smile I don't want to talk about your husband. Understood?"

"I understand."

There's an empty shack just on the other side of that hill. What do you say we take a ride up there and rest our horses a bit?"

As they rode toward the shack Beth's mind raced far ahead. This man wants to seduce me and I've done nothing to discourage him. In fact, I've been encouraging him. This was lust just as it had been with James. Martin Stone would not feel the burden of guilt as James had and turn away. If she offered herself, Martin would surely take her.

Once inside the shack Martin wasted no time but began to quickly undress while Beth stood stock still in the middle of the floor. Martin stepped out of his trousers and looked up into Beth's dazed face. In an instant he was by her side, sweeping her into his arms. I'll understand if you'd rather not."

As Beth felt the warmth of his flesh against her own all of her guilt and inhibitions were suddenly washed away and Beth surrendered to her mounting desire. She needed the feel of him to remove the longing that had become so much a part of her. Martin slowly and patiently helped Beth to undress. He spread their clothes on the dusty floor to serve as a pallet and soon they explored the mysteries of each other's bodies. He caressed and kissed every inch of Beth's body until she thought she would explode. Finally he entered her smooth sweetness and she welcomed him, wrapping her legs around his strong back and instinctively moving to the sensual rhythm of his body. Beth was shocked at the height of her own passion. Their love making was slow and patient and when it was finally over, Beth missed him as soon as the warmth of his body left her own. They spoke no words but dressed quickly and left the shack.

Martin helped Beth to mount her horse. "Shall we meet again?" he asked.

"We shouldn't," Beth answered.

"I know but I want to be with you again."

"And I you, but this is all so dangerous."

"I promise to be very careful."

"Alright, in two days I will meet you here at dawn."

"Until then, my sweet," Martin said as he kissed two of his fingers and pressed them to Beth's lips.

"Until then," she said before she turned her mare and galloped down the hill.

For days Beth was burdened with guilt. She couldn't help thinking that she had acted no better than a common whore, but almost as soon as the thought came to her she would remember that her husband left her barren and alone while he sought the sexual charms of another. Why should she feel any guilt or shame? She deserved happiness as much as anyone did, but of course, this was not happiness. Could this be revenge? She didn't know but she did know that her infatuation with Martin Stone was nothing more than lust, carnal abandon.

Even with her feelings of guilt, shame, revenge and lust, she met Martin again and again. Sometimes she could hardly wait until they could come together again. Each time he took her in his arms, each time she felt him rise at the sight of her, all her inhibitions vanished and she gave in to her desire. Though she knew that she did not love Martin, he made her feel like a desirable woman again and for that she was grateful.

*D*enny resented having Rebecca tag along with her. She was little more than a child when she was assigned to be Miss Beth's personal maid and it had taken her a couple of years to learn all of her mistresses likes and dislikes. She was nearly sixteen now and she knew exactly what to do to make her mistress happy. When things were going well, Miss Beth would give Denny time off and she would be free to visit her family in the field shacks. But she knew that those times would not come too often since she would now have to look after Rebecca. Denny knew that she was suppose to be teaching Rebecca how to be a personal maid but she wondered if that was the real reason why Rebecca had to tag along behind her. It was more likely that massa David just wanted to give the girl something to do to keep her out of everyone's hair.

The two girls were close in age but as different as dogs and cats. It seemed that no matter what the chore, Rebecca found a way to simply not comply or blame Denny when things went wrong.

One night Miss Beth asked that her bath be drawn and Denny sent Rebecca to fetch one of the men to bring up the hot water. Denny laid out fresh towels, a nightgown and slippers for her mistress while she waited for the water. After more than an hour of waiting, the water still had not come.

"Denny did you tell Jacob to bring up the water," Beth wanted to know.

"Yes Ma'am. I'll go see what's taking so long." She excused herself and went to look for Jacob. When she found him he said that he hadn't seen Rebecca and no one had told him to bring up the bath water. "You better hurry Jacob. Miss Beth's been waiting for that water for a long time."

Then Denny went to find Rebecca. She found her gorging on apple pie and milk in the kitchen house with her mother.

'Becca!" Denny yelled. "Miss Beth has been waiting for her bath water for a long time. What happened?"

"Oh," Rebecca answered nonchalantly. "I forgot."

Denny looked from mother to daughter and decided that it would not be wise to engage either in an argument. She simply turned and left the kitchen.

Later that evening Denny explained to Miss Beth that Rebecca was just not interested in learning how to be a maid and she spent most of her time in the kitchen house with her mother. The next morning Beth summoned both girls.

"Rebecca," Beth tried to keep the agitation from her voice. "You've been with Denny now for a couple of months and I think that it is time you assume some of your own chores. We'll start with the chamber pots. The pots must be emptied and cleaned four times a day." She held up four fingers to make sure the girl understood. "I never want to wake to a soiled chamber pot. You will change and wash the bed linens twice a week. Also, you will help Denny when I need dressing and I expect you to be here whenever I need you. I'll assign other duties as they come to mind. Do you understand?"

"Yes Ma'am."

"Good. Denny, I should be back in an hour or so. I intend to come directly to my room so please have a breakfast tray sent up and a bath drawn by the time I get back."

"Yes Ma'am," Denny said. Both girls curtsied and backed out of the room.

Rebecca was furious. She had come to hate Miss Beth even though Miss Beth had never been anything but kind to her. Rebecca knew that her mistress did not like her mother and she hated her for that if nothing else. As soon as Beth left she would go in and empty the chamber pots as she was told, but as soon as she could, she would escape to the empty shack on the hill. Rebecca often went to the shack. It was her castle, her promised land. There, it didn't matter if she were black or white, if she were slave or free. The shack was her world where she was Mistress. She could hide there for hours while Denny ran around doing most of the chores.

As soon as she could Rebecca headed up the hill to her castle. When she finally reached the top of the hill she could tell that someone else was there. She heard voices as she approached the shack cautiously. "I'll meet you again the day after tomorrow." Rebecca recognized the familiar voice of her mistress. She warily moved closer to the shack's window. Even through the layers of dust on the windows Rebecca could see Mr. Stone dressed in only his boots. She covered her mouth to stifle a gasp that threatened to reveal her presence.

"David should take better care of you Beth. If I were your husband I'd make sure you never had a reason to seek another," Mr. Stone said.

Beth finally stood up revealing her nakedness. Again Rebecca stifled a gasp. She watched as Mr. Stone took Beth in his arms and kissed her, his hands roaming Beth's body. Rebecca knew that she would have to hurry to get back to the big house before her mistress, so as soon as she saw Beth had begun to dress, she crept away from the shack window and ran down the hill as fast as she could. She entered the house through the back and heard Denny call her as she ran. "Rebecca! Where you been girl? Miss Beth be wanting her bath now. You better get moving."

"Alright, calm yourself Denny."

Once the hot water had been brought up, Rebecca hurried to help her mistress undress but she couldn't stop thinking about what she saw in the shack. Miss Beth had given herself to another man. If massa Vance knew he would surely send her right back to Philadelphia where she came from.

The next morning Rebecca was late in attending Beth. She rushed in with a flood of apologies. "I'm so sorry Ma'am. I promise I won't be late no more."

"It's alright Rebecca. I will do just fine dressing alone this morning."

"Yes Ma'am. I promise I won't be late again. I knows how you like to be on time for Mr. Stone." As soon as the words left her lips

Rebecca realized that she had said something wrong and she covered her face with her hands.

"What?" Beth was so shocked that she began to tremble. She grabbed the girl by the arm. "What are you talking about?"

Rebecca did not answer. She began to cry.

"Answer me, girl," Beth said as she took Rebecca by her shoulders and began to violently shake the girl.

"I saw you and Mr. Stone in the shack on the hill. I'm sorry, Ma'am. I didn't know I wasn't supposed to be there."

Beth was devastated. She pulled the girl to her and began to caress her. "Don't cry Rebecca. You didn't do anything wrong."

"But I didn't mean to see. I go there lots of times. I heard voices so I looked in the window."

"I know that you didn't mean to see us. Listen to me. Stop crying and listen to me."

"Yes," Rebecca sobbed.

"You must never tell anyone what you saw at the shack. This will be our secret. Do you understand? No one must know."

"Yes Ma'am. I won't tell anyone, I promise."

"Now stop crying. Go and tell Nan that I said you can have a slice of cherry pie. Will that make you feel better?"

"Yes Ma'am."

As soon as Rebecca left the room Beth broke into tears. How could she have been so careless? If David ever found out that she had been unfaithful she knew she would lose him to Lillian forever. How could she be sure that Rebecca would not tell what she saw to her mother or worse yet, she might go right to David? For all Beth knew she could be telling Lillian at that very moment and Beth knew that Lillian would use the information to destroy her. She couldn't let that happen. She would do everything in her power to keep David from finding out about Martin. Now she had no choice in the matter. Lillian had to go and Beth cared little for what it would take to finally and completely be rid of the woman and her meddling daughter.

Beth decided that she had to meet with Martin one last time and explain why they could not continue their affair. Martin was reluctant to end the affair and suggested that they meet less often instead of doing away with a relationship that he considered special. "You worry too much," he tried to console. "If you keep her busy she will no doubt forget all about the entire incident."

"No. You're wrong. She won't forget and what's more, she may have already told her mother. If Lillian knows, my marriage is as good as over."

"That might not be a bad thing."

"What are you saying Martin? I can't think of anything worse."

"Even if our association is made known, people will only say that David drove you to it with his flagrant disregard for your feelings. For god's sake Beth, he's been bedding one of his slaves right under your nose!"

Beth thought for a moment. That was the first time she had heard anyone actually put the entire affair in words. The more she thought about it the more she agreed that David had disregarded her feelings and why shouldn't she seek comfort from someone other than her husband? Who could blame her? "We have got to be very careful Martin."

"We will," he whispered as he took Beth in his arms and made love to her.

Beth continued to secretly meet with Martin and there was no sign that anyone on Gloria was the wiser. One brisk October morning Beth had her horse saddled and headed out over the still lush green hills of Gloria hoping to meet with Martin. She had been riding the better part of an hour when she doubled back toward the shack but she was suddenly stricken with a violent attack of dizziness and nausea. It came on so quickly that she was unable to dismount before her stomach retched. Her throat constricted and her entire body convulsed violently. The sudden movement frightened her horse and it suddenly broke into a rapid gallop across the hills. Still dizzy and weakened from the nausea Beth held tight to the reins while she struggled to control the horse. She had no idea how long her struggled lasted but without warning the horse stumbled and she was thrown headlong into a tree, losing consciousness immediately.

It was two days before Beth opened her eyes. At first she tried to sit up but her head ached so that she gave up and fell back onto the pillows. Denny, noticing that her mistress had finally regained consciousness, was overjoyed. "Massa David! massa James! Miss Beth is awake," she screamed. Denny's high-pitched voice screeched inside of Beth's aching head.

David, James and Dr. Anders all came running in response to Denny's call. David was the first to reach Beth and taking her hand in his own he knelt at her bedside. "My darling, you've given all of us quite a scare. We thought for a while that we might lose you. Does your head hurt very much?"

"Yes," Beth weakly managed.

"I'm so sorry."

"You have to be more careful Beth," James put in. "We've all gotten kind of use to having a lady around. I won't allow you to leave us just yet. We will never let you ride alone again."

"Alright, David and James, both of you move aside and let me examine my patient," the doctor said. Once alone the doctor examined Beth thoroughly before he said, 'You took quite a lump on the head. I'm sorry but you'll have that headache for a few more days. Other than that, you'll be just fine. You and David may try to begin a family again whenever you feel up to it."

"A family," Beth repeated. She couldn't believe what she was hearing. "Dr. Anders you're saying that I'm pregnant?"

"You were pregnant, dear, before that nasty fall. You didn't know?"

"No. I had no idea. Does David know?"

"Yes, of course." Dr. Anders seemed puzzled. He expected Beth to be more upset after having been married for over seven years without conceiving an heir only to have lost her first pregnancy. "I examined you shortly after you were brought home and your husband was very worried. But there is no need to worry dear. As I said, there is no permanent damage and you and your husband can begin a family whenever you like."

"Thank you doctor," Beth whispered. She turned her face to her pillow and sobbed softly.

This seem to satisfy the old doctor and he said his good byes and left.

Who had fathered the baby that she lost, Beth wondered. She and David had been together so seldom that the possibility of the baby being David's was remote at best. The baby was Martin's, she was sure.

Dr. Anders was right. After only a few days the headache disappeared but she was still left with a terrible numbness. David apologized profusely as if he had some responsibility in the lost of the child. The doctor had not told either of them how far along Beth was and David never doubted that the child was his.

Both David and James hung about Beth as if she were a small child. Their fretful attention made Beth nervous. It was as if they expected that any moment she might suddenly collapse from grief. Beth did grieve but not because of the child she lost. The realization of what could have happened had she found herself pregnant with another man's child was enough to grieve her. She wanted to go to Martin and tell him of all that had happened but how could she when she was being watched so closely. She knew that eventually Martin would hear of all that had happened. She also knew that to meet Martin again would be foolish and she never rode to the shack again.

or years after the massacre of the whites, small groups of runaway slaves and white abolitionist groups began to spring up throughout Richmond, South Hampton and Norfolk counties. Beth had heard the slaves whispering that a band of runaway slaves and abolitionists were camped in the forest near the James River. The band was led by a white man named Colonel Tate. The slaves called him simply the Colonel.

The first time Beth was to hear of this was when General Barnett came calling one fall evening. He was invited to stay for supper and after the meal was over, the men began to discuss business. The General expressed his concern about the band of abolitionists in his usual fiery tone which was not short of expletives as he raged against the growing opposition to the southern way of life. Ladies usually excused themselves when the men began to talk business but Beth feigned ignorance as she slowly sipped her wine, hoping to hear more of the abolitionist's activities. It occurred to her that this band of law breakers could somehow be instrumental in her plan to get rid of Lillian and Rebecca.

When Beth realized that the men had curtailed their conversation because of her presence, she politely excused herself and went straight to her room. She lay awake for hours thinking and planning. When she finally fell asleep, she knew exactly what she must do.

Beth had not been allowed to ride alone since her fall so she waited and prayed for an opportunity to carry out her plan. David spent most of his evenings with a bottle of brandy while James worked on the family books night after night until late in the evening. It was just such an evening that Beth decided to finally put her plan into action.

It was late February and David had drunk himself into a stupor and passed out as soon as he reached her room. Beth quietly crept out of the house and to the stables. As soon as her horse was saddled she left, walking the horse until she was far enough away from the house that she was sure she could not to be heard. Then she mounted and rode toward the river.

She tied her horse to a well-hidden tree and then picked her way toward the clearing by the river. She heard voices and knew that she traveled in the right direction.

"Shush! Someone's coming!" one of the men said. Beth stepped through the clearing to see several black and white faces huddled around a fire. The largest of the men was a white man with a long gray beard. He wore a patch over his right eye and a large earring in one ear. His one visible eye was a mere slit which made him look as if he were squinting. There was a look of unlawfulness about him and Beth thought he looked like an old pirate. She quickly contemplated a change of plans. Maybe this wasn't such a good idea she thought. But then she told herself that there was no other way to be finally rid of Lillian. All of the men looked up at her as if she were a ghost. The one eyed white man held a stick in his hand that he had been using to draw some sort of map in the dry earth. Somehow Beth knew that this must be the leader.

"Are you Colonel Tate?" she asked as she tried to hide her fear.

"Who wants to know?" He rose to his feet and walked toward Beth. Her natural response was to take a few steps backward. "Who are you?"

"My name is Elizabeth Vance."

"You're shaking like a leaf. Afraid, are you?" he grinned wide and toothless. "Take it easy Ma'am. Ain't no body gonna hurt you." He dropped down on his haunches and then turned to look up at Beth again. One of the others, a ragged black man, led her to a rock at the edge of the clearing. "Take a seat and tell us what makes a lady like you seek a band of outlaws."

All eyes turned to Beth. "I'm from the Gloria plantation," she stuttered. "I would like to hire your services, that is, the services of Colonel Tate."

"I'm the Colonel," the one eyed man said. "Just what kind of service are you talking about?" The group snickered.

"There is a slave woman and her child that I would like to set free. I thought you could help her get safe travel north."

"Why not just set the woman free and give her the proper papers?" the man questioned suspiciously.

"Well, I would but you see," Beth stumbled through her explanation. "My husband would not hear of such a thing and the woman is much too loyal to leave Gloria of her own accord. I am extremely fond of this woman and her child and I thought I might help her in this small way. I'm willing to pay you a very handsome sum.

The man gave a small laugh as he stood. "Our services are not for hire," he said bluntly. "Our mission is a God given one. We have been called upon by God to stamp out this unjust system that allows men to enslave other men. Freedom is not a commodity that you can buy like some new French fashion, Mrs. Vance."

With the one eyed man standing probably well over six feet and Beth perched on a large rock looking up at him, she felt as if she were indeed small with a small request. She stood up abruptly seizing the authority that she felt her request demanded. "Colonel, I absolutely understand that your mission is a noble one but certainly there must be a need for funds to further your cause."

"Yes Ma'am, you're quite right but I've got a feeling that if you want this woman free it's for reasons that you are not saying."

"If your mission, sir, is God given as you say, my reasons are of no importance. You will simply have aided two slaves to freedom and acquired a handsome sum of money to fund future missions. I am willing to pay you five thousand dollars sir. Surely you can find the means to accommodate my request."

"You are quite a persuasive lady Mrs. Vance. You do realize that if I accept the money you offer it will buy a lot of guns and ammunition that will, in time, be used to forge an end to your way of life."

"Yes Colonel, I am quite aware of that and I do agree that it is an unjust and inhumane system. I could stand here and lament the evils of slavery but that would not serve my purpose at this time. Do we have a deal Colonel?"

"Would you mind giving me a moment to confer with my men?"

"Not at all," Beth said as she sat down to wait for the Colonel's decision. Colonel Tate and his men moved into the trees leaving Beth alone in the clearing.

Though it was only a few moments Beth began to again feel uneasy as she waited. Then she knew from the moment she saw the look on the men's faces that the Colonel had decided to accept her offer. Beth relaxed as she stood to shake the Colonel's hand and thank him.

"Thank you. I can't tell you how grateful I am sir. There is just one problem."

"I figured as much," the Colonel said.

"The woman doesn't know a thing about this and even if she did she wouldn't want to leave Gloria."

"You're suggesting that we steal her away from the plantation?"

"Exactly, that is the only way that she would ever leave."

"Where do we find her, what's her name?"

"Her name is Lillian. Are you familiar with the Gloria plantation?"

"I know that it is a few miles north of here."

"Yes, well, there is a supply shed approximately a hundred yards or so behind the main house. At exactly eight tomorrow evening I will send Lillian to the shed. A few minutes later I will send her daughter after her."

"Can we expect any interference?"

"Not if you're there at exactly eight. My husband and brother -in-law usually travel to Richmond for supplies at the end of each month. Neither will be at home and the Overseer's cabin is miles away from the shed. He shouldn't be able to hear you." Beth put her hand down into her boot and withdrew a folded kerchief containing the crisp new bills. The Colonel quickly fanned the bills before stuffing them into the inside of his coat. He then presented Beth his hand and she gratefully accepted it, sealing their deal.

In less than thirty minutes Beth was back at Gloria and no one suspected that she'd ever left.

The next morning David and James left the plantation before dawn just as Beth expected. The rest of the day seemed to drag on as Beth waited anxiously. She had imagined the entire incident. After Lillian was gone David would certainly grieve for a time. He would probably be so distraught over Lillian's runaway that he would turn to Beth for comfort. She would forgive him for all the hurt and happily accept him back. Then he would finally be hers alone.

The day seemed to move very slowly, almost dragging. Beth tried to occupy her time so as not to appear anxious but she was in fact so anxious that she caught herself wringing her hands more than once. After the evening meal was served, she locked herself up in the library and tried to read as she waited for the appropriate time.

At half past seven Beth sent Denny to summon Lillian and

Rebecca to the downstairs parlor. A short time later they both appeared and Beth could tell that they must have been sleeping. The girl, who was rarely called upon, shyly hung behind her mother. "Yes Ma'am, you wanted to see me?" Lillian asked.

"Yes. I wish to speak to you about Rebecca."

"Why? Has she done something?"

Beth sat in her chair facing the fire with her back to the two slaves. "Not exactly. I have already spoken to David and he agrees that Rebecca needs more supervision than Denny. Besides Denny has her own chores and I prefer Denny as my personal maid to Rebecca."

"Is that all?"

"No. Your daughter was made chamber maid some months ago. As you know, her responsibility was to empty and clean the chamber pots several times a day. She was also responsible for changing the beds and generally keeping the rooms upstairs free of dust. She has not as yet handled her responsibility to my satisfaction. She needs supervision," Beth paused and turned to look at Lillian. "That will be your responsibility. You are to teach the child to handle those chores responsibly. You will begin first thing tomorrow morning, five a.m."

"Have you forgotten," Lillian said smugly. "Ma'am has forbidden me to be in the house other than the dinning areas. I can't very well teach Rebecca of household chores if I am not allowed in the house."

Beth quickly turned to face the fire again. "No I have not forgotten. I've simply changed my mind. Do you understand?"

"Yes, but who will be responsible for the cooking and serving?"

"You will. There's been no change to the kitchen help."

"Is that all?"

"Yes. You may go. " Beth dismissed Lillian with a wave of her hand but Lillian did not move for several minutes while Beth continued to sit with her back to Lillian.

She was up to something, Lillian thought. Why would she summon Rebecca and me at this late hour, Lillian wondered? Had she seen David leave her shack a couple of days ago? Lillian didn't know what it was but she was sure that something was amiss. As she turned to leave the parlor she heard her mistress say, "Wait!" I knew it, Lillian thought.

"There isn't a single fresh candle in the entire house. Will you please fetch a box of candles from the supply shed? Rebecca can wait here until you return."

Lillian paused wondering again what Beth was up to. She knew that she could not disobey Beth so she simply hurried off to the supply shed for the candles.

Beth was becoming increasingly nervous. If the Colonel was off by one minute it would ruin everything. She began to pace back and forth while Rebecca eyed her suspiciously from her hiding place behind the curtain. For as long as Beth could remember Rebecca was always watching from some hiding place in the house. At times Beth had even thought that the girl was spying on her. The girl made Beth even more nervous.

The pacing stopped so abruptly that Rebecca was startled and she jumped at the sound of Beth's voice. "Your mother seems to be taking much longer than necessary just to fetch a few candles. Go and see what's keeping her."

Rebecca darted from behind the drapes and ran off to find her mother.

Beth wanted desperately to see if Colonel Tate had kept his word but she knew that she must appear to be totally unaware of the slave's disappearance. Beth listened intently but she could hear nothing. Had something gone wrong, she wondered? Maybe the Colonel had changed his mind or maybe the Colonel and his band of outlaws had been captured since she last spoke with them.

Neither Rebecca nor Lillian returned to the house and after hours of waiting Beth was finally overcome with her need to know if her plan had worked. The house was completely quiet and shrouded in darkness as Beth slowly crept to the back of the house. If something had gone wrong surely Lillian would have come back with the candles, she thought. Then Beth heard the hoof beat of many horses and she knew that she had succeeded. Lillian and Rebecca were finally gone.

Chapter 11

🍁

GLORIA
The Vance Plantation
Richmond, Virginia

Beth's strange behavior did not escape Lillian and the more she thought about it the more she knew that something just wasn't right. She took a lamp from the wall at the back of the house to light her way to the supply shed. She tried remembering if she had ever been summoned at such a late hour just to get candles from the shed. It was a strange request, all the more reason to think that her mistress was up to something, but what? The back of the house was pitch dark and the lamp Lillian held hardly lit her way but it did cast eerie shadows on the walls. Lillian was careful as she left the back of the house and headed for the shed. Just a few steps from the back door she heard the snapping of a twig. Someone was out there. Lillian froze in her tracks as she listened closely. Only a few seconds passed before she saw a large white man picking his way through the bushes behind the shed. Lillian quickly blew out the lamp and moved back into the shadow of the house. The door squeaked loudly and Lillian prayed that the man hadn't heard the noise. Inside the house she watched from the window.

The white man was dressed in a military uniform and was followed by several ragged black men who led their horses toward the shed. Lillian did not recognize the men from either Gloria or any of the neighboring plantations. Something told her that the men were looking for her. She watched as some of the men went inside the shed and the others seemed to be searching the ground behind the house and around the shed. After a few minutes the men in the shed came out to join the others. "There ain't no sign of them Colonel," one of the men whispered.

"Guess that pretty lady changed her mind," said another.

"Maybe," the white man acknowledged. "In any case we can't afford to wait around here while she makes up her pretty little mind. Let's move out."

Someone touched Lillian on the shoulder and she gasped and jumped in fear before she realized that it was Rebecca. "Ma'am says you taking too long with them candles."

"Shush," Lillian warned. "Ma'am don't really need no candles, child. What she wants is for them men out there to kill us both."

"Mama?"

"Shush! Look out there. Can't you see them? I think Miss Beth sent them here for us. That's why she's got me going to the shed for candles this late."

Rebecca peeped over her mother's shoulder and watched as the group of about ten men led their horses toward the river and away from Gloria. "Mama, Miss Beth would never do such a thing. Nan says she's the kindest white woman she ever seen."

"Nan doesn't know what she's talking about, now hush."

They were both quiet until they were sure the men were far enough away from the house not to see them. "I think that fall Miss Beth took must have knocked her senses loose," Lillian said. "No matter though, you and me have got to leave Gloria. It just ain't safe here no more."

"Mama we can't go anywhere. Where we gone go?"

"I don't know baby, I just know that we can't stay here anymore. That woman has finally lost her mind and she means to get rid of us both. We can't let that happen. Come on." Lillian left the house by the back door with Rebecca close behind her. "I knew she was up to something. I could see the devil right in her eyes but I never thought she'd go this far."

"But, why Mama?"

"Jealousy."

"Why would a woman who has everything in this world be jealous of a slave?"

"It may seem like she has everything but she doesn't. She doesn't have the one thing that she wants most of all. Now stop asking so many questions."

Lillian and Rebecca went directly to their shack. Lillian reached under the bed and pulled out the old carpetbag that had once belonged to the late Mrs. Vance. The sight of the bag brought back the memory of how it came to be in her possession. The bag had been a gift from Big Bill.

It was a sort of peace offering. He'd felt a twinge of guilt at having taken the little girl who had whimpered and cried softly as he satisfied himself. Lillian remembered that when it was over she felt dirty and worthless. She ran down to the river hoping that the cool water would make her feel clean again. She washed her body again and again but she still felt dirty. Back at her own shack her mother tried to console her by telling her of the rewards she would reap if the master liked her. He would certainly like her even more because she was obedient. It didn't make Lillian feel any better. She didn't think at the time that anything would ever make her feel better. She couldn't take back what the massa had taken from her.

A little while later old man Vance came to the shack with the bag as a gift. He'd somehow thought the bag would make her happy but it only saddened her even more. How could he think that this old beat up bag could make her feel better? What use would she have for a bag like this? The bag was cheap and useless and it only sickened Lillian to think that her virtue had no more worth than an old beat up carpetbag.

This is no time for sentiment, Lillian told herself while blinking back the tears that stung her eyes. She stuffed the bag with a few treasured items and a change of clothes for herself and Rebecca. For most of her life she'd heard stories of Negroes who found freedom in the north but she had no idea how long it would take to reach the north. She only knew that she must leave Gloria as quickly as she could.

After the bag was packed she went to the kitchen house and packed a small pot, some tea, the biscuits she had baked earlier the day before, a bag of grits and a chunk of cooked beef.

She and Rebecca crept behind the slave shacks and ran under of the cover of darkness to the woods. It was near dawn when they finally reached the end of Gloria land and the main road.

"Which way do we go now, Mama?" Rebecca questioned.

"Don't know baby. I think that maybe it would be best to wait for night before traveling any further. At least at night we'll be able to see the North Star."

"What's that?"

"People say it's the brightest star in the sky. As soon as we see the star we can follow it."

"Follow it where?"

"North," Lillian said as if the question was ridiculous. "Just north, folks like us be free in the north."

Knowing that it would be safer to travel at night, she knew that she should find a place where they could hide themselves during the day light hours. She searched through the woods until she found a small cave just off the main road. She and Rebecca spent most of the morning covering the opening with twigs and bushes. Inside they ate some of the beef and biscuits. Lillian made a fire and they both drank hot cups of strong tea.

The night had been a tiring experience for both mother and daughter and they both slept soundly. Lillian woke up sometime in late afternoon. She peeped outside through the facade of shrubbery that they had pushed in front of the opening of the cave. Clouds gathered across the sky above and she wondered if they would be able to see the star through the dense clouds. She roused Rebecca and they ate more biscuits and drank tea. She then anxiously positioned herself at the cave's opening and waited for the sun to go down. Soon the sky became the color of a ripe peach as the sun set over the hills, its brightness veiled behind the ominous clouds. When darkness finally covered the sky, not a single star was visible and Lillian continued to wait.

On the third night the wind gently blew in cooler temperatures and Rebecca was cold and restless. "Mama lets just go back," she pleaded.

"No. We can't go back now. Don't you know what happens to run-aways?"

"Mama, you know massa David ain't gone allow no one to beat us. Why can't we just go back?"

"It ain't massa David I'm worrying about. Maybe he wouldn't beat us but the missus and massa James would. I ain't gone take that chance. Besides, Miss Beth probably thinks we're both dead so she ain't likely to send a party looking for us just yet. That gives us just a little more time to reach north."

"Mama you don't even know where north is and I'm cold and hungry. I want to go back."

"No! Now stop your winning. I promise we are going to be alright. I promise."

Lillian refused to give up hope. On the fourth night Lillian again positioned herself at the cave opening and watched the sky. A calm wind rustled the foliage and Lillian could see that the wind was slowly moving the clouds across the sky revealing a single bright star. "It's there, baby," she said to Rebecca. "Come and see."

"I see it," Rebecca said sharing in Lillian's excitement.

"Come on. We got to be moving out."

When Rebecca looked again she couldn't see the star. "Mama, the star is gone. Now what are we going to do?"

"It ain't gone. It's just hiding behind some clouds but they're moving fast. You'll see."

After they had gathered their belongs Lillian took a leafless twig and brushed the dry ground inside the cave so no one would be able to tell that anyone had stayed in the cave. Then she made sure that no one was outside the cave before she and Rebecca headed for the road.

"I see it, Mama," Rebecca said excitedly. "It sure is bright."

"That star is so bright its gone light our way to freedom."

Under the cover of night Rebecca and Lillian traveled north. They stayed far enough off the main roads not to be seen by other travelers. Lillian moved so fast that Rebecca could hardly keep up. She was always alert for the sound of approaching carriages, wagons or riders on horseback. Sometimes she would scramble behind a tree or huddle under the coverage of the foliage until she was sure that they would not be seen.

What little sleep they got was during the daylight hours but Lillian was always ready to move. She didn't want to stay in any one place too long. The wind continued to softly blow making Lillian even more anxious. She had lived in Virginia her entire life and she could tell by the taste and smell of the wind that behind its gentle breeze swirled a fierce fall storm. What was worse, the winds moved in the same direction they traveled, north. There was no doubt that the storm would travel the same path. At first Lillian was fearful of the coming storm but her fear would be lessened when she realized that a storm would mean fewer travelers on the roads. She soon realized that she and Rebecca would be able to cover a good amount of ground during the storm.

Soon the storm caught up to them. The winds swirled wildly pushing a driving hard rain. The ground became sodden making every step an effort. Still, the two slaves trudged on.

Once the storm had passed, each morning as the sun began to rise Lillian would look for a place to hide for a couple of hours of rest. They slept under bridges, in abandoned shacks and anywhere Lillian thought they would be safe. The nights became colder and Lillian knew that if they didn't keep moving they would surely freeze to death if they did not find shelter before winter.

Soon the winds began to blow again and Lillian knew that another storm was pushing its way north.

Six days had passed and their food was beginning to dwindle and Lillian tried to conserve what little was left. She cursed herself for not bringing a weapon to kill small game. By the eighth day there was only tea left.

"Mama, I'm hungry," Rebecca complained.

They were deep in the forest where rabbits and squirrels were abundant and ran freely. Using the only spoon she had brought along, Lillian dug a hole in the earth about a foot and a half deep. Then she used a rock to sharpen several sticks. Three were pushed in the ground in the bottom of the hole. She covered the hole with grass and other plants and then waited for some small game to fall into her makeshift trap.

The wait was short. Soon they heard the squealing protest of a rabbit caught in her trap. Lillian then used the fourth sharpened stick as a knife. She skinned and gutted the rabbit before impaling it on her stick to hold over the fire she made to roast the animal. The rabbit made a tasty meal that lasted for the next few days.

The next day it began to drizzle. By nightfall the drizzle had become freezing rain and soon a torrential cold rain was completely upon them. They continued to move north although walking became increasingly difficult on the muddied and in places, ice slicked ground.

Soon they came upon a hole in the ground. The hole was as deep as a grave but not as long. She guessed that it must have been some sort of animal trap much like the one she had made. Lillian instructed Rebecca to help her gather some large rocks, branches and leaves. They threw the rocks down into the hole before they climbed in. Lillian stacked the rocks to make it easy to climb out of the hole. Standing on top of the stacked rocks, Lillian covered the opening of the hole with the branches and leaves that she had gathered. It wasn't perfect but it would serve to hide them until the storm passed or at least lessened in intensity. Inside the hole was cold and damp and rain dripped through the foliage. Lillian and Rebecca huddled together under the few blankets Lillian had packed.

Rebecca fell asleep quickly but Lillian was unable to sleep for most of night and well into the next day. She thought about what might happen if she were able to finally reach the north and safety but mostly she thought about David and all that had happened from the first time their eyes had met when they were both only children. Some time after midday Lillian fell into a fitful sleep marred by dreams of the past. Her last waking thought was a revelation that she did not really love David.

In her dreams Lillian saw David, weak and dependent. David was even more dependent on her than she ever was on him. In her dream she didn't love David. How could she possibly love a man as weak and pathetic as David Vance? In fact, she hated David Vance and everything he and others like him stood for. What she loved was controlling him just as he and his family had controlled her and her family for generations. She smiled in her sleepy self-conscious as she saw the gallant southern gentlemen humbled into a whimpering, spineless jellyfish at her feet.

Why couldn't they see that? Why couldn't Miss Beth see that she didn't really want to take her husband? She only wanted to use him as he used her. She didn't love David Vance anymore than she had loved his hateful father.

She then thought about the respectable brother, massa James? She saw how James looked at Miss Beth and knew that he wanted her for himself. She knew now what she had only wondered about before. Massa James wanted Miss Beth to see her and David together. He probably thought that Miss Beth would come running right to him. But she didn't, of course. The silly woman still wanted her weak husband.

Lillian awoke to the sound of footsteps as the wet soil was trampled beneath the heels of men and horses. Afraid that Rebecca would make some small sound that would reveal their presence, Lillian gently placed her hand over her daughter's mouth while she held her own breath and prayed that the travelers would quickly move on. When she heard the men talking she was relieved to find out that they were not looking for her but that relief quickly faded when she realized that it didn't matter if they looked for her or not. If she and Rebecca were caught without papers they would either be sold at auction or returned to Gloria. Lillian didn't know which was worse.

Finally, she heard the men move in the opposite direction. Fearful that the men might return she quickly prepared to leave and continue her journey northward. The wet ground made movement slow and cumbersome but Lillian knew that they must not stop.

Hidden deep in the forest Lillian came upon a small clearing where a tiny white house stood. The house seemed so out of place that Lillian thought she might be delirious. Why would any one build a house in the middle of a forest, she wondered. But she only gave that question a smidgen of time as no matter how odd it may have seemed the house could offer shelter and maybe something to eat.

The first thing Lillian noticed was that there were no carriages or horses in front of the house. She looked over at Rebecca whose color was a motley gray. Lillian put her hand to the girl's forehead. Rebecca was feverish and had probably caught a chill. Lillian knew that she had no choice but to take advantage of the temporary shelter the house offered.

She ordered Rebecca to stay at the edge of the clearing while she went to see if the house was empty. Carefully, Lillian made her way to the other side of the house and peered into one of its windows. The house was completely furnished with a smoldering fire in the hearth. Lillian hurried back to her daughter and they both sought refuge in the tiny white house.

Lillian took some wood logs from the side of the house and she carried enough inside to rekindle the fire. In the small kitchen she found a half-eaten kettle of soup. The kettle was still warm and Lillian knew that the owner of the house had not long ago left. She propped Rebecca up in front of the fire and began to feed her the warm soup. She took very little for herself. She found a few clean blankets in a cedar chest and she packed them into her bag discarding the dirty wet blankets that she'd brought from Gloria. As soon as Rebecca was warm and fed they prepared to leave. The last thing Lillian needed was to be caught stealing from a white man or woman. She took some tea and bread and left the house as quickly and as quietly as she had come.

They waited in the forest until nightfall and then continued their journey north. Just before dawn they came to the end of the forest. It had never occurred to Lillian that the forest would end before they reached their destination. She looked out over a wide open plain that stretched for miles. There were no trees to use for cover and Lillian knew that once they started out over the land they would-

n't be able to stop until they reached another wooded area. She decided that they should camp at the edge of the forest and set out
again when the sun went down.

The chill Rebecca caught was getting worse and she burned
with fever. Although the little house that they'd found had provided
something to eat, that was a couple of days ago and they were both
hungry again. Lillian sat with her back against a tree and Rebecca's
head in her lap. She stroked the girls long raven hair as she prayed
softly.

Lillian had never been a religious woman. For years the only
preacher she ever heard was the white preacher that preached in the
little chapel on the plantation. Every Sunday the slaves were herded
into the one room church that Big Bill had built for them. The white
preacher told them that God had made them slaves and put the white
man over the black man because, in God's infinite wisdom, He knew
that blacks were like little children and needed instruction and discipline. Since this was all by God's doing, it was obviously His will and
how dare we disagree with God's will? The preacher would scream
and pound his fist on the podium as he spoke. He'd say that if you
disobeyed massa, you disobeyed God. And when the massa punished
or beat you it was because God had given him the right to do so.
Lillian had often seen that same preacher clutching his worn bible as
some slave was having his flesh torn from his back. She refused to
believe in a God who would sentence his own creations to suffer and
toil for a lifetime with no means of redemption.

One day, when Lillian was about sixteen, a tobacco buyer
came from New York. One of the men traveling with him was a free
black man named Reverend John Thomas. Reverend Thomas had
learned how to read and write in the north and when he read the
Bible he told the slaves about a different God, a God who loved all
men who loved Him. This God had once freed other slaves called Hebrews. This was all familiar to Lillian and even some of the other
slaves. The God she prayed to now be the God that her mother, Bell,

Nan and Jacob, talked of. Her mother told her stories about how God loved his people so much that he sent his Son to redeem them and the only thing we had to do was believe in Him and in His son.

After Reverend Thomas left Gloria, everyone was hungry to know more about the God that loved black people. One day, old Jake asked the white preacher about the God that freed other slaves called Hebrews. The preacher turned red in the face and yelled at old Jake. "Jake," he said. "God ain't never freed black slaves. Why, you even asking such a question is blasphemous and blasphemy is a terrible sin against God. That thought is straight from the devil himself and if you don't want to go to hell, you'd better get them devilish thoughts out of your head. All of you!"

A few years pass and massa buys a slave named Boaz. He had been taught how to read by the young massa of a plantation in Louisiana. He was the only one who could read from the book that Reverend Thomas had left behind. The slaves began to have secret church meetings to learn more about that special God. This was the God Lillian prayed to now. "Help me Father. I know that I've done really terrible things in my life and I am truly sorry. But Father, I never stop believing in you or your son and now I need your protection. Don't take Rebecca from me. Please heal her with your special power, Father. Help me to find freedom like you did for them Hebrews. Show me how to find Freedom, Father. Amen."

In the distance Lillian heard the beat of hooves. She couldn't tell how many but she knew that men galloped behind her and the great open plain stretched before her. There was no place to hide and no where to run and Lillian knew that her journey had come to an end. Weak, cold and hungry Lillian pulled her daughter even closer as she waited for her captures.

"Well look at what we got here," a large white man said a he spat a stream of black tobacco juice onto the ground. He smiled revealing a mouth full of rotted teeth. "Looks like there's one for you and one for me, Fitch," the man said. His partner was only a boy who looked to Lillian to be no more than seventeen.

The man Fitch swung his leg over his horse and jumped down to get a better look. He leaned down and looked at Lillian. "Why if it weren't for them rags tied around your head I could have mistook you for a white woman, the girl too.

Lillian scrambled to her feet helping Rebecca up and pushing the girl behind her. She stepped forward meeting the man's gaze with her usual defiance. He smiled back. It was an ugly hateful smile that told Lillian she had much to fear.

"You take the girl," the man ordered his younger comrade but the boy didn't move a muscle. He started licking his dry lips as if he saw something mouth watering.

The man pushed Lillian hard against the tree and began to undo his trousers. He lifted her skirts and began to roughly tear at her under garments. Lillian did not fight him and he took her there at the edge of the forest, her head and back smacking hard against the rough bark of the tree. Her nostrils filled with the stench of him and she gasped and tried to hold her breath. She wanted to spit on him but she knew that it would only make things worse. He finished his business quickly and began to adjust his clothing as he smirked in satisfaction. "What's the matter wit you boy? Take the girl. Ain't no one here to stop you."

Fitch still did not move. Finally he said more to Lillian than his comrade, "There ain't nothing I wants from a nigger."

"You got free papers?" The man asked Lillian.

"No sir."

"Well, I guess finding you two is about the luckiest thing that's happen to me in a long time."

"How you figure Earl? Ain't a damn thing lucky about niggers. It's a curse is what it is."

"I don't know Fitch. If we can get these two to Richmond by

the end of the month we could sell them at auction. I bet the young one would fetch a couple of hundred dollars. I'd say that's pretty lucky."

That night Lillian and Rebecca were kept in an old barn at the edge of the forest only a couple of miles from where they'd been captured. Rebecca was still burning with fever and now Lillian wished she had never left Gloria. When young Fitch came with two plates of food Lillian asked for medicine for her daughter but the boy only laughed.

"Listen to me, boy," Lillian said. "You tell your Pa, or whoever that man is, a sick or dead nigger don't sell. Do you hear what I'm saying, boy? My daughter needs medicine, now."

Later the man came to the barn and gave Lillian a small brown bottle. "See that the girl takes this," he said.

Lillian gave Rebecca the medicine. She was sweating so profusely that Lillian began to wrap her head and shoulders with cool wet rags. She repeated the process through the night and by morning Lillian thanked God that Rebecca's fever had finally broken.

Later the next day the two slaves were bound together by their waist while each was tied securely by hand and foot. The end of the rope that encircled their waist was held by Earl as he rode while pulling Lillian and Rebecca behind his horse. Lillian's boot was worn clean through the sole and the ground scarred and tore at her feet as she walked toward Richmond. Rebecca, still dazed from three days of fever, was simply pulled along. Twice she had fallen and her legs seemed to become weaker with every step. Her captors showed no mercy. "Get that girl on her feet," Earl yelled.

After four days they came to the city of Richmond. The scene was so common place that no one seemed to notice the two female slaves bound together and being pulled down Main Street of the sprawling city of Richmond. The city was alive with activity as many people filled its streets and sidewalks. There were vendors everywhere, peddling everything from brooms to medicine. The medley of so many different people and voices was alluring to the young Rebecca and she longed to see the city but was too tired to even lift her head. The rope around her waist tore into her flesh and her head ached from hunger, fear and fever.

Lillian seemed dazed as well as she stumbled along silently. When they finally stopped, Lillian lifted her head to see where they were. Earl went to speak with another man leaving Fitch to watch over the women. He returned a short time later gleefully waving a hand full of bills for his young partner to see.

"Cut em loose," he said. Lillian watched as the two men danced in the street waving their crisp new bills in the air and she knew that she and Rebecca had been sold.

They were led to a barn like building right in the middle of town and shoved inside. The building was filled with other people, other slaves just like themselves. Men, women and children of all ages were packed into the barn. Some were standing, some sat while others were lying down on the dirt and straw covered floor. Some were clothed and others were in only rags. All of the slaves were bound in some way or another. Some were bound at the ankles and wrist while others were bound by the throat or waist. Some of them had tightly curled kinky hair and some had hair that was long and flowing, a sure sign of mixed breeding. Some of them had deep scars on their backs and legs from years of whippings while others had cuts into the flesh of their faces as if they were some sort of tribal markings.

After Lillian and Rebecca were bound again, this time by the ankles, she settled herself and her daughter on the straw covered floor. "You a run-away?" A stout black woman with a deep chocolate complexion wanted to know.

"Yes," Lillian answered.

"Thought so. I can always tell who is a run-away and whose

just been sold. I'm a run-away too. This is my fourth time trying to get free. Each time I gets a little further away. Gone keep on trying too. Gone keep on trying till I makes it to freedom or they kills me for trying."

"Have you been here before?"

"Yep."

"What will they do to us?" Lillian asked.

"Sell ya to the highest bidder. They'll clean you up first then put you out there on the auction block." The woman eyed Rebecca. "This your girl?"

"Yes."

"Better love her all you can right now cause I can bet she ain't gone be with you after the sellin is done."

Lillian cringed. She hadn't thought of losing Rebecca. "What do you mean? I'm her mother, they wouldn't separate us."

The woman chuckled a little. "What I mean is," she moved closer. "I pray that they don't but don't you be forgetting that they could. Ain't no need to fret about it now. There ain't a thing you could do to change whatever they decide to do."

"Why would they do that? A girl needs her mother."

The woman looked shocked at Lillian's comments. "Where you been, girl? I guess you was one of them house niggers. You got that pretty yellow complexion and I guess you been in the white man's house so long that you forgot you was a nigger."

"I haven't forgotten anything. I know who and what I am."

"Then you should know that to white folks you ain't no mother. You just a nigger woman, a slave who can make more slaves. That's all your girl is to them too."

Lillian wanted to be able to dispute the woman's claims but she knew in her heart that the woman was right. She had been on Gloria her entire life and enjoyed far more privilege than most of the other slaves on Gloria. Again, she wished that she had never left Gloria.

Lillian and Rebecca lived in the barn behind the auction building for over three weeks. They were fed only once a day and were not allowed the privacy of relieving themselves which contributed to the awful stench of the barn. The air was laden with vomit and excrement.

Once a week after being fed a small portion of grits, the slaves were stripped naked. Lillian had never been made to undress in the presence of other men and women and it embarrassed her to stand stark naked in a room full of other men, women and children, all under the watchful eyes of five large, white men with guns.

Once all of them were naked they would be doused with buckets of water to wash themselves. They were given no soap, rags, or brushes for their hair. It was just cold water thrown at their naked bodies. After the washing, the slaves were made to dress in whatever garments they possessed and made ready for auction.

One at a time they were led into a room full of jeering white men and sometimes a few women. They were made to stand on a block of wood in the center of the room while the auctioneer shouted their attributes as if he were selling horse flesh.

Some of the buyers would even come up to the block to examine the slaves more closely; looking at their gums and under their eye lids. There were days when Lillian would pray to be sold just to escape the filthy conditions of the auction house. On other days she was grateful when no buyer found her or Rebecca appealing. Lillian noticed that the slaves who sold the fastest were the strongest and healthiest of the lot. She thought that if she could somehow appear to be less than healthy she could avoid being sold. She hadn't considered what fate that might bring but she began to bury the small portions of food given out each day. She took only water for Rebecca and herself.

At the end of the three weeks Lillian was indeed frail in appearance and when she was brought to the auction block she was almost delirious from malnutrition. "This here is a fine nigger wench," Lillian heard the auctioneer shout. "She speaks better than most niggers and she ain't hard to look at either." Lillian looked out over the room, the faces of the men blurred and the rhythm of her heart seemed to slow as if it would stop at any minute. She closed her eyes and opened them again to clear her blurred vision. She thought she saw David but her legs suddenly seemed unwilling to support her and her vision became even more blurred.

Lillian blinked again and felt her body sinking toward the floor. She tried to stop from falling but she was just too weak. She blinked one last time before loosing consciousness and she was sure she saw David Vance in the crowd.

Chapter 12

🍁

GLORIA
Richmond, Virginia

*I*t had been only a couple of days since Lillian and Rebecca seemingly disappeared from Gloria. There was much whispering among the slaves concerning their whereabouts. They had bravely escaped to the north and freedom was one of the rumors circulating. One man even said that he had come upon the two in a nearby cave on the very night of their escape. Although all of the accounts of Lillian's brave escape seemed plausible, Beth knew that David would never believe that Lillian willingly left him.

Beth sat quietly in front of a smoldering fire as she anxiously awaited David and James return from Richmond. She expected that there would be some confrontation once David learned that Lillian was gone and she knew that that confrontation must not take place in the house where they would surely be overheard by the house slaves. She would have to find a place far away from Gloria's tale bearers. She thought of Lillian's empty shack, what better place to meet and tell David of Lillian's disappearance? The more she thought of it the better the idea seemed. David would probably go straight to

Lillian's shack and she would be there to greet him.

Beth waited until she heard the squeak of wagon wheels along the road through Gloria's front gates before she went to Lillian's shack. The shack was cold and damp. Beth lit a single candle on the table but its small flame did little to brighten the dankness of the shack. A gusty wind blew outside and whistled through the cracks of the uneven wood planked walls making the dust from the dirt floor whirl around Beth's feet. She looked around the one room shack and shivered at the thought of spending even one night in the dismal hovel. The sudden light of the candle sent a rat scurrying across the dirt floor and into one of the many holes under the wood planks. Beth couldn't help feeling a tinge of guilt. After all, it was she who had banished Lillian and Rebecca from the house and into this hell hole. They were two women in love with the same man and the empathy that Beth felt for the slaves hadn't stopped her from hating Lillian. Beth consoled herself with the thought that she had helped Lillian escape to freedom. She would not only be free from David but she would be free from a lifetime of misery and servitude.

A light tap on the door brought Beth's attention back to the situation at hand. "Lil," David softly called. Beth did not answer. "Lil," David said again as he entered the shack and closed the door behind him. It took David a few moments to adjust his eyes to the dim light and then he saw not his beloved Lillian but his wife, Beth.

"She isn't here anymore David," Beth said evenly.

David's face began to twist and distort and he did not try to disguise his anger and alarm. His eyes quickly scanned the shack. "What happened?" his voice was low and menacing. "Where is she? What's happened?" His questions came almost frantically.

Beth moved closer to her husband. "She's gone David," Beth said flatly. "She left Gloria and she has taken Rebecca with her. Now what will you do? Who will you turn to now that your precious Lillian has left you?" she taunted.

David was angry. Beads of perspiration began to dot his fore-head and he held clenched fist at his sides as he began to tremble with rage. "What do you mean she's gone? Where?" His anger seemed to grow with each passing second as he advanced even closer to his wife. "I promise that if you have hurt either of them in any way I'll . . ."

"You'll what?" Beth cut in. "What will you do? Your promise means little because I've done nothing to hurt your precious mistress and your bastard child. Why is it so hard for you to believe that she wanted freedom more than she wanted you? Face it David, she has been gone for a couple of days now. She isn't coming back and there is nothing that you can do about it now."

David lurched forward reaching for Beth as he screamed, "You're lying!"

Beth quickly moved out of his reach and he stumbled for-ward in his attack. "You know where she is. What have you done, Beth? I know that you've done something. Lillian would never leave Gloria."

"Maybe you don't know her quite as well as you think David. You see, she has run off. She not only left Gloria David, she left you. It might be, my dear husband, that the allure of freedom was much more appealing than a lifetime of unrewarded servitude to you. She's gone David. Blaming me won't bring her back."

"I don't believe you." David's eyes narrowed but Beth could see that they were filled with bitter hatred and she was suddenly afraid. Maybe she had underestimated David from the very begin-ning. She knew that David would be upset and she even expected him to brood for a while but eventually realize that life would go on without Lillian. There was no way she could have anticipated the murderous hatred that she saw etched into his face at that moment. David lurched forward again, this time his fist came crashing down on the table toppling the candle to the floor. The light was quickly extinguished and Beth used the opportunity to hurry past David and out of the shack.

Beth ran toward the house with David only a few steps behind her. She entered the house through the back and hurried past the library toward the main staircase. Just as she reached the steps she heard the back door and knew that David had come inside also. She went straight to her room and locked the door. Pressing her back against the door, her heart pounded frantically as she expected David to come crashing through the door at any second. After a few minutes Beth breathed a sign of relief as she realized that once in the house, David had probably been intercepted by James.

Hours passed and Beth thanked God that David would by now have calmed down. Maybe he had gone to look for Lillian or maybe he just needed time to face the fact that Lillian had left Gloria and he would probably never see her again. There was nothing Beth could do but wait.

She didn't know how long she been in her room but she awoke to a knock at the door that startled her. "Who is it?"

"I'm sorry to wake you but I think we should talk."

Beth opened the door. "What is it James?"

"It's David." James swept into the room as he spoke. "I found him sprawled on the library floor. He must have drunk an entire bottle of brandy. The room reeked of the stuff. I've already put him to bed. I just couldn't believe that he'd gotten drunk again. It has only been a few months, but he was doing so well. Something must have set him off. I've got to know what's going on. Did you two have a fight?"

"Lillian, James. It's the same thing that is always going on in this house. It's Lillian."

"Lillian? What are you talking about Beth?"

"She's run off James."

"No. Lillian would never leave Gloria."

Beth exhaled in frustration. "Well, she has James. She left and she took her daughter with her. When I told David he flew into a rage and I left him there, in Lillian's shack."

James did not answer right away. He only had to look at his sister-in-law to know that there was more to this story than she was saying. "Beth," James kept his voice as even as he could. "David knows that Lillian would never leave Gloria on her own accord. I don't know what really happened here but it doesn't matter much. He will surely blame you for Lillian's absence. I'm not sure you realize the effect this will have on him. He will never forgive you Beth."

"Forgive me? What about me? Am I to forgive him for sleeping with that woman right under my nose since the day he brought me here? I've done nothing to be forgiven for James and he will get over this. In time he'll forget all about Lillian and when he does I'll be right here. I'll be the only one here for him."

"Beth, you've changed so much over the years. Sometimes I'm not even sure that you are the same shy young woman that my brother brought home. Are you sure you even want the same things? Do you really want David or is it that you just don't want him to want Lillian?"

Beth turned away from James and went to sit down on the bed. "I've always wanted David. Oh, I admit that at first it was just a marriage of convenience and I was willing to settle for that. But I fell in love with David and I fell in love with being his wife. I thought I could satisfy him and he wouldn't want Lillian any more but he always seemed to choose Lillian over me. He flaunted her as if I should just accept it. He made me feel inferior and inadequate. It began to feel as if I were his mistress and she was his true love and I hated them both for that."

"Yes, I can see that," James said sympathetically. "But Beth, I think David has become your obsession much the same as Lillian is his."

Beth turned away. She could no longer look into James' accusing eyes. "Maybe David is my obsession but I'm his wife. Lillian can never be any more than she is at this moment, his slave."

"Be careful Beth. You aren't the only one who has changed. I know that at one time I told you that David would eventually get over Lillian. I'm not so sure about that anymore. In fact, there are a lot of things about my brother that I'm no longer sure of."

Beth swung around to face him again. "What are you saying James? Is there something I should know about?"

James remained silent and Beth was sure that he knew something he wasn't saying. "Beth you know as well as I do that David really tried to fight this thing with Lillian. I saw how hard he was trying but there's just something in him that won't let him leave her alone but he still tried with everything in him. He gave it all he could and he did that for you. When he had nothing left, no power to change things he turned to the bottle which was the worse thing he could do. Before we knew what was happening he couldn't stay away from the brandy or Lillian. He doesn't think straight. He's not rational any more."

"He's never been rational where Lillian is concerned."

"It's more than that. He's been very little help on the plantation for more than a year. He is seldom able to make any decisions and when he has, he changes his mind on the matter within minutes. These are not the actions of a sane man Beth."

"Oh, come on James. So he has trouble making decisions. He's not the first man to go through a difficult period in his life. You're not suggesting that David is insane are you?"

"It's much more than just not being able to make decisions Beth. He forgets things. When he drinks heavily he usually blacks out and forgets long spaces of time. This has been going on or a long time now. In one of his more lucid moments I was finally able to convince him that the brandy was killing him and he's been able to keep sober for a while. Now this. I'm just afraid of what this will do to him now."

"It doesn't matter, James. He drank because of Lillian but she is gone now."

"I'm not sure he can get through this."

"Why on earth not? It's not as if he's alone. We're both here and we both love David. We'll help him through this, you'll see. I'm sure of it."

"I hope you're right. I have my doubts Beth. I think that this could be the push that finally sends David over the edge. His sanity is definitely in question."

"Nonsense, he'll get over Lillian and when he does I'll be right here."

David did not get over Lillian as Beth had predicted. After James had gone to bed, Beth went into the library where David was sprawled on the floor again. She got down on the floor and lifted his head into her lap. She gently ran her fingers through his mass of thick curls smoothing the touches of gray at his temples. James was right, David had changed. Beth wondered why she hadn't noticed before now. This man was far different from the southern gentleman she met at Madam Renee's. Beth remembered thinking at the time that David was the strongest and most handsome man she'd ever seen. Now he looked every bit the part of a beaten man. His body had lost the tone and stature that had made him appear dashing. He'd lost that sun darkened complexion and now looked sallow and sickly. The result of his drinking more and more and eating less was etched in the lines in his face. Beth continued to stroke him even though his breathing was uneasy and his snoring was harsh and foul smelling. It was well past dawn when David finally opened his eyes.

"What are you doing here?" he stammered.

"You were drunk and upset. I just wanted to be sure that you were all right. I wanted to be near in case you needed me for any-thing."

David pushed Beth's hands away before he struggled to get to his feet. "I've been drunk before, I don't remember your concern then."

"I know dear," Beth said in a fretful voice. "This time I was worried about you."

"Worried?" He swung around to face his wife. His legs were unsteady and weak. "I don't need your pity Beth."

"No, no, of course I didn't mean that I pity you David. I was just concerned. I wasn't sure how you'd adjust to Lillian not being here."

"You were concerned," he repeated sarcastically. "I find that hard to believe Beth."

"Why? I'm your wife David." She reached for his hand and he pulled away. "There is no reason for you to be angry with me David. I haven't done anything. I only wanted to be here for you. I'm your wife."

"Do you think I don't know what you did?"

"What are you talking about?"

"Alright, I admit I don't really know what happened while James and I were in Richmond but I do know that Lillian would not leave Gloria. You sent her away or maybe you sold her. I don't know what you did but I do know that you had something to do with her leaving Gloria."

"You're upset David, you don't know what you are saying."

"I know exactly what I'm saying and you're right. I am upset. Do you know what I thought when I came in here last night?"

Beth turned away and walked toward the window. "No," she whispered.

David sat down to pull his boots on. "I wondered why, in all these years, I have been torn between Lillian and you. I never wanted to hurt you so I tried to be honest about our relationship. I never promised to love you. I told you from the beginning that this marriage would be a marriage of convenience. But somehow you turned my honesty into some sort of game, a challenge between you and Lillian. It was never supposed to be that way."

"You're wrong David. You did make promises to me and you gave me this Sapphire necklace to remind me that you would do anything to be the husband I deserved. Don't you remember?"

"Yes, I do remember and I have been burdened with guilt for not living up to that promise but no more. I don't have to worry about that because the husband you deserve is exactly what I intend to be. You have connived and schemed until you drove Lillian away. That makes you no better than me."

"David, please," Beth knew that there was nothing she could say to change his mind now.

"I'm going to find her Beth. I'm going to find her and bring her back to Gloria where she belongs."

"You can't be serious."

"You have no idea how serious I am."

"Why, David?" Beth swung around to face her husband as he continued to dress. "Why are you going to bring her back, to be your slave? She can never be more than that David. Don't you realize that now? I am your wife David."

"I know who you are Beth, I don't need to be reminded. Everyday for the past seven years I've regretted bringing you here. At first I was sure that a wife would set things right but I soon found out that didn't change anything. I regretted bringing you here because I knew that I could never be a real husband to you."

"We can try again." Beth began to sob softly.

"I have tried. Believe me Beth, I have tried and tried again. Maybe I'm cursed, I don't know but I know that I can't live without her."

"Please let us try again David. I know things will be different this time. With Lillian gone, there is nothing to stand in the way of our happiness."

"You don't understand Beth. Hell, I don't even understand, why should I expect you to understand?"

Beth was not willing to give up hope and she ran into David's arms. "But I do understand darling. You can get over this, I know it. I'll help you. Look at me David. Why do you need her? I'm your wife!"

David gently took her by the shoulders and pushed her away from him. "Nothing has ever been able to replace Lillian. No other women could dull my need for her, not brandy and not even you Beth. I must get Lillian back."

Beth turned away. "I don't want to hear anymore," she said. Tears stung at her eyes as David continued to confess his love for Lillian. "Stop it," Beth yelled. "I don't want to hear another word."

"I know you don't want to hear it Beth but I've got to say it. It's time the truth came out so we can stop hurting each other." He moved close behind Beth and with both hands resting on her trembling shoulders he said, "If you want to leave I'll understand. I'll arrange for your passage to Philadelphia as soon as possible."

"Are you sending me away?"

"No. You are still my wife and mistress of Gloria. I would never send you away but if you stay you must accept me as I am. You must accept my weaknesses for what they are, a part of me. I can't change now Beth. I realize that now. I will never be able to live up to the romantic fantasy that you've created."

"Are you asking me to accept your relationship with Lillian?"

"You don't have much choice at this point. Stay here and continue to be my wife and Gloria's mistress."

"You are asking me to continue to be your wife while you continue to sleep with Lillian? You are asking me to continue to be the fool while you flaunt your mistress in my face? No thank you, David." With tears streaming freely down her face, Beth lashed out at David striking him repeatedly in the chest with her fist. "Go then! Go and find your precious black whore but I will not wait for your return. My only hope is that retribution comes quickly for you and your precious Lillian. I hope you both burn in hell."

For a moment David felt ashamed. When he had brought Beth to Gloria she had been a naïve young woman full of romantic dreams but time had transformed her into an unscrupulous woman who would stop at nothing to get what she wanted out of life. David was responsible for the woman Beth had become. "I'm sorry Beth," he whispered before he left.

Beth went on screaming obscenities but David no longer heard her outrage. His only thought was of how he would get Lillian back. All of Beth's resolve crumbled as David grabbed his hat and jacket and strode from the library leaving Beth alone and in tears.

avid had no idea where to begin his search. If Lillian left of her own accord as Beth had said, he knew that she would travel north. He stopped at every farm house, shack and plantation along the way to inquire about a mulatto woman and child. No one remembered seeing the two. He slept in the back of the wagon at night and rose early each morning. After several weeks on the trail David was beginning to lose hope and track of time. Finally he reached the Pennsylvania border and decided that it would be futile to go further. He doubted if Lillian could have gotten this far on foot. Feeling defeated and weary David turned his buckboard around and headed for home.

The days and nights he spent on the trail provided countless hours of solitude, making it difficult to escape the torturous thoughts that ran through his mind. How had he come to this? How had he let a woman so completely control him? Lillian filled his thoughts both day and night. Night was the worse because he would be carried back in time to where it had all begun. In his mind's eye he saw the boy who had fallen in love with Lillian from the first moment he saw her. He remembered thinking that she was the most beautiful woman in the world. No other female, black or white, slave or free, compared to his Lillian. Even as a girl she moved with grace and elegance. Confidence exuded from her every move. Lillian possessed all of the characteristics that he lacked and loving her had weakened him even more. Though he had been told time and time again that what he felt for Lillian was not love, he knew in his heart, then and now, that love was the only word to describe the feelings he held for Lillian. What he felt for Lillian was the deepest and most sincere love the world has ever known. He wondered if they had been born in a different time and place, where their love was not forbidden by class and race, would he still want Lillian as he did now. Would loving her hurt as it did at that moment?

In the beginning no one paid much attention to the two children who were somehow been drawn together. They spent hours in absolute awe of the extreme differences between them but as they grew older Big Bill was embarrassed by his son's relationship with the young girl. He soon forbids his son from spending so much time with her. David was well aware of the consequences of disobedience and he tried to obey his father but his desire to be with Lillian far outweighed his fear of Big Bill.

They had a special place down by the river and whenever they could get away they would meet there. Most of their time was spent talking and laughing together. David had even taught Lillian the alphabet and later to read. Sometimes he would bring a book and read to her for hours. Lillian would lose herself in the stories David read, imagining herself as the heroine and he, the gallant hero.

On one particularly hot August afternoon when David was fourteen and his young body was beginning to mature into manhood, Lillian suggested that they take a swim in the river to cool off. Before David could protest Lillian stripped off her clothing and ran down the steep bank to the river leaving David to struggle with his high leather boots and britches. The sight of Lillian's sleek bronze body excited him and he gave little thought to what the consequences would be if they were caught. David could also not control his excitement and the effect it had on his maturing body. He looked down in astonishment and quickly turned away from Lillian.

"What's the matter?" she yelled playfully.

David held his shirt in front of him as he turned back to Lillian.

"Don't you want to swim?" Lillian asked.

"Yes, of course I do."

"Then come on, the water will cool you." Lillian ducked her head under the water and swam toward the middle of the river while David stood watching her duck beneath the water and then bounce up again in joyful play. Her breasts were full and round and her hips slender. "Come on David," she yelled again.

"I'm coming." He threw off his shirt and ran into the water. When they had finished their swim and laid on the grass in the shade David leaned over and kissed Lillian. He had wanted to do that so many times but this time something in him would not let him hold back. Feeling awkward and inexperienced he leaned closer to her and Lillian sensed his desire and met his lips with her own. She took his hands and gently guided him through the seduction of his dreams and his first taste of the drug that would enslave him for the rest of his life. She opened her legs to accommodate his manhood and David trembled as he entered her softness. They were lost in the ecstasy of lovemaking and did not hear the approaching footsteps of an intruder. Both jolted in surprise as they finally heard the sound of a whip as it sliced through the air. Before they could untangle themselves the whip slashed through the flesh on David's back and he rolled away from Lillian leaving her at the mercy of Big Bill. She curled her body into a small ball as Big Bill's whip whistled through the air striking her again and again while calling her a nigger whore. David charged his father in a futile attempt to save his beloved Lillian but the old man was as strong as an ox. With just a wave of his hand he slung David's fragile body aside and continued his tirade against the girl. Lillian crawled behind a tree and David lunged at his father a second time. This time Big Bill did not see David coming and the jolt sent the whip flying through the air to a spot at the river's edge. Both father and son scrambled down the bank after the whip. Lillian grabbed her clothes and ran. David reached the whip first and threw it far out into the middle of the river. The old man glared at his son before he landed a crushing blow to the side of David's face knocking him off of his feet. "If I ever catch you with that nigger whore again I'll make you wish you were never born." Bill turned and walked away.

That evening, while David was locked in his room, Lillian was summoned by Big Bill to perform her usual carnal duties. Her body was bruised and sore and she winced with each painful touch but knew that she could not refuse him nor would he show any sympathy.

David, like everyone else he knew, respected Big Bill. There was no doubt that he feared his father but in spite of his fear, his respect was now lessened. His one afternoon with Lillian changed all of that. He felt powerless and small in the old man's presence. He could not take Lillian away from Gloria and could not protect her here. His respect for his father quickly turned to distrust and soon even hate.

It never occurred to David that his father's bitterness toward the relationship he shared with Lillian was anything more than pure racist hatred until now. Only now as he lay beneath the stars dreaming of times long past and missing his beloved Lillian did he consider that Big Bill loved Lillian also.

David remembered early one spring morning he'd gone to his father's room to ask permission to travel to Richmond for writing supplies. He opened the door of the master bedroom with casual abandon, calling his father as he went. "Father, are you awake?"

The sheer curtains that hung around the large canopied bed had been drawn but did little to hind the sight of his father's rear end as he humped like a wild animal on the small body of a girl. David stood motionless for several seconds before he backed out of his father's room and closed the door. He stood with his back against the wall in the corridor and waited. He heard Big Bill's loud moan of delight and knew that he had finished his business. It was several minutes before Lillian emerged from the room. With her head down she didn't even see David until she bumped into him.

"David?"

"Lillian," he took her by the shoulders and held her away from him to look at her. "What has he done to you? Are you hurt? Did he hurt you?"

"No, I'm alright. Let me go David. He can't see us together. Please let me go."

David was outraged. How could his father do this when he knew how he felt about Lillian? It wasn't enough that he'd taken to giving Lillian out as some sort of hospitality gift to his business associates, but now he had to have her for himself. What kind of man does something so evil?

One look into Lillian's drawn and embarrassed face told David that this was not the first time and probably would not be the last time she was with his father. David released his hold on Lillian's shoulder as if the feel of her was suddenly hot enough to burn him. He took a step backward and let her pass him down the corridor. David had forgotten that day until now.

He blinked his moist eyes. His heart was bitter as he remembered the things that he had been too young to understand at the time. The sound of rustling dead leaves brought his attention quickly to the present. The sound came again and this time he assumed that some small animal had scurried by. When the sound came again he grabbed his rifle and slowly got to his feet. He listened closely as the intruder approached. Suddenly there was a sound directly behind him and he turned slowly. The cold barrel of a shot gun was placed at the back of his head. A white boy no more than eighteen appeared in the clearing but he could not see the face of the man that held the gun to his head.

"You can drop that gun Mister. Ain't no cause for alarm. Me and the boy here just want to share your supper," said the voice of the man with the gun.

David dropped his rifle on the ground and slowly raised his hands. "This isn't necessary you know? I've got plenty of food and you're both welcome to it."

The boy was going through David's bundle. "Well, that's mighty kind of you Mister," the older man said while he motioned the boy to check all of the bags.

David stood very still as the boy dumped his belongings onto the ground.

"Ain't no money here Earl," the boy said.

"What do you mean no money? Fancy man like this has got to have some money on him. He ain't travelin' empty."

"No Earl, I'm telling you there ain't no money in them bags."

As man and boy argued back and forth David felt the barrel of the gun at his head lower just a fraction and he knew that the man was so busy with his young fellow thief that he had relaxed. David swung himself quickly around knocking the man to the ground and kicking his gun from his hand and out of his reach. He then grabbed his own gun. The boy stood motionless while the man tried to raise himself from the ground, his face wet with fresh blood. "Get over there!" David shoved the man into the boy. "You ought to be ashamed of yourself teaching a young boy to rob and steal."

With his rifle still aimed at the two thieves David took a rope from his wagon and bound the two together with their hands behind them. "You gone kill us?" the boy asked.

"No one would fault me if I did but, no. I've no intention of soiling myself with your blood. I'll drop you both at the Sheriffs office in Richmond." After he was sure that both men were tightly bound David began to pack his saddle bags and roll his bundle again for traveling.

"I told you Earl. I told you we got enough money to settle down for a while after we sold those niggers but you had to go and lose it all. Now were headed back to jail."

NIGGERS? The word roared in David's head and he stopped his packing. Picking up his rifle again he moved closer to his captives. "You two sold slaves?"

"Yeah," the boy said.

"Where?"

"Take these ropes off and let us go and I'll tell you," the boy said.

"Men or women?" David asked ignoring the boy's request.

"A woman and a girl," the old man offered. "But I tells you no more till you free us from these ropes."

David hit the man hard across the face with the butt of his gun and the man groaned in pain and spat blood on the ground. "Where did you sell them?" David asked calmly.

His head still spinning from the blow, the old man lifted his head and spat a fresh glob of blood onto David's boot. "What's it to you? Does she belong to you?"

"Where did you sell them?" David asked again.

"Can't say as I blame you for wanting her back, she is a

mighty fine filly. Those round hips is almost like she was made for riding. She took me and my boy here real well, the young one too."

Rage replaced reason and David lifted his rifle and struck the man again and again until he was barely recognizable.

"Stop!" the boy yelled. "Stop, you're going to kill him. I'll tell you whatever you want Mister," the boy said. "We sold them to the Richmond auction house."

By the time David reached Richmond he was exhausted. He promptly took the two thieves to the Sheriff's office just as he'd promised. Then he checked himself into the nearest hotel, grateful to be able to stretch out on a real bed. The room was scantly furnished and the bed covers smelled of moth and mildew. The wallpaper was cracked and pealing and so old and dirty that its original pattern was hardly discernable. Although he was weary from travel and pure mental exhaustion he found sleep impossible. Loud laughter and carousing floated up from the saloon below. Lying on his back with his arms folded behind his head he tried to block out the sounds. He studied the faded papered walls and could see that the paper was once pale pink with little roses in a striped pattern up and down the wall. He longed for a drink but instead he began to count the tiny roses on the wall. If he could have just one drink, it would be enough to get him through the night he thought. Finally, David could resist no longer. He dressed and went down to the saloon. Seating himself at an empty table, he ordered a drink of brandy and instructed the saloon keeper not to leave the bottle. The single glass of light brown liquid sat on the table just inches from his hand. For several minutes David just starred at the glass. An empty feeling washed over him and he gradually felt as if his very soul had abandoned him. With a trembling hand David reached for the glass. His hands shook so violently that the liquid sprinkled droplets over the table as he brought the glass to his lips. He tossed the brandy into his mouth and its potency burned a path to his stomach. Closing his eyes he waited for the numbing effects of the alcohol, desperately wanting to rid himself of the visions of Lillian and Beth. His tormented mind cried out for relief and as had happened so many times before, one drink was hardly enough. David summoned the saloon keeper again, this time asking that he leave the bottle.

When David finally awoke from his stupor in his hotel room, he didn't at first know where he was or how he had gotten there. It took a few minutes before he recognized the rented room. He tried to raise himself, but his head ached so dreadfully that he was forced back onto the dingy pillows. A slow grumbling rose from the pit of his stomach and he knew that he would be sick. Crawling on his hands and knees, he searched for the commode. The brandy he had consumed made its way up from the pit of his stomach and he retched violently. His throat burned, his rib cage felt as if it were so bruised and battered that it might collapse with each breath. With his energy spent, his head throbbing and his mouth filled with the sour taste of vomit, he lay on the floor by the commode and slept. It would take David two full days to nurse himself back to health.

*D*avid pushed his way down the crowded streets of Richmond to see where the auctions were being held. It didn't take long to find the auctions. A crowd of people were gathered outside a barn-like building in the middle of town. A signed tacked above its entrance read: AUCTIONS: STRONG HEALTHY SLAVES FOR SALE TO THE HIGHEST BIDDER.

David had no way of knowing if Lillian and Rebecca were the slaves that the thieves had sold but he knew that it was a great possibility that Lillian would not have been able to get out of the county without being caught. He knew that if she had been caught on the roads without free papers it was a good chance that she would have been brought here. He checked his watch. It was near four and he knew that the selling would soon end for the day. Full of new hope and visions of Lillian he hurried to the auction house only to find that it was closed for the day.

He dreaded having to spend another night in that god for-saken hotel room but the possibility that he might actually find Lillian and Rebecca made it easier to stay sober. He took only his meals in the saloon and afterwards went straight to his room. He visited the auction house every afternoon. By the fifth day he was beginning to lose hope. He'd watched slave after slave being led to the block and paraded before the eager buyers. A frail haggard woman was led to the block. Her eyes were sullen and her hair was tied up in a dirty cloth. She was apparently ill and was unable to stand on her own. When the woman was led to the center of the block and left on her own her she collapsed and dropped to the floor. "My God, it's Lillian," David whispered.

The auctioneer's attention was drawn to a gentleman in a blue jacket who had just bid five hundred dollars for Lillian. David was in no mood to haggle. All he wanted was to buy Lillian and Re-becca back and take them home to Gloria. He stepped right up to the auctioneer's podium, "Two thousand dollars." The room fell silent for several minutes as Lillian lifted her head, seeing David for the first time. He stood only inches away. She reached out a feeble hand to-ward him and then fainted.

"Two thousand once, twice, sold!"

David paid the two thousand dollars for Lillian and one thou-sand for Rebecca. Both were severely malnourished and Rebecca was still coughing up clots of phlegm. Lillian's once beautiful hair was now matted to her head. She was so thin that the outline of her ribs could be seen through the ragged clothes that hung on her body.

Her eyes were sullen and dark and rolled back often as she slipped in and out of consciousness. David took them to his hotel but the desk clerk refused to let him take them up to his room. The shed at the back of the hotel was all that the clerk would offer with strict orders that neither was to enter the hotel through the front door. The shed was small and cold but David made two beds of straw on the dusty floor. He was thankful that there was a small wood stove in the center of the shed. At least it would provide some heat.

David spent the next two weeks in Richmond shuffling back and forth between the shed, his room and the general store where he could buy the necessary supplies to nurse Lillian and Rebecca back to good health. For the first couple of days Lillian was too weak to speak. The only sounds she made were groans. She would stare in space for short periods of time and then lose consciousness again. On the fourth day of her convalesces she opened her eyes and gazed into David's face as if seeing him for the first time. "It's alright," he assured her as he stroked the softness of her cheek.

He patiently feed mother and daughter and kept them warm until both gradually regained their strength. When Lillian finally became alert David stared down into her sullen face. Her eyes brightened as she recognized him. "I knew you would come for me," she said. "Your missus sent some men to kill me and Rebecca. I just took my baby and ran. I didn't know what else to do. I thought I could find my way free in the north but we got caught."

"I knew you wouldn't run away without a good reason." He kissed her forehead. "You get some sleep sweetheart. As soon as you're well enough we'll leave for Gloria."

Lillian was suddenly afraid. "Gloria? Oh no, we can't go back there. She'll kill us, you know that. Massa, please don't make me go back."

"There's nothing to worry about, love. My wife is by now, on her way back to Philadelphia. Everything will be just fine. There is no need for you or Rebecca to be afraid."

"You don't understand. Even now, you really don't understand. It can't ever be fine, massa."

"Lillian do you think that I would have come after you if I weren't going to take you home with me? All of our lives people have been trying to keep us apart. That's not going to happen anymore. I'm taking you home to Gloria to live in the house, to wear beautiful clothes and to be with me always. Isn't that what you want?" Lillian gazed into David's eyes in alarm. The smile that David expected to see was not there. "Lillian," he said again. "Isn't that what you want?"

"At one time," she began. "I was foolish enough to want that and I really thought that it could happen. I'm not so foolish anymore. I think massa, that you are foolish for believing that such a thing could be so. Your daddy always said you were foolish, now I believe him."

"What are you saying?"

"You think that because your daddy is dead and your wife has done run off that the whole world is gone bless you and me? No massa. If you take me back to Gloria I will always be your slave and you will always be my massa. It is foolishness to go on dreaming about things that can't ever be. This world ain't gone ever let us be together the way you say. They will surely kill us both before that could happen."

David knew that what Lillian said was true and he cursed himself for offering something that they both knew he was unable to give. He would take Lillian back to Gloria and she would continue to be his slave and he her master but at least they would be together.

As soon as Lillian and Rebecca were well enough to travel, he bundled the two in blankets in the back of the wagon to keep them warm and started the long journey home.

Chapter 13

♥

GLORIA
Richmond, Virginia

Beth reluctantly prepared to return to Philadelphia. There was no family or friend that would look forward to her return. There would be no one to greet her when she arrived as Mr. Thornton had passed long ago. She took comfort in the fact that she would return to Philadelphia in much better circumstances than she had left. She left Philadelphia as a chambermaid in a brothel and would return as a wealthy southern lady.

She supervised the packing of her belongings with little enthusiasm. The sapphire necklace that David had given her on the night of the ball so long ago lay in her open jewel case. She took the necklace in her palm and pressed it close to her heart as she remembered the promises David had made to her that night. Her marriage had been nothing but a farce from the very beginning. She could not remember a single moment in her entire married life when she wasn't trying desperately to hold onto her husband. David had never provided the comfort and security that most husbands did without a thought. She had stupidly accepted his slights as a husband, always hoping to overcome the obstacles, so that a happy marriage would prevail. How foolish she had been. David was the smart one. He knew that for his plan to succeed, he needed a young woman that was more than just naive. She had to be totally incapable of putting an end to the peculiar relationship he had with his slave. He obviously saw some weakness in her from the very beginning. She had wanted nothing more than to have her husband all to herself and now she only wanted to be free of this insane union. Sending Lillian and Rebecca away had been her last desperate act for the only man she had ever loved. She had risked everything just to have David all to herself. It never occurred to her that David would not want her after she sent Lillian away.

It was a gamble and now she wondered if it had even been worth the effort. Why couldn't she have just accepted the situation as it was? After all, David wouldn't have been the first man to have a mistress or to carry on an affair with a slave. She had learned over the years that it was the notion of a superior character that allowed southern ladies to never acknowledge their failings, even in marriage. Affairs went on right under their noses but no one would ever suspect that that lady had even the slightest idea that her husband was not the most faithful. Why couldn't she have been more accepting, she wondered.

She had never considered that she would be the one to lose, the one to be asked to leave Gloria. But she had lost. She lost David to a slave woman and she would accept her loss with all the dignity she could muster. She would no longer be mistress of this vast southern dynasty and her only hope was that she could leave Gloria before David returned with his beloved mistress.

James was not at all surprised that David had gone off to find Lillian. During David's absence James spent most of his time in the tobacco fields. He would return very late in the evening and take his meals alone in the study complaining that David's absence had over burdened him with the running of the plantation. Sometimes he would saddle his horse and ride off never telling Beth where he went and she never asked. She and James spent very little time together and they almost never spoke to one another. During the early days just after she had come to Gloria, James had gone out of his way to be a good friend and was often her only support when she had been deserted by her husband. She knew that their friendship ended the night she offered herself to James. Now James seemed detached, withdrawn and Beth thought that she had not only lost her husband but also a very dear friend in James.

It was early April now and the sky was overcast but a warm breeze brushed Beth's face as she entered the garden. Gloria's rose gardens had always been a place of peace and serenity for Beth and she decided to take a walk through the garden one last time. The rose bushes that had once been alive and colorful were transformed by the change of seasons and were bare and brittle. It would only be a matter of weeks before they would burst into color and eventually full bloom again. The awesome power of God would restore them to their original beauty year after year. Beth was suddenly struck by the enormous power of God over his every creation. She prayed softly, asking God to restore her just as she knew he would restore Gloria's rose garden.

"Couldn't leave without one last look, ah?" James asked.

"How did you know?"

"Maybe because I know that you've spent countless hours in this little garden over the years."

"You're right. I don't know why but this garden helps me to think." She turned to look at James. "Did you also come here to think?"

"No, I came to find you."

"Why? Is there something wrong?"

James did not answer right away. He starred at his sister-in-law with an expression that Beth thought was odd and she became alarmed again. "What is it James? What's happened?"

"There is something that I must tell you."

"James, if you're going to try to persuade me not to leave Gloria you'll be wasting your time. I've already made up my mind. There is nothing I want more than to be as far away from Gloria as possible. I couldn't bear to look at David again and I refuse to live with Lillian as a wedge between my husband and me. I've got no choice James. I have to leave Gloria."

"You may not want to leave after I tell you what I've come to say."

"Why? What is it?"

"This is not something that I should just blurt out. Let's go inside and have a cup of tea where we can discus this mater comfortably and privately."

"Alright James, if that's what you want."

Moments later James and Beth sat in the parlor sipping their tea. Beth noticed that James wore the same odd expression on his face. He didn't seem angry yet his brows were knitted together and his mouth was set in a sort of frown. It was several minutes before he spoke. "Beth, it's very important to me that I share this with you. I've been walking around with this thing for weeks not knowing what, if anything, I should do about it. I kept debating whether to tell you or not and I apologize that it's taken me this long to come to you."

"James, if you don't tell me this instant I think I might explode. What is it, for God's sake?"

"All right. Shortly after my father passed, his belongings, mostly books and journals, were stored away. I knew that I should have gone through them but I just never seemed to have the time. Recently I made the time. I'm not sure what prompted me but for some strange reason I felt compelled to go through those crates and I did just that."

"What has that got to do with me?" I didn't even know your father."

"It's got nothing to do with you but it has everything to do with Lillian and David. Apparently my father kept a journal for most of his life. I found several volumes of his personal journal, written in his own hand. Most of them are filled with business and just a passing phrase of his personal life. There are others that present a detailed account of his personal life. In fact, they are too detailed for me to simply relay what I've read to you. It would be better if you read them yourself."

"I still don't understand what this has to do with me James."

"Just read them Beth. You'll understand everything, I promise you. I've had Denny place four journals in your upstairs parlor. We'll speak again after you've read the journals." Beth did not answer and the two continued to sip their tea in silence.

Later that evening when all of Gloria was quiet Beth sat in her small sitting room and began to read the first of the four journals.

May 20, 1803. My beautiful Gloria, so fragile is she that I am often afraid to make love to her. She winces and cries and I curse myself for hurting the only woman I could ever love. I'm often left feeling like a monster when all I've done is exercise my rights as her husband. I hope that in time she will come to enjoy our love making for I am not sure how a man is to live with a wife who cannot perform the duties that God has plainly set for her.

June 25, 1803. I have been married for just a little over thirty days and my loins ache with desire as I watch my beautiful young wife across the table. Her eyes are so blue; her skin so pale, her long blond hair is swept up in a role of curls at the back of her head. How delicate she is. My desire never fails to heighten at the sight of her beauty. But once again I will be forced to suffer my desires without relief for she is ill again with one of her many ailments. I desire no other woman but God only knows how long I can go on like this.

August 30, 1803. The end of the month shopping trip to Richmond was profitable to say the least. Our tobacco harvest for this quarter was plentiful and I was able to sell the entire harvest at auction for a generous profit. I had intended to purchase a couple of additional bucks for the fields but instead I bought one buck and one girl. I knew that the girl was too slight to be of much help on the plantation but I couldn't keep my eyes away from her. She starred directly at me from the auction block and I even thought she winked at me. Imagine that, a nigger woman brave enough to wink at a white man from the auction block. I've never seen anything like that before or since. I guess that's why I just couldn't turn away from the girl. She wasn't hard to look at either. She was a very dark skinned girl with a smile that could light up the world. Maybe I'm getting soft but whatever the reason, I bought her.

September 3, 1803. Cursed is the man who marries a frail woman for although I know that Gloria is the most beautiful woman that I've ever seen, I fear that she will never be able to bear me strong sons. She is a fragile woman who is weak and sick much of the time. The smell of tobacco sickens her and she is plagued with many other ailments and bouts of nausea. I've taken to sleeping in another room so as not to disturb her. I go to my wife each night before going to my own room, hoping that she will welcome me into her bed. But never am I invited. Sometimes when she is not feeling too poorly I come to her bed uninvited. My passion is never returned as she lies there with her eyes wide open and never daring to move a muscle except the occasional wince as I relieve myself. I am cursed.

September 17, 1803. I was right in my assumption that the girl, Mamie would be of little use in the fields but she has proven herself to be well worth the price I paid for her. She is slightly built with big brown searching eyes. To my surprise she is a skilled temptress, very apt at fulfilling all of my sexual desires. She works with diligence to bring me slowly to the height of sexual ecstasy, until I am left spent of all energy but with an overwhelming feeling of relief. Our encounters are not frequent but often enough to allow me the release I need and to spare Gloria many nights of tears."

There were many other entries scrawled in the old man's strong hand detailing business transactions, deals that brought great profits. There were countless entries detailing illnesses suffered by Gloria Vance and her husband's apparent anxiety regarding her ill health. Beth scanned the rest of the journal until she reached one entry that was printed in bold angry letters.

December 30, 1803. I am bewildered, filled
with guilt and remorse but unable to free myself of the
curse. Following the lust of my loins I have unwittingly
allowed myself to become ensnared in the web of the
temptress. She silently beckons to me day and night
and my own lust renders me incapable of rational
thought. I am obedient to her call. God help me!

It seems that David is more like his father than any of us
could have imagined, Beth thought as she closed the first journal. She
wondered why James would think that anything in the journals could
change her mind about leaving Gloria. So far there was nothing new
here. Southern men have been sleeping with their slaves since the
first slave ship docked in the Americas. Some of them had actually
loved their slave mistresses but Beth had never heard of any southern gentlemen who had risked social disgrace for an illicit affair with
his slave. Beth opened the second journal and began to read.

July 11, 1804. Although Gloria is great with
our first child I doubt if she will be able to carry the
child until birth. I had become accustomed to seeing
her bright and cheerful face when I return home in the
evenings but now she rarely leaves her room. Her
hands and ankles swell, making movement laborious
for her. It is apparent that her small frame has great
difficulty with the extra weight of the child. Six months
of pregnancy has been demanding for Gloria as is evi-
denced in her haggard appearance. I curse myself
each time I look into her sullen eyes. How could I have
done this to her? Mamie is also with child but unlike
my wife, she seems to thrive in her condition and is

even more beautiful and just as vital.

December 21, 1804. Mamie delivered a healthy ten pound boy whose wail was strong and deep as he flung his tiny arms in protest at being forced into the world. I watched with great joy as he left his mother's body. After the baby was cleaned and placed into Mamie's waiting arms, I moved closer hoping to get a better look at the boy. To my surprise Mamie pulled the baby away from my gaze and to her breast as if she sought to hide the child from me. I was able to glimpse the child's pink complexion and a head covered in dark curls. "I'll not take him," I tried to assure her but she still held the baby close to her breast. "This boy be yours massa just like all the chillin' here on your land but he is my son," she said. I didn't know what the girl meant. I could not understand her fear but I was in no mood to indulge in the idiotic superstitions of slaves. I promptly left the shack.

When I reached the big house, I learned that Gloria was also in labor. I climbed the stairs two at a time, eager to be with my wife during her delivery of our first child. She was propped upon several pillows and her thin blond hair was plastered to her face and neck with perspiration. Her lips were blue and the rest of her skin was paler than I'd ever seen it. She looked as if she were dying. I had hired the most skilled midwives in the county and even they could not offer any hope that Gloria would be able to survive the delivery. I promptly sent for the doctor. Upon the doctor's arrival, some two hours later, I was quickly ushered out of the room to wait in the downstairs parlor. Gloria's labor lasted for over twenty hours and she screamed and cried out the entire time. Each scream pierced the air and my heart as well. Finally I was summoned to her room. "It's a boy," I said. "Only a boy would be so stubborn."

"It seems as though your son does not want to be born," Gloria said. I looked up at the doctor hoping for some confirmation that everything was going to be alright. "It won't be long now," he assured me.

After twenty hours of labor Gloria finally delivered a stillborn baby boy and immediately passed into unconsciousness. One of the midwives wrapped the baby in a cloth and took it from the room. I sat down looking at my wife's colorless face as she slept. There was a hint of a smile on her pale face, and I knew that she was pleased with herself, having thought she had given me the boy I desired. I hated the thought that I would have to tell her that there was no baby boy.

I was beside myself with grief. My beautiful wife, as fragile and as delicate as a rose pedal, had suffered through nine months of hell to give me the desires of my heart, only to deliver a stillborn baby. For all that I had put her through, how could I ever look into those big blue eyes again, without feeling the burden of guilt?

I left the room and went straight to my study where I could be alone to contemplate how I could tell Gloria that she had lost our son. That's when it occurred to me that Mamie had also delivered a son less than twenty-four hours earlier. At that moment I knew what I must do to save my Gloria from any fur-

ther pain. As I left the house that cold December morning, I knew that I was about to commit an unspeakable act, but I was convinced that this was the only way to save my wife from a truth that I was certain would kill her. Her happiness meant more to me than any earthly pleasure, and I would do anything in my power to see her happy again.

As I came to the top of the hill I could see the light of torches and I knew that the slaves went to bury my son. I rode as fast as I could to catch up with them. I ordered them not to bury the child in the white graveyard but in front of the main house with nothing to mark the grave. When spring came they were to plant a tree that would serve as the only marker.

It was dawn and the sky was spitting tiny crystal slivers of sleet. The winds blew north promising a great storm but I took little notice. When the baby was finally buried I rode to Mamie's shack. By the time I reached the shack a fierce blizzard was completely upon us and the entire landscape was covered in heavy wet snow. The wind blew at hurricane force. As soon as my hand touched the door of the shack the wind snatched the door from my grip and blew it open with uncommon force. Mamie lay crouched on a cot against the wall with the baby at her breast. She screamed when she saw me. I remembered how afraid Mamie was the night the child was born. I now wondered how she could have known that I would come to take her child. As I stood over her looking down at the child, who looked as white as any white child, I knew that this was the only way to keep Gloria from finding out that her child was stillborn. I *leaned closer and Mamie started to scream. "No massa! No! No!" she screamed.*

"I'm sorry Mamie. I've got to take him," I told her but she continued to scream and tried to hold onto the child. "Give him to me Mamie," I said. I tried to pull the baby from her arms but she refused to release her hold on the child.

"He ain't white massa. Please don't take him," she pleaded as she continued to hold the child close with tears streaming down her brown face.

"Mamie!" I shouted. "I don't want to hurt you girl. Just let the boy go," I said calmly. But Mamie just kept screaming that the child wasn't white. The door that had blown open allowed the wind to rush into the shack, bringing with it burst of wet snow. "No one can hear you girl and even if they could no one could stop me." Finally fed up with the struggle, I slapped her hard across the face and she reeled backward against the wall, releasing her grip on the small bundle. "I'm sorry Mamie," I said as I sheltered the child inside my coat. "This is the best thing that could happen to your child. I promise you that this boy will have a wonderful life. He will never work in the fields or feel the lash of the whip. Don't you understand? I'm not taking your boy Mamie, I'm saving him."

She stopped crying for moment as she considered what I said. "You think just cause the child looks white you can pass him off as a white child? Maybe so, but no lie stays secret forever. One day he gone know what he is and who his mother is and then even you won't be able to protect him," she said.

"No one will ever know," I assured her as I left

the cabin with the baby tucked warmly inside my coat.

The child was washed and dressed in the clothes Gloria had been sewing for our child since the first sign of her pregnancy. He was placed in the bassinet beside my wife's bed. He was a beautiful little boy with a round face and a head full of curly black hair.

The next time I saw the child he was at my wife's breast and he suckled greedily. "Look Bill," Gloria said. 'He has your green eyes. I think I shall call him David after King David."

I was feeling the weight of my sins upon my shoulders, but the minute I saw Gloria with the child, all of my guilt vanished. Gloria's happiness was my only concern and I knew that as long as she was happy I would have no trouble living with the things I had done.

The journal went on to tell of the years of David's growing up and how his father feared that one day his blackness would be revealed and they would all be ruined. Big Bill protected him because he feared him. After perusing the third journal Beth was weary and even more confused. The one fact that stood out was that David was half black and not the rightful heir to Gloria. Did this mean that her marriage was not legal and what about David's relationship with Lillian? As far as Beth could tell this might be good news for David. He could finally be with the woman he loved, but where. This news would certainly change the relationship David had with his brother.

The fourth journal was unopened on the night table and Beth briefly considered not reading it at all. It was late and she was tired, the journal could wait until morning, she thought. But then there was a light tap at her door and she knew it must be James.

"Come in."

James came in carrying a tray with a fresh pot of tea and some small sandwiches. "I thought you might be hungry," he said.

"Thank you."

"How far have you read?"

"I've read three of the journals."

"Then you know about David?"

"Yes," Beth eyed James closely but his expression did not change. "How do you feel about it?"

"I don't know really." James settled himself on the small sofa opposite Beth. "I've loved David as my brother all of my life and he is still my brother. If I feel anything at all it is more contempt for my father. On one hand, I understand his actions. He was only trying to please my mother. On the other hand, I think what he did was despicable."

"He must have loved your mother very much. I wonder if David loves Lillian as much." Once again Beth was struck by the odd expression that came over James' face. "What is it?" she asked.

"Nothing really, I was just thinking. There's no need for you to read the last journal. I'll tell you what it says." He stood up and thrust his hands deep into the pockets of his trousers and began to pace the small sitting room. Beth waited patiently as James took the space of her room in two easy strides then turned on his heels in the opposite direction. His pacing went on for several seconds while she waited patiently. He finally came to a stop in the middle of the room, his expression grim as he turned to face Beth. In a low voice he said, "Mamie had a daughter five years later. That baby was also of mixed blood but my father writes that he was not the child's father."

"Lillian?"

James began to pace again for a few minutes. Suddenly he flung himself onto the sofa and dropped his head into his hands in defeat. "Don't you see, Beth? Lillian and David are half brother and sister. They have the same mother."

"Oh my God!" Beth said. "James, you can't tell him. This will destroy him."

"I've got to tell him."

"Is it because you are the rightful heir to Gloria?"

"No! I don't care about that."

"Then don't tell him. This will only devastate him."

"I've got no choice. I can't let him continue with this thing he has for Lillian. It just isn't right. I have to tell him."

"This is why your father was so opposed to Lillian and David in the first place."

"Yes. There's more. After my mother died the old man was lonely. I think my mother's passing is what made him so mean. Then there was Lillian. My father was in love with Lillian himself. He didn't love Mamie but when Lillian was a girl she reminded him of Mamie. When he found out that the girl was in love with David and he with her, he was furious. That's why he drove David away. He figured that David would make a way for himself away from Gloria and his real parentage would be secret forever and he would have Lillian all to himself. But Lillian wouldn't love the old man. She hated him for sending David away. He knew that she loved David and he tried to punish her for it for the rest of his life."

It was finally all out and James shoulders seemed to lift as he shed himself of the burden. "Oh, one more thing, there is the possibility that Rebecca is my father's child. I guess we'll never really know."

"James, you can't tell David any of this."

"I don't have a choice, Beth. Maybe, this is just what he needs to pull him up and he can finally be a man."

Epilogue

A Time To Heal

"Often times have I heard you speak of
one who commits a wrong as though
he were not one of you . . .
But I say that even as the holy and the righteous
cannot rise beyond the highest which is in each of you,
so the wicked and the weak
cannot fall lower than the lowest which is in you also."

Kahilil Gibran, The Prophet (1923)

Chapter 14
❧

G L O R I A
Richmond, Virginia

*S*oon after his wagon entered the front gates of Gloria, David saw that his brother had come out onto the porch. Just as the wagon came to a stop, Beth also came out onto the porch. David had not expected to see his wife. He thought that she would have tried to leave Gloria before his return. One look at their grim faces and he knew that something was wrong. "I hadn't expected such a welcome," he said. Neither of them answered. David swung his long legs down from the wagon and began to help Lillian and Rebecca down.

Beth ordered Denny to help Lillian and Rebecca to their shack. Lillian took one last pleading look at David before she jumped down from the wagon. She refused Denny's help. "See what I say, massa. Ain't nothin' gone ever change." With the blanket wrapped around her shoulders she pulled Rebecca to her and the two walked slowly away.

David turned to his brother whose face was drawn and his forehead was creased with tension. One look at James' face was enough to know that something was dreadfully wrong and David's apprehension grew. Beth stood close to his brother, her auburn hair hung loose around her shoulders and her face also held a dismal expression. David dropped the reins and jumped down from the driver's seat. "What is it?" he asked. "What's happened?"

Beth spoke first. "Nothing has happened. It's just that your brother and I would like to discuss something with you. However, I'm sure you must be tired from your journey and our discussion can wait until you've had time to bath and rest."

David turned away from Beth and looked toward James for answers. "What's going on here James? What the hell is she talking about?"

"We'll be waiting for you in the library when you're ready David," was all James said before he disappeared behind the large oak doors leaving Beth and her husband alone on the porch.

Awkward moments passed. "I'll have a bath drawn for you. Are you hungry?"

In two long strides David was face to face with Beth and he grabbed her forcibly by the arm. "I want to know what's going on here Beth."

"As I said, there is nothing going on. Your brother would like to discuss a family matter with you. Now if you're hungry I would be happy to have a tray brought up to you." She turned to walk away again and again David grabbed her by the arm.

"Why are you still here? I thought you would be half way to Philadelphia by now."

"I thought it best to stay until you returned."

"Why?"

"James will explain everything to you."

"If my brother wants to discuss a family matter, what has that got to do with you? You are no longer part of this family. Did you think I would take you back after you tried to have Lillian and Rebecca killed?"

"I did not try to have your precious Lillian killed. I tried to give her freedom. I tried to get her away from Gloria. Yes, I may have been foolish to think that you could finally be a husband to me if she were not here. Maybe I was even foolish enough to believe that you could forget her but you've proven that you can do neither. I have finally accepted the fact that you will never be a husband to me. I only hope that you can live with the truth once you've heard it." Beth did not give him time to answer. She pulled away from his grasp and hurried inside the house leaving David alone and bewildered.

Minutes later David stormed into the library where James and Beth sat. "What the hell is going on here? One of you had better tell me now!" Beth got up to leave. "Where are you going," David yelled.

"I was going to have a plate prepared for you."

"I don't want to eat anything until I find out what you are hiding from me."

Beth glanced over at James and she could tell that he was in as much agony as David. "David, please calm down and have a seat. James will explain everything." She turned to leave them alone but David blocked her way.

"I don't want you to leave now. Whatever James has to tell me, must be pretty important. Apparently it was important enough that you changed your plans about leaving. I think I want you right here until I've heard the whole story."

"Alright David, if that's what you want," she said.

When all three were seated James began. "There is no easy way to say this so I'll just come right out with it," James said. "Do you remember that I told you about some crates our father stored in the attic?"

"Yes. You said that they were business journals and you would go through them to see if he'd stored anything of importance."

"Yes but unfortunately I did not take the time to go through those journals until just about a month ago."

"Alright, what's the point?"

"The point is that while you were off searching for Lillian I went through those crates and they contained a great deal more than business journals. It seems that our father also kept personal journals, very detailed personal journals. They contained some pretty startling things about our family, Dave."

"What!"

"David, you are my half brother. Gloria Vance was not your mother."

James waited for David to grasp what he'd said and David just stared blankly. "I don't believe you. What are you trying to pull here?"

"It's true but that's only half the story."

"Well, get on with it!" David said impatiently.

"Lillian is your half sister. You and she have the same mother."

"Is this some sort of joke? I don't understand what's happening here."

"It's true David. It's all recorded right here in Big Bill's own hand." James handed his brother one of the journals but David refused to take it. "If Big Bill had not written it all down we may have never known any of this."

"I don't believe you. How could that be?"

"I'm sorry David," Beth said.

"I don't believe you little brother. I'm not sure why but for some reason you're trying to keep Lillian and me apart just as everyone has for as long as I can remember."

"You're right David. I am trying to keep the two of you apart just like Big Bill did and now we know why," James said as he thrust the journal at David's chest. "Read it for yourself David. Gloria was not your mother. You and Lillian were both born to a slave woman named Mamie."

David sat down and opened the journal at the place where James had placed a marker. He quickly scanned page after page, tears welling in his eyes. Finally, he threw the book in the middle of the floor and jumped to his feet. "It's a lie! I won't believe it, it just can't be true."

"No David. It is all true and Big Bill must have somehow known that his secret would one day destroy this family. As long as he was alive and could protect us from the truth and we would be secure in our future. He wrote everything down because he knew that once he was no longer here to protect us we would have to learn the truth. His secret was buried for over thirty years and there is no reason why anyone should learn of it now. You're my brother and you always have been. There is no reason for that to change. We can burn these journals and their secrets will disappear into the flames."

"Why would you do that?"

"It's simple. You're my brother. I don't care who your mother was or was not. I only know that I love you as my brother and that will never change," James tried to reassure his brother.

David was in shock and he could only stand there with his body rigid from anger and disbelief. "How could he have done this to us?" he whispered.

"I know that this is a lot to digest. We're going to leave you alone for a while. We can talk again after you've had time to read the journals."

James gently closed the library door and turned to Beth. "Someone should tell Lillian."

"You're right of course but I hope you aren't suggesting that I speak with her. She'll never accept this news from me. She'll probably think it's just a ploy to win David again. Maybe David should tell her if he can."

"I'm not sure he can. I guess we'll just have to wait and see what happens next."

Beth took her evening meal in her room. She was exhausted both physically and emotionally. How strange it was that the lives of an entire family could be changed forever in the span of only a few days, she thought. Lillian had spent her entire life in pursuit of a man that she could never have totally. Beth realized that she actually felt empathy for Lillian's situation. The two women had been bitter rivals since their first meeting but now because of circumstances beyond their control their battle had ended. For seven years Beth had tried to keep her husband away from Lillian and now that she knew that their separation was inevitable and permanent Beth felt no victory. Lillian was no longer her rival for David's affections but simply a woman, a victim of love. Both she and Lillian were suffering from the loss of their first and only love and Beth could not hate her anymore.

Beth looked around her room. It was the same beautiful room only it no longer felt like her room. Her trunks were all packed and ready for her departure to Philadelphia. James had assumed that she would change her plans and stay on at Gloria but Beth had no wish to stay. Even though she knew that David had no choice but to end his relationship with Lillian, Beth had no wish to remain Mrs. David Vance. James assumed that her decision was based on finding out that David's real mother was a black slave but in truth that had nothing to do with Beth's decision to leave Gloria. She loved David with all her heart and knew that she would probably love him for the rest of her life. But when David left to go find Lillian, Beth knew that he could never love her as he loved Lillian. If she stayed she would only be a substitute and she simply could not live with that knowledge. She would only stay until things had settled down a bit and life on Gloria could return to some semblance of normalcy.

Just as Beth was getting ready for bed James came to tell her that David had not taken the news well. In fact, David had not left the library since their meeting earlier that evening. "He must still be reading the journals," Beth tried to reassure James. "Maybe we should just wait."

When David did not come out of the library for the next three hours Beth thought it was time to see him. She went to James first just to let him know that she was on her way to the library.

She tapped on the library door but there was no answer so she went inside anyway. David sat stone faced in front of a smoldering fire. A cold wind blew through the terrace doors. The tray of food that she'd had brought in for David earlier had been left untouched. "David," Beth whispered. "May I come in?"

"You're already in."

Beth ignored his sarcasm and went to close the terrace doors. She pulled a chair up close to where David sat on the floor. "I am so sorry David."

"Why? What do you have to be sorry about? Sorry you married a nigger? Oh, but of course you didn't know I was a nigger when you married me or you would never have married me, right?"

"David, I know that this is very difficult but . . ."

"You don't know anything," he cut in.

"That's not fair David. You can't blame me for any of this. You can't even blame yourself. None of us had anything to do with this."

"Is that right? Well Mrs. Vance, just who do you suggest I blame?"

"There is no one to blame David. Try to be reasonable."

"Why would he do this Beth? Why?"

"You know I can't answer that question." Beth watched as the strong, self-assured man she had married crumbled at life's final blow. His eyes filled with tears and he finally hung his head in total defeat. "Why?" he softly asked.

"Don't judge your father too harshly David. He had good rea-

sons for what he did. We may never fully understand all that lead to
his deception but we know that he must have loved your mother
very much. It was her happiness that drove him to such lengths."

"Listen to you. You're still talking as if Gloria Vance was my
mother. He didn't do anything for my mother except steal her son."

"Gloria Vance died thinking that you were her son. She loved
and cared for you because as far as she knew, you were her son. And
your real mother Mamie, watched you grow into a fine young man
with all the advantages life had to offer, advantages that she knew
she could never have given you. She had to find some joy in that."

"That doesn't change anything."

"It doesn't have to because none of it matters now. You don't
need to make any changes in your life. Your brother is still your
brother and you are still the first born son of Big Bill Vance. You
could go on living and running one of the largest tobacco plantations
in the state just as you have. You could live as if those journals never
existed."

"But they do exist, Beth."

"Destroy them!"

"Don't you see Beth? I'm not who I thought I was. Things will
never be the same. African blood runs through my veins and that
changes everything. Will I stand by and watch a slave flogged for disobedience now that I know that it could just as easily have been me.
I'm not Moses Beth. I can't take on the sins of the races. I can't free
them and I can't be one of them."

"It isn't nearly as complicated as that, David. We can burn
those journals and with them anything that could ever hurt you in
the future. No one need ever know."

"I'll know and what about Lillian. Have you and James considered the fact that I've been sleeping with my own sister since I
was fifteen? How am I supposed to feel about that? My love for
Lillian has turned into something sordid and dirty. How will Lillian

feel once she's heard the truth? She'll hate me Beth. She will hate me as much as I hate myself at this moment."

"Set her free David. The kindest thing that you could possibly do for her is to give her and Rebecca their freedom. Let them go David so that she can be allowed to make a life for herself and Rebecca away from Gloria."

David did not answer.

"If you agree, I will tell her this and give her two signed declarations of freedom." Beth placed her hand over David's shoulder briefly considering an embrace but David pulled away from her touch.

For as long as she had been David's wife she had been appalled at his dependence on alcohol but now she sought only to ease his pain. She went to the cabinet and returned with a bottle of brandy and a glass. She poured a generous amount into the glass and pushed it across the desk toward David. "Here. Maybe this will help."

David starred for a few moments at both the bottle and the glass that Beth had placed before him and then turned away. He thought of the familiar taste and the oblivion that would follow but it did not beckon to him as it had so many times before. For the second time in the past few weeks he found that he did not want to escape his thoughts. "No," he said. "I don't want a drink."

"Alright," Beth said calmly. "I see you haven't eaten. Aren't you hungry?"

"I don't want to eat Beth and I certainly don't want to drink. All I want at this moment is to understand why or how my father could do such a thing to me, to all of us."

"It doesn't matter anymore David. What matters is what we all do from now on, from this moment forward. Give Lillian her freedom David. It's the only right thing to do under the circumstances."

Beth pulled two sheets of Vance embossed stationary from the top drawer of the desk. In her elegant hand she wrote out the

two declarations of freedom and pushed them toward David for his
signature. Without hesitation David signed them both. Beth folded
the two sheets and placed them in an envelope and sealed them. "If
you wish I will give these to Lillian first thing in the morning."

"No," David said. "I'll take them to her now."

Moments later David stood outside of Lillian's shack. He
couldn't help but remember the many times he had come to find
comfort in Lillian's arms. She hadn't always welcomed him but when
she did he was allowed to escape into a world where being in her
arms was right. It always felt as if being with Lillian was where he
should be. Now their special world had been turned into something
sordid and perverse. Their love had been crushed, not by their own
sins but by the sins of the past.

He didn't knock. As he pushed the door open he was again
stirred by memories of their love. Lillian turned at the sound of the
door. She jumped to her feet and ran to David. "Massa, I knew you
would come," she whispered the familiar phrase.

"Lillian we need to talk."

"Oh yes massa. There is talk that the Missus really is leaving
Gloria just like you said. Maybe it won't be so bad. I can move back
into the big house and everything will be just fine." Lillian rambled
on, her excitement at the prospect of having David all to herself again
made her much more talkative than usual.

"Sit down Lillian." David's expression was grave and Lillian
suddenly heard the seriousness in his voice.

"What's wrong? What's happened?" She put out her hand to
touch his face but David turned away. When she reached for him a
second time David stopped her by taking both of her hands into his
own and firmly pushing her down into the chair.

"I'm sorry Lillian. I want you to know that I will always love
you," he began.

"You're going to sell me, aren't you? Your Missus is making

you sell me. Is that what you come to tell me?"

"No, no, I'm not going to sell you. I told you that I would never do that and I won't."

"Then what?"

"I'm going to give you and Rebecca your freedom."

Lillian didn't understand. Fear slowly spread over her face as her eyes bore into David. "I'm giving you your freedom," he said again. "You will no longer be a slave to me or anyone else." He fished the envelope from his pocket and handed it to Lillian. "The papers in this envelope say that you and Rebecca are free. Do you understand?"

"Why?"

"Do you really have to know why?"

"Yes. I want to know why you don't want me no more. What have I done?"

"You haven't done anything. We have my father to thank for this."

"I don't understand massa."

"Don't call me that anymore. I am not your master. You are free."

"Why? You must tell me why."

"I know that my father was very mean to you and your mother and I know that Mamie hated him most of her life but did she ever tell you why she hated him so?"

Lillian stood up and walked closer to David. "She hated him for the same reasons I hated him. He took her when she was just a girl and when she was a woman he took her baby boy away. He sold him the same day he came into this world."

"He didn't sell the child Lillian. He was the child's father."

"I don't understand what this has to do with me and Rebecca. I be here all of my life and I seen many children on Gloria that your daddy fathered. That ain't no reason to send me and Rebecca away."

David sighed in frustration. "I guess there's no easy way to say this. Lillian I am the child that Big Bill took from Mamie and my father tried to keep us apart not because you were a slave but because you are my sister, half sister."

Lillian backed away from David and sank onto the chair. "That can't be so," she whispered.

"Yes. It's true Lillian. Mamie was my mother."

Lillian sat quiet for a moment trying to understand exactly what David was saying and what it meant to her. Tears began to stream down her face and she wiped at them with the back of her hand. "So you ain't freein' me because you want to, you just don't want me around to remind you of who you really are." It was more of a question than a declaration as Lillian sought to find a reason why she should have to leave Gloria.

"No, that's not true."

"Then why do I have to leave? I ain't gone ever tell no one, I promise. I been here on Gloria all of my life. I don't know nothin' about the rest of this world. You can't free me, cause I got no place to go."

"You're wrong Lillian. I'm not doing this to hurt you. I loved you as a woman and I will probably always love you but until just a few hours ago I did not know that we had the same mother. Now that I know, we just can't go on like this. It just isn't right. I'm giving you freedom because I know that I will never be able to see you as anything but the woman I've loved my entire life. I know that I cannot live with this new reality. Don't you understand, Lillian? We have the same mother."

"What will I do?" Lillian sobbed.

"You and Rebecca will leave Gloria in the morning. I'll give you enough money to get you to the northern states and a letter of introduction that will probably help you to find a place to live and work."

"But I don't want to leave."

"I know you don't. We can't change the past Lillian but I am trying to give you a better future."

"There ain't no future for me. You are just making me free so another white man can make me his slave. Them papers don't mean nothin'. The first white man that sees them will tear them to shreds." Lillian was angry now. "Why don't you just sell me?"

Lillian was angry and hurt and there was nothing that David could say or do to change their situation or how she felt about it. He leaned over and kissed her soft brown tear stained face as she hung her head and sobbed softly.

"Isn't there anything I can say that would convince you to stay?" James said to Beth.

"No James. I really must leave Gloria. I'll never be able to find peace and happiness here after all that's happened."

"It's not safe for an unattached female these days. What will people think?"

"I'm not concerned with what people think. Besides, I'm not an unattached female. David and I are still married and he promised to provide for me until I marry again. I'm sure I'll be just fine."

"But, why Philadelphia? You don't have any family there now."

"It's the only city besides Richmond that I know, its familiar. Besides, Philadelphia is much different from Virginia. Some of the women there actually own businesses. It's a big city with lots to offer. I just need to take some time to figure out what I want to do with the rest of my life. Who knows, maybe I'll marry again."

The last of her trunks were being loaded on the wagon as she and James exchanged their farewells in front of the house. "Aren't you going to say good-bye to your husband?"

"I haven't seen David. I went to his room earlier this morning but he didn't answer my knock. I left him a letter in the study. You will be sure he gets it, won't you?"

"Of course I will. Promise me that you'll keep in touch and maybe after the wounds have healed you can come back for a visit."

"That sounds wonderful. Goodbye James." Beth leaned forward and kissed him on the cheek. "Thank you James. I'm not sure I would have survived all of this if you hadn't been there for me."

"Goodbye Beth. Take care of yourself.'

James helped Beth into the carriage and in a moments time the carriage lurched forward. Beth couldn't resist one last look at the beautiful southern mansion that had been her home.

After several minutes of riding the carriage slowly came to a stop and Beth knew that they had reached the front gate. Beth knew that it should have taken the driver only a minute or two to open the gate but after several minutes had gone by she began to wonder what was taking so long. "Jake, is there something wrong?" she yelled from the window. As she leaned her head out of the carriage window she could see that Lillian and Rebecca were standing by the front gate. Their ragged bundles tied to their backs. Jake swung himself back into the driver's seat and prepared to move the horses forward. "Wait!" Beth said. She opened the door and climbed down.

"Where are you going Lillian?" Beth asked.

"I don't know. I'm just going." Lillian had not turned to face her former mistress.

"I'd like to help, if you'll allow me."

Lillian stopped and turned to face Beth. "Why?"

"Lillian, you're not the only person who has been hurt by all of this. I've lost a husband and my home. We've both suffered heartbreak. The one thing that kept the two of us at odds with each other is no longer an issue. Maybe we can put all of this behind us and help each other." Lillian didn't answer. "Look," Beth said in exasperation as her patience faded. "It will be much safer for you and Rebecca if you travel with me rather than alone. No one has to know that you are a free woman until we have traveled far enough north, for it not to matter."

Lillian considered this and decided that Beth was right. She untied the pack from her back and let it fall to the ground. Beth took the gesture as a sign of acceptance. "Jake! Please put Miss Lillian and her daughter's things in the back of the carriage with mine. We'll be traveling together." The old man smiled as he ambled down from the driver's seat.

Once inside the carriage Lillian asked again. "Why would you want to help me? I don't deserve it."

"I don't think either of us has deserved the hardships life has given us thus far. Maybe together we can both find out what we do deserve."

"Don't you hate me?"

"I'll be honest with you Lillian. I hated the control you had over David. In all the years that we were married I only wanted him to give me a chance to be a real wife to him. Now I realize that you couldn't have control over David if he did not love you so. There is no reason I should hate you. If I must place blame or hate I would have to place it on my own naiveté. I really thought I could make him love me."

The carriage finally went forward at a steady pace and Beth settled back into the seat happy and contented that she would at last find peace. Suddenly the carriage stopped again. This time an uneasy feeling swept over Beth. "What is it Jake? Why have we stopped?"

"There's something blocking the road Miss."

"What?"

"It's a man."

"Do you mean a man is lying across the road?" Beth questioned.

"No Ma'am. He's hanging from a tree."

"Oh my god!" Beth said as she leaned her head out of the window trying to see.

"Ma'am, please don't look. It ain't right for a lady to see such a sight," Jake said.

"Who is it?" Lillian asked

"I don't know." Beth answered.

"Ma'am. It looks like massa Dave. He's done hung himself."

Jake pulled hard on the reins to steer the carriage around the tree. As the carriage began to move forward again Beth couldn't help looking out of the window as it passed the tree where David's limp body swung back and forth from a low hanging branch. Beth winced and turned away.

Lillian didn't even bother to look. She put her hand over Rebecca's eyes to spare the girl the sight.

Tears clouded the eyes of both women. "I never expected him to do such a thing," Beth said and she began to softly sob.

Lillian leaned over and took Beth's hand. "Don't cry ma'am. I guess we're all free now."

THE END